He has high expectations. And she exceeds every one.

Seth Barlow picks his teeth with the bones of secretaries he's chewed up and spit out. Except Tessa Edwards. She's completely unruffled by his bad attitude--and completely undone by his touch.

But Tessa is balancing on a high wire with no safety net. Her job is the only thing that keeps her from losing custody of her little brother to her money-hungry aunt and uncle, who care less for the dyslexic child than for the hefty trust fund that comes with him.

When ten thousand dollars goes missing from Barrett Newspapers and shows up in Tessa's personal bank account, not even her budding relationship with Seth can help Tessa keep her job...or her little brother.

Books by Laura Browning

Winning Heart

The Barlow-Barretts: An American Dynasty
Bittersweet, Book One
Balancing Act, Book Two
Remember Me, Book Three
Broken Heart, Book Four

Published by Kensington Publishing Corporation

Balancing Act

The Barlow-Barretts: An American Dynasty, Book Two

Laura Browning

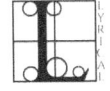

LYRICAL PRESS
Kensington Publishing Corp.
www.kensingtonbooks.com

Lyrical Press books are published by
Kensington Publishing Corp. 119 West 40th Street New York, NY 10018

All Kensington titles, imprints, and distributed lines are available at special quantity discounts for bulk purchases for sales promotion, premiums, fundraising, and educational or institutional use.

Special book excerpts or customized printings can also be created to fit specific needs. For details, write or phone the office of the Kensington Special Sales Manager:
Kensington Publishing Corp.
119 West 40th Street
New York, NY 10018
Attn. Special Sales Department. Phone: 1-800-221-2647.

Kensington and the K logo Reg. U.S. Pat. & TM Off.
Lyrical Press and the L logo are trademarks of Kensington Publishing Corp.

First Electronic Edition: September 2012
eISBN-13: 978-1-61650-403-8
eISBN-10: 1-61650-403-X

First Print Edition: September 2012
ISBN-13: 978-1-61650-849-4
ISBN-10: 1-61650-849-3

Printed in the United States of America

To every teacher out there who takes the time and makes the effort to encourage struggling students and give them hope. Your efforts are noticed.

Chapter 1

Tessa stared at the steel and glass monstrosity that housed the headquarters of Barrett Newspapers. It reminded her of the blue-blooded snobbery she had vowed to leave behind, but in the end, a job was a job. Right now she was in need of a steady, well-paid position as opposed to part-time social work with juvenile offenders. Not only did she need to be the picture of stability, but also the additional income working for Barrett Newspapers would provide.

She entered the building at barely seven AM, but a security guard already sat with his elbows propped on the reception desk. Tessa hadn't batted an eye when the personnel director told her how early she would be expected to arrive. She had yet to work any job with truly traditional hours. If the bear of the Barrett family was an early riser, well then, so was she.

"Good morning. I'm Tessa Edwards, Seth Barlow-Barrett's new executive assistant."

"Should I congratulate you or commiserate?" the guard asked.

Tessa tilted her head. Another confirmation of what she'd already heard. The company's chief operating officer had a reputation other employees were more than willing to share. Even the personnel director who hired her warned her in advance. Seth Barlow-Barrett was dictatorial and demanding. He was cruel and cantankerous. The bottom line of everyone's description was he was impossible to work for, and he had a history of secretarial resignations to back that up, so much so they didn't even bother to have him interview any of the candidates anymore. They never lasted long enough for it to matter.

She would be different.

She grinned at the security guard. "May I get back to you at the end of the day?"

He snorted. "If you're still here by the end of the day, you'll have outlasted several of them. Elevators are just ahead. The express elevator's the one on the far right in case you want to leave in a hurry."

Tessa glanced at the tightly sealed steel doors and shuddered. "No thanks. I like to take the stairs. Keeps me fit."

She dashed up the steps to the ninth floor. Used to the exertion, she was barely out of breath when she stepped from the stairwell into the carpeted luxury of Seth Barrett's floor. Well, Seth and his brother Brandon's. It appeared sole occupancy of a floor was reserved for the patriarch, their father. Tessa sniggered.

The personnel director had told her where her desk would be and what her duties were. She'd also warned her Seth Barrett normally arrived around six in the morning, so he would be there already, and she should introduce herself when she arrived.

It seemed odd that no one really wanted to face him. Only the favorite son in a family-owned empire could get away with such terrible behavior in this day and age, but surely no one was that bad--even the lordling of the mighty Barlow-Barrett empire.

After setting down her belongings, Tessa checked her appearance in the small mirror she kept in her purse. She'd pulled her hair back in a smooth chignon at the base of her neck. It made her look mature and conservative, the image she was trying hard to project. Young and inexperienced was not the impression she wanted to make. Taking a deep breath, she knocked on the partially open door.

"What is it?"

What not who, as though he were too busy to be bothered by ordinary mortals. Tessa raised her brows at the decided bark in that deep voice, but when she stepped into his office, she'd composed her expression.

"Who are you?" The man standing near the windows eyed her with a mixture of irritation and impatience.

The first thing that struck her was how big he was, not fat, just big. He had to be somewhere around six-foot-five, give or take a couple inches, and possessed incredibly broad shoulders that tapered down to lean hips and long, long legs. Not a bear in his den, as she'd been led to believe, but a different animal entirely. His appearance reminded her of a sleek and dangerous lion, ready to attack at any moment.

"I'm your new secretary, Tessa Edwards."

Even the eyes were feline. The color of gold, they still managed to be cold as they assessed her. "Coffee, Teresa."

"Tessa," she corrected with amused patience. No way was she going to bite on his deliberate baiting.

"Coffee, Tessa." The deep voice dripped sarcasm.

She kept her expression controlled until she left his office, and then she smiled. He was as bad as everyone said. Maybe worse. He had the personality of the building in which he worked, she decided. All glitz and sharp edges, but no substance. Expensively cut hair, hand-tailored suits and the arrogant air that went hand-in-hand with his name. No wonder the man went through so many secretaries. But she--Tessa gave herself a pep talk--would not be one of them. She knew his type. She had grown up around a dozen or more people just like him, and she could handle his blue-blooded arrogance. She might avoid her father's relatives, but that didn't mean she hadn't learned from them over the years.

She needed this job too much to let some old-money ogre scare her away. If she had to pull out her own pedigree to do it, she would. In court next month, she had to represent the epitome of security and stability because if she didn't, she could lose custody of Zach.

Her smile slipped for a second. Public school last year had been a disaster for her little brother, but she'd found a school that could help him. Now she had to make sure they stayed together. The job with Barrett would provide enough money to pay his tuition, and help keep Aunt Kathleen and Uncle Edwin at bay.

As long as she could prove she was providing the best home for her brother, they didn't have a leg to stand on. She knew the only reason they wanted custody was because of the trust her parents had left behind. If they had guardianship, they could tap it for expenses. She could imagine how expensive Zach's lifestyle would become.

All Tessa had to do was wait it out. One more year, and she would be old enough to use the trust as her parents had intended--for her brother. The problem was, and always had been, that her aunt and uncle could access it right now, but only if they were Zach's legal guardians. If she could show the court how secure her employment was, they would never dream of taking him....

"Is that coffee arriving by mule from Colombia, Tina?" Barrett barked over the intercom.

Tessa grimaced at the speaker. Who on earth still had one of those squawk boxes, in this day and age?

She hadn't asked him how he liked his coffee. She looked at the supplies next to the coffee maker. The creamer was untouched. She checked the small fridge right next to it. Mountain Dew lined the shelves. The man must be a caffeine addict, though he hardly seemed to need anything that would make him testier. No sign of cream. He must take it black. The sugar had been opened and some had spilled. Shaking hands trying to get the ogre's coffee ready? Tessa made a face and added one teaspoon of sugar. He would want it sweet, but not too sweet. Maybe that was to help make up for a very sour personality.

She pushed down a button on the intercom and said, "Coming right up, Mr. Barrett."

He sat behind a very large, cherry desk with a gleaming finish. The papers on it were arranged with almost pinpoint precision. He looked up as she approached his desk, his scowl locked in place. Did the man never smile?

"It's about time. What secretarial school are you from…the Slowpoke Rodriguez School?"

"I didn't attend secretarial school, sir. I graduated from Smith," Tessa replied. That seemed to give him pause for a moment, and she managed not to laugh out loud. Oh, yes, his snobby background was showing now. She'd bet he had a girlfriend named Muffy or Priss filed neatly somewhere in his life. A small chuckle escaped.

For the first time that morning, her new boss slowed down to really look at her.

"I amuse you?"

"Not at all, sir."

His glittering, golden gaze lifted and bore into her this time instead of skating over her. Tessa could now understand how he made other secretaries uncomfortable, but she was not other secretaries and she would not be intimidated. If this was an undeclared war, she was more than willing to plant her flag and stand her ground.

He looked her up and down. "What was your major?"

"Social Work."

"Ah, a do-gooder," he dismissed her. "Why are you here? Has personnel decided I need counseling? Someone who can ask open-ended questions and get me to reveal how society has damaged me? Are you here to save me from myself, Tessa? Help me reveal my inner child?"

She kept her temper under control. "I think you credit them with way too much interest in the position as your secretary. You have a job. I need one. As to your inner child, I believe that answer should be obvious to you. It seems to me you need no assistance with that…sir."

One thick brow slowly arched. "Can you type?"

"Seventy-five words a minute."

"Dictation?"

"Transcription…while you talk."

"How are you with computers?"

Tessa shrugged. "I do well enough."

No way would she tell him about hacking into her high school's computer system when she was fourteen and changing the principal's appointment book so he showed up to a non-existent meeting with the superintendent. Some things were better left in the past.

The rest of the day passed like volleys in a naval battle. Barrett never asked her to do things, he barked orders at her, as if firing missiles over her bow.

Early in the afternoon, the intercom bleated, "I need you in here for some transcription."

She took her laptop and set it up at the conference table, watching as he paced. She was already half-convinced he was just another rich prick riding on his family's fortune. If she didn't need the steadiness and income this job offered, she'd walk like everyone else.

Then he began to speak. Her fingers flew as he talked through the plan he had apparently wrestled with all day long. As he outlined his strategy to acquire several struggling Midwest publications, Tessa acknowledged what he had developed was brilliant. Even more important, the acquisitions he designed wouldn't cost jobs. She felt a new level of respect for the man, but didn't dare let that show in her face. He still had an arrogant and overbearing attitude toward his personnel that would never be tolerated in any company where he wasn't family.

At three, he abruptly stopped and stared hard at her.

"Go home," he growled as he tossed a Mountain Dew can in the basket next to his desk. When she arched one brow at him, he added, "Be back tomorrow morning at seven."

He had dismissed her, but not fired her. From what she heard, that meant she was a success. Tessa packed the laptop and headed for the door.

"Thanks, Teresa."

"Tessa," she corrected.

"Tessa."

As she left the building, she gave the surprised security guard a thumbs-up.

* * * *

By Friday, she began to think Barrett was an automaton programmed only to work and bent on driving her crazy. She could see why he had a reputation for chewing secretaries to bits and spitting them back out. His mind worked at light speed, so keeping up with him was a challenge, but Tessa had managed.

She never saw him smile. She wondered if he had no personality or if he just hated what he was doing. Neither option boded well for either long-term employment or pleasant working conditions. He was bound to lose his temper with her at some point.

A package arrived after lunch on Friday. Or rather, Tessa found it sitting on her desk right after lunch with Seth Barrett's name scrawled on it.

"I have a package for you, sir," she said over the intercom.

"How many times have I told you not to use that damn intercom? Bring it in."

Tessa grinned. He told her not to use it almost the same number of times he told her to stop barging in on him and use the intercom instead. She took the package and handed it to him. As she turned to go, he spoke.

"Take the rest of the day off. We're done."

Tessa stopped and stared. She supposed the amazement must have shown in her expression.

"Go!" he barked.

Tessa grinned as she tidied up her desk, locking drawers and file cabinets. She was always meticulous about her work area, probably a good thing with Mr. Psycho Clean on the other side of the door. A muffled sound from Barrett's office followed by a crash stopped her just as she was about to depart for the day. She hesitated for only a second before she pushed the door open and stepped back into his inner sanctum.

He sat unmoving in the chair behind his desk, staring out the window. His face was pale, and his jaw clenched and unclenched as if he were working hard to get his emotions under control. An expensive sculpture that had perched on his desk now lay on the floor in pieces.

"Mr. Barrett?" Tessa murmured. He must be furious at having smashed the artwork. He turned eyes on her that burned with such intense golden fire, she took a half step back, but she would not retreat. "Can I help you with anything else, sir?"

For a moment, she thought he might throw something at her, but she refused to be intimidated. He raked a hand through his thick, blond hair and blinked a couple times as if he were trying to fight his way through whatever disturbed him and focus on what she'd said.

"Check my calendar for this weekend."

She didn't need to check, she'd memorized it. "You have a Sigma Delta Chi dinner at which you are the keynote speaker this evening. The rest of the weekend is clear."

"Damn!" He stood up and paced his office, once again reminding her of a wild animal trapped in a cage not of his own choosing. He paused at the corner and looked back at her.

"Where's the jet?"

"Brandon Barrett has it, sir, in Puerto Rico."

"Then get me the first commercial flight you can after that damn dinner to Durham, North Carolina. First-class. There's never enough leg-room anywhere else."

Tessa had already logged off her computer. She gestured toward Seth's. "May I?"

"Yes." He waved her toward the oversized leather chair. She felt almost like a child sitting in it, her legs very nearly dangling without touching the floor.

It took a few minutes, and Barrett's gaze seemed to bore into her the entire time. The man was an expert at looming. It hadn't taken her long to figure out most of his attitude was not directed at her. The biting temper was who he was allowed to be. The arrogance, she was sure, was inbred at this point.

The controlled anger that bubbled up now and then was another matter, but not her problem. If Seth Barlow-Barrett was unhappy in what he did, that was too bad. There must be a lot that more than made up for it. Financial gain, for one thing. Right now, in her book, that was a pretty fair trade-off. With a couple more keystrokes, she turned to him.

"You leave National at five-fifteen a.m. and arrive at Raleigh-Durham at six AM Saturday morning," she said at last. "A rental car will be waiting for you. When would you like to return?"

"Sunday."

She punched a few more keys. "I can get you on a noon flight back."

"Book it. Use my travel account. The number's there next to the keyboard."

A couple more minutes and Tessa was pulling his ticket voucher off the computer printer.

"Done."

She crossed the room and handed him the voucher, and then Barrett did do something that caught her off-guard. He smiled. It transformed the lean features of his face and made him look years younger.

"Thank you, Tessa."

Now he'd rattled her. A smile and her correct name. She knew she was staring at him, probably with her mouth gaping, but she couldn't help it and could only nod in response.

"Go home. Enjoy your weekend."

She smiled back. "Thank you."

* * * *

Seth watched the door close behind her. Tessa Edwards. She'd made it through the first week, and that was an accomplishment in and of itself. It had taken him a few days to notice, but she was stunning in her own way. Hers was not a stand up and smack you in the face kind of pretty, but a harmonious blend of classic bone structure and subtle curves with the staying power pretty women seldom had. Not until she smiled at someone else had he seen the vivid personality to go with the flamboyant coloring. Fiery red hair, thick and straight, and the most unusual ice-blue eyes. Yes, he'd noticed Tessa Edwards, not just for her looks, but for the grit and unflappable serenity she'd demonstrated all week long.

He needed that right now, especially after the little nuclear bomb she'd unknowingly dropped in his lap with that package. Seth tapped his fingers on his desk.

He was not an easy man. He knew that. In fact, many of the people who had faced him across a negotiating table described him as a Class-A bastard who made his father look like a blessed saint. Seth knew what people thought, what some even voiced behind his back, but didn't care. He was what his father had molded him to be. He had taken over daily operations of Barrett Newspapers four years after college. When all was said and done, he was a Barlow-Barrett and couldn't drop that responsibility from his shoulders to pursue his own desires.

One soft spot remained in the armor he'd built around himself over the years. That was his sister Anna. He and Brandon were the only ones who called her that, yet that was the name she now chose to use in her professional life. Little Anna, the veterinarian. So different from the rest of them, yet she was the embodiment of what he longed to be. She was his heart, and he would do anything to protect her. He knew she viewed herself as the ugly duckling, but he saw her as the one Barlow-Barrett who had dared to be different, inside and out. When the rest of them had followed like sheep in the family footsteps, Anna had walked away. Phillip, his youngest brother, had taken a slight detour into law, but he was still right in the family fold. Anna was the rebel, and he admired her to no end.

His eyes lifted to the DVD player and the disc he still hadn't removed. Watching even a portion of it had made him almost sick. Then the anger had exploded, costing him a piece of artwork he'd paid through the nose for. He wanted not only the blackmailers who'd sent the video, but the fucker on the disc with her.

Chapter 2

Tessa pushed thoughts of Seth from her mind as soon as she arrived at her neighbor's apartment to pick up Zach. His freckled face split into a huge grin when he saw her and he leaped up from the video game he played. She laughed and hugged him. He was the joy in her life and had been ever since his birth. Their parents' deaths had served to draw them even closer.

"Tessa! I got to the third level of Space Zombies."

"That's great, Zach." Tessa grinned back at him.

Reading might be a problem, but he was a real whiz when it came to math or anything resembling computers. They had bought this latest video game just yesterday. If she allowed it, he would play all the time, but Tessa tried to make sure they spent time doing other things when they were together.

She read to him and took him out in the country as much as possible.

"Why are you home so early? Was your boss as bad as everyone told you and you quit?"

"No. He told me I could leave. You know what that means?"

Zach's eyes widened. "We're going to the beach today?" At her nod, he tossed down his game remote and danced around the room. "Yes! It's almost like getting a whole 'nother day."

Zach talked almost non-stop as they packed their camping gear, fishing poles and plenty of snacks. Tessa knew he got bored over the summer. As much as he disliked school, it still offered a change of scenery from the neighbor's apartment.

"Do you think we can catch any sharks?"

"Sharks!" Tessa laughed. "Who's going to take them off the hooks?"

"I can," Zach reassured her with an air of importance. "Remember, I did last year."

Tessa smiled. They had caught some baby sharks that Zach insisted on taking off the hooks. Tessa had let him. It made him feel like the man of the family to have his hands on a shark, even one a foot and a half long. They'd marveled at the sandpapery feel of the little sharks' skins. Tessa much preferred it to handling a slippery fish. She wasn't keen on fishing, but Zach enjoyed it, so she indulged him as much as she could.

As they neared the campground at the shore late in the afternoon, Zach drifted off to sleep. Tessa glanced at him and smiled. His hair was as red as hers, but his eyes were dark blue, and he'd gotten the freckles that somehow missed her creamy skin. She knew he took ribbing about his looks. What redhead hadn't? Add in the freckles and it just made it worse. He'd also inherited a double dose of intelligence, and a severe reading disability that made life at school miserable. Her mother and stepfather had worked with him and had him tested. Things had been getting better until last year when the call came about their parents.

Tessa had broken the news to Zach. He had been quiet to start, but then the problems began at school. Tessa worked with the counselors and a psychologist. She took the first job she could find in her field to be near him. The job was part-time and kept her away many evenings. That was when the trouble with Aunt Kathleen and Uncle Edwin had first started. They claimed she shuffled Zach from one sitter to another and was too young and irresponsible to have custody. Tessa feared their grumbling would soon evolve into more than idle threats.

It wasn't her brother they wanted, just the trust fund that came with him, so she couldn't afford to give them any fuel. They would crush Zach. He didn't need more humiliation. He needed to have the talents he possessed nurtured. They would never understand the way his mind worked. Tessa could because hers worked much the same way, so she understood how important it was to get him away from everything now and then.

Zach fished all evening from the pier. Tessa helped bait hooks in between watching other people and, she had to admit, thinking about her new boss.

She had seen many of Seth's moods during this first week, most of them unpleasant, but today something had rattled him. Whatever was in that envelope she had given him wasn't good. She checked off what she knew. One of his sisters lived in North Carolina--she'd seen the address in the computer file. Preston. No. Anna was what it had said. Dr. Anna Barlow, without the Barrett attached. Something in that envelope must have involved her. It had shaken Seth. While he often growled orders and paced around like a caged animal, she'd never seen that look of angry frustration.

Tessa didn't like unsolved puzzles. Her mind went back to the package. The size, the weight. A plain manila envelope with Seth's name typed on the outside. A CD or DVD? And if so, of what? Something involving Anna. What else did she know from the computer contact information? There was a child, she remembered. A baby.

"Tessa!" Zach interrupted her thoughts. "I've caught something. Come help."

She jumped up and coached him through landing the fish he had on the line--a bluefish that put up a good fight. Not huge as fish went, but he worked the line enough it turned Zach into one happy ten-year-old. That was enough for Tessa.

By the time they headed home Sunday afternoon, they were both tired. Zach pulled out his Gameboy and played it, more out of habit than actual interest.

They were about halfway home when he looked up, game forgotten for the moment.

"Will I have to go live with Aunt Kathleen and Uncle Edwin?"

Tessa was used to the questions that often seemed to come out of nowhere. She glanced over at him, then turned back to the road. What on earth had started him worrying about that? Sometimes she wondered at the depths at which his brain was always working. It bothered her that a ten-year-old should even have to consider where he might be forced to live.

"No," she said with more confidence than she felt. "You'll stay with me. That's what you want, isn't it?"

"Yeah. Aunt Kathleen smells like that porta-potty perfume, and Uncle Edwin smokes cigars. Yuck."

Tessa laughed. Zach had a way of making her look at things on the most basic level. She reached over and ruffled his hair, and he grinned back at her. They were covered in salt spray, flushed from the sun, and Tessa was happier than she'd been in a long time.

Those feelings of peace and contentment lingered as she ran up the stairs Monday morning. She slipped her heels back on before she left the stairwell and smoothed the skirt and jacket of her business suit. In a matter of minutes, she carried a steaming mug of coffee to Seth.

He sat at his desk, an ever-growing pile of snapped-in-half pencils lying in front of him. When she set the cup down, he grunted. As she started to remove the pile of broken pencils, he snapped, "Leave them. Leave me. I don't want to be disturbed."

Tessa, unruffled, turned on her heel to go.

"Will there be anything else this morning, sir?" From the relative safety of the doorway, she figured he wouldn't dare throw anything at her--not that he had, but she'd heard rumors of such things happening to some of her predecessors.

Seth glanced at her from under thick blond brows drawn together in a forbidding frown. "No. As I said, I don't want to be disturbed."

Whatever had so upset him Friday afternoon must still be an issue, even after the visit to North Carolina. Tessa went to work on several reports in the works. There was another trip to arrange for Seth later that week. Since his brother, Brandon, wasn't expected back until the end of the week, she would have to book a commercial flight. She scribbled the number for his travel account down on the back of an envelope as she began to work on the trip, but was prevented from doing anything else when the elevator doors opened and an athletically built man with wheaten hair and gray eyes stepped off. He was dressed in a navy sport coat and tie, not in the formal, conservative suits Seth preferred.

"I'd like to see Barrett," the man said. "Please tell him it's Chris Stevenson. He'll want to see me. It's about his sister Anna."

Tessa invited him to take a seat as she stalled for time. Then she punched the intercom button.

"Mr. Barrett?"

"What?" he snapped back. "I thought I told you I was not to be disturbed this morning."

Tessa grimaced. A gut-feeling told her this visit was tied to that package. She pushed open the door and stepped into Seth's office.

"What the hell is it, Teresa?"

"Tessa," she corrected him, knowing he was provoking her on purpose. "It's Tessa, sir."

"Whatever."

"I think you will wish to see this visitor," she added.

"Someone gave you permission to think?" Seth goaded her. She knew it, but she wasn't rising to the bait. One temperamental person on this floor was enough. Instead, she glared right back at him.

"His name is Chris Stevenson. He said he wished to see you about Anna."

Seth stood up. He towered over her, but she didn't give ground.

"Why the hell didn't you say so?"

"Because you didn't give me a chance?" she suggested.

Seth frowned. She frowned back.

"Show him in."

She smiled as sweetly as she could. "Right away, Mr. Barrett. Shall I bring you both coffee?"

"No, but you might want the first aid kit handy."

Tessa did pause then, casting a questioning look at him. He was serious. Okay, maybe his temper was as bad as rumor had it.

She glanced back at Chris Stevenson and said, "Mr. Barrett will see you now."

With a silent blessing on the man's continued good health, she held the door for him and then shut it as he walked into the office. Even from outside, she heard Seth. His words left her in no doubt both what it was about and that finding the first aid kit was a necessity. She also located an ice pack to be on the safe side. God knew, she had gained experience dealing with fights while she worked with juveniles. And this seemed to be a very similar occasion.

She had gathered all the supplies when Seth's voice came over the intercom.

"Tessa?" He added emphasis on her name. "Please bring two cups of coffee and a bag of ice. Oh, you better bring the first aid kit too."

"Yes, sir."

Tessa refused to show any surprise at all upon seeing the bloody handkerchief Stevenson held to his nose. She handed him an ice pack, keeping her expression the same as if she had been giving him a letter to sign.

Seth almost smiled. "Thanks, Tessa. That will be all."

"Yes, sir, Mr. Barrett."

Tessa returned to her desk and shoved her personal mail back into her oversize purse before she returned to what she was working on. Arrangements for the trip for Seth. She looked up the account number again and soon had everything booked. He would take the corporate jet later that week instead of a commercial flight, so all she needed to manage were rental cars and the hotel suite.

Chris Stevenson left a short while later, the ice pack still on his nose. Tessa watched him with curiosity until he disappeared in the elevator.

"Tessa!" Seth barked over the intercom. She started. "Get in here. Bring the laptop."

Seth worked like a demon until lunch. Whatever had distracted him was now forgotten.

"Check my calendar."

Tessa replied without needing to think. "You have a one o'clock appointment with Barrett senior and a supplier is coming in to make a pitch at three."

He stared at her, narrow-eyed, but Tessa just returned his look with a bland expression.

"I don't even want to know how you do that. It's a little scary." He stared out the window for a moment. "Cancel the supplier. Damn. I don't suppose there's any way you can make that one o'clock with my father disappear."

She tilted her head and gave him a steady look. "I can, if you're serious." At his nod, she asked, "May I use your computer, sir?"

Seth stood up and moved from behind the desk. "Help yourself."

Tessa sat down and logged into the company system. She moved through several different screens, alternating between typing and clicking the mouse until his father's calendar popped up. A minute later Tessa sat back.

"There. The one o'clock is rescheduled for Wednesday and it will look like his secretary entered it that way last week. Is that okay?"

Seth arched an eyebrow at her. "Something you learned at Smith?"

"High school."

"Hmm. I suppose you were a straight-A student."

Tessa slanted a sideways glance at him as she stood up and started to move past him. "Yes. Legitimate A's."

Seth locked up his desk and closed his briefcase. "I'll be gone the rest of the afternoon. If you'd like to take the day off, you may."

Tessa smiled. "Thank you, Mr. Barrett, but I believe I'll get those reports finished for you before your trip."

"Yes, right."

Seth was in a better frame of mind the rest of the week. He left Thursday morning for Chicago and Minneapolis and wasn't scheduled to be back in the office until Monday morning. So Tessa at last had a chance to become acquainted with her workspace. She learned her way around the filing system and reorganized it. The revolving door of secretaries had left things in a shambles.

She was tidying up her desk before going out to lunch when Brandon came out of his office down the hall. Instead of heading straight for the elevators, he strode toward her. Tessa glanced at him, finding him a less vibrant version of his brother. Though they were almost the same size, his eyes were hazel rather than the gold of Seth's, and his hair was darker, as if his blond was attributable to the sun rather than heredity.

"I was going out to grab some lunch. Want to come with me?" His voice was pleasant, not the bark of his elder brother.

Tessa smiled. "I don't think that would be a good idea, Mr. Barrett."

His brows lifted. "Afraid of what others will think? Or afraid Mr. Cantankerous will bite your head off?"

Tessa arched a brow in return. "Neither. I just see no need to wave the red cape in front of any of the bulls in this building."

Brandon grinned, then broke into a full-fledged laugh. "You are so exactly what my brother needs. Please don't leave. Now, all kidding aside, I'm running down to the deli on the corner. Can I get you anything?"

"A chef salad would be great." She started to reach for her purse.

"My treat. Call it a reward for putting up with Seth." With a wave of his hand, he turned for the elevator. "Be right back."

* * * *

By Friday, she was feeling much more secure in her office space. She had finished setting up workable systems and getting things organized when her personal line rang late in the day.

"Good afternoon. Tessa Edwards here."

"Tessa. I'm glad I caught you." It was her attorney. "The judge moved the custody hearing up. I at least got them to give me a time Monday afternoon. Can you make that?"

Tessa's hand trembled. She had to catch her breath before she responded, "Yes. I'll be there. What time?"

"One PM."

Seth had rescheduled his supplier for that time and she knew he would want her in on the meeting, but this was more important. She would just have to convince Seth of that. After all, she didn't have much choice, and she was not going to be the one making waves about the timing of the court date.

She arrived extra early Monday morning. Even so, he was already in the office. Sometimes Tessa wondered if he lived there. She knew he kept extra dress shirts and ties in his coat closet. She'd seen that one day over lunch when the dry cleaner showed up with laundered shirts to put there. She brought him a cup of coffee, but instead of leaving after setting it down like she did other mornings, Tessa stood in front of his desk.

Seth was working at his computer. He had a habit of hyper-concentrating like Zach. A bomb could go off around her brother when he was absorbed in something. Seth appeared to be no different. He grabbed the coffee, his mind still elsewhere, and that's when he noticed her.

"What?" he barked. She'd already begun to realize some of his tone was sheer reaction to having his concentration broken.

Tessa kept tight control over her nervousness. She had yet to ask him for anything.

"I need to leave at lunchtime today."

Seth regarded her out of hooded eyes. "You're free to do as you please with your lunch hour."

Tessa shifted. "I'm sorry. I expressed myself badly. I mean I will need to leave for the day."

"You know I've got that one o'clock that I canceled last week, and I need you to take notes. It will have to wait." A note of impatience threaded through his voice.

Tessa felt like a child being raked over the coals, but outside she was as cool and composed as ever.

"It's a personal matter, sir. It came up without much warning. I have to go to court. It's a custody hearing for my little brother."

Seth leaned back in his chair and crossed one long, elegant leg over the other as he regarded her. "You currently have custody?"

"Yes."

"Who wants him?"

Tessa raised one eyebrow at him, but somehow she knew she shouldn't be surprised he asked such a personal question. If he wanted information, he wouldn't let the fact he might be prying get in the way.

"Aunt Kathleen and Uncle Edwin," she said. "Kathleen is my mother's older sister."

"What happened to your parents?"

Tessa avoided his gaze and looked out the window. "They were killed in a car accident a little over a year ago. I have custody, but no access until I'm twenty-five to the trust fund my stepfather left for Zach. You see, they didn't expect it to be a problem."

"But it is one." His voice lost its inquisitorial tone and revealed only concern. The sudden change took her off-guard.

She nodded.

"Sit down, Tessa."

She sat. Seth being nice threatened to dissolve her composure with far greater ease than his usual taciturn manner ever could have.

"Is it money?" he asked "Do you not have enough?"

Tessa shook her head. "I make more than enough to support Zach and me. I even make enough now I can send Zach to a school where he can get help with his learning disability."

"Then what's the issue?"

Tessa hesitated. She was still reluctant to air the family laundry. She started to tell him it was none of his business, but Seth being understanding was a lot harder to withstand. In fact, he was impossible to withstand.

"It's Aunt Kathleen and Uncle Edwin. They don't want Zach. They want access to his trust fund, which they would have if they had custody right now. I can only access it when I reach the age of twenty-five--or by getting married. Since my getting married isn't a factor, they've been working to prove I can't take care of Zach, trying to split us up before I come of age."

Her voice broke at the end of the last sentence, the stress getting the best of her. She bit her bottom lip to stop it from trembling. As Seth continued to regard her, Tessa curled her fingers into fists.

"May I go?"

"To the hearing or away from me?" His voice was gravelly.

Tessa darted a glance at him, catching a soft expression on his face that was unexpected. Her nervousness left as fast as it had come. She smiled. "Both."

Seth studied her. "Reschedule the supplier again. I'll go with you."

"There's no need," she began, but he ignored her.

"What time do we leave?"

Tessa sighed in resignation. "Noon."

When Seth emerged from his office with his suit jacket on right before noon, Tessa was waiting on him. She followed him without thinking right to the elevator. As the doors opened and he entered, she darted a glance at the stairwell door.

"Well?" he prompted. "Let's go."

Tessa stepped in and over to the far side, away from Seth's looming form. As the doors slid shut, her breathing tightened. This was a mistake. All she could do was stare at the doors as they hissed together. Although she knew it wasn't logical, her heart beat faster in fear the doors wouldn't open again. The elevator lurched into its descent, and Tessa fought back the roaring in her ears.

"Tessa? Are you all right?"

She clutched the polished wooden wall rail and nodded without looking at him. No way was she going to admit to this man she was petrified of any tight spaces. Mercifully the elevator was an express that went straight from Seth's floor to the lobby below.

Seth took her elbow without a word and led her out to his black SUV. He helped her into the passenger seat before going around to the driver's side. Tessa's breathing eased and her heart quit racing.

* * * *

"Why did you get on the damn elevator if you're claustrophobic?" Seth snapped as he keyed the ignition. Did he really intimidate everyone to the point they would fail to mention a fear on the level of a phobia? "All you had to do was say something. We could have taken the stairs."

"I'm sorry," Tessa said. "I didn't think. It won't happen again, Mr. Barrett."

Seth raked one hand through his hair and pressed his lips together, biting back the need to tell her to stop being so damn polite. He'd seen her eyes flash a couple of times when he'd baited her, so he knew there was a temper tamped down in there somewhere beneath her ice queen exterior. He scowled at her. "Where are we going?"

"Juvenile and Domestic Relations Court in Alexandria."

"I know it. What about your brother? Do we need to pick him up from somewhere?"

"My attorney's bringing him," she replied, already distracted, it would seem, by what lay ahead.

When they arrived at the courthouse, Seth steered Tessa away from the elevators and up the stairs. She had looked ready to pass out, and she didn't need to go through that again right before going into court. He glanced at her as she climbed the steps. His office was on the ninth floor of a ten-story building. Did she tackle nine flights every day? It would account for her shapely legs and derriere, some of the first things he'd noticed about her aside from that hair. It burned with highlights so fiery he wondered sometimes if he would singe his fingers if he touched a lock.

When they reached the top of the stairs, a slender redheaded boy stared in their direction. Seth would have known the little boy was Tessa's brother even if he hadn't come sprinting down the hall toward her.

"Tessa!"

While the lawyer stood near the elevator doors, her brother knew her well enough--his eyes had been on the stairwell. The boy slowed down as he reached Tessa and threw his arms around her. She bent her head and pecked him on the cheek. Both had the same amazing red hair, but where Tessa's skin was a creamy light tan, the boy had hundreds of freckles.

"Hey, Zach! Have you been good for Mr. Stanley?"

"Yes."

Seth was taken aback again when Tessa smiled at her little brother. It lighted her expression with such beauty it was startling. Gone was the seriousness he was accustomed to. In its place her face softened and her eyes shone with warmth and love. She could make a man melt if she looked at one that way, he thought, an odd tightness in his chest.

The attorney motioned to them from the other end of the hall.

"Tessa," Seth prompted. "I think your case is being called."

As she looked down the hall, the cool mask she so often wore slipped back into place. Even though she appeared calm, he felt the tension in her as he cupped her elbow so they could hurry toward the courtroom.

One glance at the couple who must be Aunt Kathleen and Uncle Edwin showed Seth all he needed to know. He'd seen plenty of their kind over the years. They peppered the clubs and restaurants he'd frequented since he was a child. Kathleen and Edwin Price dripped designer clothes and expensive jewelry. If his suspicions were correct, they regarded Zach as a way to finance their lifestyle.

His gaze shifted to Tessa. Her long hair was slicked back into a French twist. The dark navy suit she wore was stylish but conservative. He knew from looking at her when she'd stood before his desk that morning, the only jewelry she wore were pearl studs and a thin gold chain.

Seth listened, along with the judge, to both sides. So far the attorneys had done all the talking. At last the judge turned to Tessa.

"This petition was brought while you were employed as a counselor and social worker for a juvenile services facility. I understand from documents filed by your attorney you have new employment. Would you please describe your job for the court?"

Tessa nodded and stood up. "I am executive assistant to Mr. Seth Barlow-Barrett, COO of Barrett Newspapers."

The judge looked up, spotted Seth and gave an imperceptible nod. Seth's face was impassive. They had attended the same military school years before and met a few times since then at one social event or another.

"How long have you held that position?"

Tessa's chin rose. "Two weeks, your honor."

"Not a very long employment history," her aunt and uncle's attorney interjected.

Tessa turned and looked the man up and down. "It is if you work for Seth Barrett. His last three assistants left within the first week."

The judge coughed to cover his laughter and put a hand over his mouth. "Mr. Barrett," he said at last, "is what Ms. Edwards says true?"

Seth arched one thick blond brow at Tessa's back and drawled, "Yes, your honor. What Ms. Edwards says is indeed true, both about her employment and the length of employment of my previous assistants. I might also add she has proven herself to be a very valuable employee. She shows remarkable responsibility and maturity for her age."

The judge nodded and turned his attention to Zach. He rose from his seat and said, "Why don't you join me in chambers for a few minutes so we can talk man-to-man?"

Zach stepped forward and followed the judge into his office off the courtroom. Tessa turned to look at Seth where he lounged in the row right behind her. While her facial features remained serene, her eyes were a little wider than normal. It was enough to betray her anxiety.

"You'll be fine," Seth reassured her. "Trust me on this one."

In a couple minutes, Zach and the judge returned to the courtroom. The boy had a sucker stuck in his cheek and a smile that seemed to go from ear to ear.

"I see no reason to separate this young man from his sister," the judge said, staring at Tessa before turning his attention to her aunt and uncle. "She's shown over the past year she's putting the needs of her brother first and providing a nurturing home environment. Petition to grant custody to Kathleen and Edwin Price is denied."

Tessa laughed and hugged her brother to her. As she closed her eyes next to the boy's thick red hair, Seth saw one small tear trickle from the corner of her left eye. He swallowed. He understood how close the bond between brother and sister could be. He had often filled the role of protector for Anna. The sad part, he thought, was it was very often against their parents.

He caught Kathleen and Edwin Price glaring at Tessa and him. Seth arched a brow and stared at them. In a few seconds, they hurried from the courtroom.

"Why don't I take you both out to a late lunch to celebrate?"

Zach nodded with enthusiasm, but Tessa shook her head. "You don't need to do that, Mr. Barrett."

"One thing you need to realize about me, Tessa, is I do nothing I don't want to do." A startled blue gaze flicked his way. He had shaken her composure. He smiled.

Chapter 3

Tessa watched Seth in amazement as he engaged Zach in conversation. She was seeing a side to the man she'd never seen before. Seth seldom smiled, but Zach still responded to the way her boss treated him. He listened to the boy as if what Zach told him about the Avatar game was the most interesting thing he had heard all day. Tessa half expected Seth to take them to some stuffy, expensive restaurant, so when they pulled into a popular burger joint, she interrupted.

"Mr. Barrett, you don't have to eat here because Zach's with us."

Seth turned his piercing gaze on her. "I'm not. I always please myself. I like burgers, and I would kill for a chocolate shake right about now."

"Let's eat outside at the picnic tables," Zach piped up from the back seat.

"You're the boss today," Seth replied. As they got out of the car, he took off his suit coat and folded it across the back of his seat.

It was hot out. Tessa unbuttoned her jacket. She hadn't intended taking it off, but perspiration was already beading on her forehead, so she slid it off to reveal an ice blue sleeveless silk top that plunged in a deep V in front and back. She caught Seth staring at her full breasts where the silk pulled across them. Heat spread over her cheeks. It was the only time she felt he'd seen her as a woman, and it made her even warmer than she already was. He didn't look at her like that again, and Tessa was able to relax. By the end of the meal, she and Zach were both laughing, and even her taciturn boss grinned.

He took them home. Tessa seldom drove her car, taking the train because it was easier and more economical. She leased an apartment, part of an older converted house. It gave Zach a small yard for play. The home was in a working-class neighborhood where neighbors were still careful to maintain what they owned. It was a far cry from the area where they'd lived before her parents' car crash, but it worked well for her to get to and from her job. She was sure it wasn't anywhere near what Seth was accustomed to, but she could afford it, and it was safe.

"Would you like to come in?" Tessa invited, keeping her tone polite.

"No. I still have some work to finish at home tonight."

He put the SUV in park and came around to help her down. As he took her hand, Tessa met his eyes. "Thank you so much for today. It meant a lot to Zach, and," she murmured, "it meant a lot to me."

Seth still held her hand, his hooded gaze a little searching. His mouth quirked. "Don't expect it every day."

Tessa nodded. "Thanks again, sir."

"Seth," he corrected. "My name's Seth."

Tessa's heart kicked up a notch. "Seth."

She stared after the SUV as it disappeared down the street. Call him Seth? No way. He was Mr. Barrett, and it was going to stay that way, even if his glance sometimes made her stomach flutter. Nevertheless, she took extra care with her appearance the next morning as she got ready for work. She settled on a salmon-colored linen dress with a bolero jacket to cover the spaghetti straps. It was one of those outfits that could go from day to evening. Not that she ever had occasion for that to happen. Living with a ten-year-old had ended her dating life, and she'd never had much of one to begin with.

Tessa felt reassured when she opened the heavy doors into Seth's office to take coffee to him, and he was back to grunting monosyllabic directions at her. He hardly spared a glance at her when she entered. While she was relieved, some small part of her felt disappointed he hadn't noticed her. It was better like this. Yesterday had been an afternoon out of time, in which she and Seth had met on equal footing and he'd been human. Heaven knew that was unlikely to occur again.

He worked her like a treadmill right up to lunchtime, then asked, "Can you go with me to a dinner tonight?"

Tessa stopped on her way out of his office. "Pardon me?"

Seth scowled. "Would you go with me to a dinner tonight, Tessa?"

"Zach..."

The latest unfortunate pencil snapped in his fingers. Seth sighed. "I know. I shouldn't have asked. My mother is involved with Habitat for Humanity. They're holding a charity dinner tonight I agreed to go to last minute."

Tessa paused. She had worked on several Habitat projects while she was an undergraduate, some as far away as South America. "I...I can get my neighbor to watch Zach. She won't mind."

Laura Browning

Seth looked up from the papers on his desk he'd been frowning at and smiled. Tessa's breath caught in her throat. It transformed his face. He was beautiful. It wasn't something she would say about a man as a rule, but it applied to Seth. When he smiled, he metamorphosed from a jungle cat into an angel.

"Thank you, Tessa."

When she returned from lunch, he was back to the lion with a thorn in his foot. At four, he sat back and stretched.

"Do you need to change?"

Tessa shook her head. "I just need a few minutes to do something with my hair."

"Right." Seth stood and rubbed a hand across his cheek. "I'll shave and put on a fresh shirt."

Even as he said the words, he loosened his tie and pulled his shirt free of his suit pants. It was an intimate gesture from a man who always seemed so formal. Tessa averted her gaze as she got up to leave.

"I'll be ready in a few minutes, sir."

"Tessa," he called.

"Yes, Mr. Barrett?" She turned back to see him clad in a sleeveless undershirt. The muscles of his arms were large and defined, as was his chest she noticed. Heat rushed to her cheeks again, which flustered her more. The atmosphere was far too intimate.

"Call me Seth. I'm supposed to be bringing a date."

"Yes, Seth."

Tessa hurried from his office and down the hall to the women's restroom. She leaned against the door after it closed and took a deep breath. Seth was disturbing enough in his dark, formal suits. Seeing him in an undershirt had thrown her and made her far too aware of him as an attractive, single male. His chest had been sprinkled with golden hair. For some reason she had always pictured blond men as smooth, but she should have guessed from the thick mane of hair on his head that he would be different. His beard was heavy enough that by the end of the day, he always looked in need of a shave.

Tessa walked over to the mirror and went to work. She loosened the sleek chignon she had worn during the day and instead piled her hair higher but more loosely on her head. After pulling a couple of tendrils loose at her temples where they curled, she redid her makeup and added a touch of perfume between her breasts. Lastly, she removed the bolero jacket to reveal the form-fitting top of the dress. It outlined her full breasts, while still leaving the delicate bones of her shoulders bare. Maybe she'd been psychic when she'd donned it that morning.

She returned to Seth's office, knocking before entering.

"Come on in, Tessa," Seth said and turned from where he was standing at the window. His eyes widened as he took in her appearance. "You look lovely."

Tessa stared at a point over his shoulder, determined to keep things businesslike. "Thank you." She still couldn't quite get his name out, but she would work on it.

He crossed the room and took her arm. "Come on, let's go. There're drinks at my parents' home before we go to the country club. You okay with that?"

Was there no end to his last minute addendums to this dinner? Tessa glared at him. "Do I have a choice?"

Seth paused to stare at her for a moment, his eyes shuttered. "No," he said and walked on.

When they passed the door to the stairwell, Tessa frowned at Seth's back.

"Mr....Seth... The stairs."

Seth turned a cool look on her. "We're going to use my father's private elevator."

"But..."

"Trust me."

Seth inserted the key at the side of the gold double doors at the end of the hall. Tessa stood next to him. Her heartbeat had already accelerated. She closed her eyes as she heard the doors slide open.

"Open your eyes, Tessa," Seth prompted. Was there just a trace of humor in his tone?

"Oh."

Alexander Barlow-Barrett's elevator was built into the outside wall of the building. The far wall looked right outside.

"Try it." Seth urged. "If it works, I'll give you my key."

She stepped inside, fighting the slight unease as the doors shut. She kept her gaze fixed on the view beyond the glass wall. While her heart beat a little faster, her breathing stayed normal and she didn't feel as though she was about to pass out.

"How was that?" Seth asked as they reached the bottom.

"Much better. Thank you." She didn't think she could handle it if Barrett were a high-rise, but such a quick ride might be okay.

They were both quiet as he headed out of the district into Fairfax. The roads narrowed and emptied. The passing scenery switched from offices and strip malls to rolling fields and trees, until Seth turned down a long, oak-lined drive. It opened up to reveal a sprawling three-story house sitting atop a grass-covered hill.

"This is it," Seth said in a tone that did nothing to express any real pleasure. "The house where I grew up."

"It's beautiful," Tessa said.

"Hmph." Seth was back to grunting. "I should warn you, my mother can be more of a dragon sometimes than my father."

Tessa swallowed. Great. Seth was carnivorous enough without facing an entire family of meat eaters. The vision of his father and a no doubt equally intimidating matriarch picking their teeth with her bones was not in the least humorous, at least not at the moment.

He helped her out of the SUV and then held her elbow as if he feared she might run. A uniformed butler opened the door as they approached. Tessa's eyes widened slightly. A butler? Who on earth still had a butler? Good Lord, even her father's family wasn't that snobbish.

"Tessa." Seth growled the warning under his breath, somehow aware of her reaction and the likelihood she might voice it out loud, along with a pronouncement on how pretentious it was.

"Mr. Seth," the butler intoned in a crisp British accent. "How good to see you. Shall I announce you and the young lady?"

Seth grimaced. "No, Forbes. I'll take care of it."

As they walked down the hallway, Tessa whispered, "A butler?"

Seth looked around to make sure they were alone before he stopped and turned her to face him. "What else did you expect, Tessa? You've met my father and Tallmadge. Did you think it would be any less stuffy at his home?"

Tessa looked up at him. She'd always thought he resembled a dangerous, caged animal, but what she saw in those eyes at Barrett Newspapers was nothing compared to what she saw now. At the moment, he looked more hunted than caged.

She remembered that feeling. It had been years since she'd experienced it, but she still vividly recalled it. Without thinking, she raised her hand to touch his chest. "I'm sorry."

Seth covered her slender fingers with his big hand and squeezed. Some of the hunted look left his expression.

"It's okay." He leaned closer to her. "Look, my mother is trying to match me up with some horse-faced debutante from the club. I know it's asking a lot, Tessa, but if you could make it seem..." He trailed off in what appeared to be embarrassment.

"Like we're romantically involved?" Tessa supplied, gaining confidence even as he seemed to lose it.

Seth ran a finger around his collar. "Well, yes."

"Okay."

"Okay?"

"That's what I said." As she heard someone approach the doorway they were standing outside, she stepped closer to Seth and slid her hand around his neck to pull his head down to her. She meant only to brush his lips with hers, but the difference in their heights, even with her heels, threw her off balance. Her body rested against his, her breasts crushed to his chest. As if by instinct, Seth brought his hands to her waist, but instead of just balancing her, he pulled her closer and slanted his firm mouth across hers. A delicate cough sent the two of them apart. Seth still maintained a casual arm around Tessa's waist.

"Good evening, Mother." He greeted her as if they hadn't been caught in the act of exchanging a heated kiss. "Allow me to present Miss Tessa Edwards."

Plucked brows arched with an inbred haughtiness, his mother eyed Tessa, who heard his soft groan. She realized the woman was about to pull out all the blueblood stops. No doubt she would try to freeze her to death with politeness.

"Are you from the Loudoun Edwards family?" his mother asked with a tone that seemed to imply the utter impossibility of such a thing.

Tessa smiled, deciding she was going to enjoy this. "Yes, ma'am, I am." She ignored the warning squeeze she felt from Seth's hand at her waist. It was obvious to Tessa that Mrs. Barlow-Barrett wanted a pedigree, so she would give her one. "My daddy was Robert Edwards of Mont Clair Park."

From the corner of her eyes, Tessa saw Seth's open-mouthed amazement. Even better, she watched as his mother thawed completely and smiled, speculation now replacing the haughtiness. "Welcome, dear. You must call me Tricia."

"And I'm Tessa."

* * * *

Seth watched in complete awe as Tessa worked everyone in the room. Gone was the ice queen of the office. In her place was a sparkling debutante to rival anything ever dangled in front of him before. Seth wasn't sure what to think. The thought even crossed his mind that Tessa had gotten the job as his assistant through some nefarious plot on the part of his parents. As they drove to the country club, he glanced at her in confusion.

"Did you make all that up back there?" he asked at last.

Tessa looked at him. "Make what up?"

"That bit about Robert Edwards?"

Tessa stared at him. "No. He was my father. He died of cancer when I was five. I don't remember him all that well."

"Hmph."

"Stop grunting, Seth."

"Do you have any other surprises for me?" he growled as they pulled into the club parking lot.

Tessa brushed a speck of lint from her skirt. "Not that I know of."

He watched her through dinner. She charmed everyone, from Habitat do-gooders to the dilettantes who always seemed to be hanging around somewhere. Seth stayed close to her side, because he realized it wasn't just the women she affected. He'd never given it much thought while they worked, but Tessa Edwards was a beautiful, intelligent woman who possessed a natural magnetism that drew people of both sexes to her.

As they waited for the valet to bring up his SUV, Seth studied her. She was beginning to droop.

"If you come from the Loudoun Edwards, why do you need to work to support Zach?"

Tessa looked at him, her eyes shuttered. "My father had a pedigree, not money. It was something he had a hard time dealing with, according to my mother. I don't care about either one. I want to earn a decent living until I can get Zach situated."

"Then what do you want?" Seth probed.

For the first time, he saw some of the same feelings reflected in her eyes that he'd experienced. That feeling of being caged.

"I don't know. I haven't had the chance to figure that out. I hadn't imagined being responsible for a child before I was twenty-five."

He helped her into the car and then strode around to get in on his side. They didn't speak again for a while. She was a surprise. More than that, Tessa Edwards was an enigma, and for the first time in a long while, Seth discovered he was intrigued enough to want to know more.

* * * *

"Tessa." Seth's voice came from a distance. "Tessa, wake up." Closer now. In fact, very near her ear. "Come on, Tess, wake up."

Tessa smiled. She was having the loveliest dream of the ocean complete with the feel of salt spray in her face. She and Zach were laughing.

"Tessa," Seth prompted again. "You're home."

There was laughter in his voice and his breath was a whisper against her cheeks. She turned her head at the same time she opened her eyes.

"You're home," Seth said again. Silence stretched as they continued to stare at one another. Seth's gaze drifted to her mouth, and Tessa self-consciously licked her lips. Their eyes met again.

"I should go in," she whispered, but she made no move to leave.

Seth's large hand came up and he brushed the backs of his fingers against her cheek.

"Thank you, Tessa."

"For what?" she asked in confusion, staring at his wide, firm mouth.

"For agreeing to go with me tonight. For giving up some of your own time." Seth quit talking for a moment. "I am about to make a very big mistake." He slid his hand behind her head and leaned closer. "Tell me to stop," he whispered as his mouth brushed hers.

"Seth." His name came out on a breath as her heart thudded in her chest. The saner part of her agreed with him. It was a mistake. Sanity prevailed. She leaned back. As soon as she pressed against his hand, he released her and sat back.

"I'm sorry," he said in his usual gruff voice. "That should never have happened."

He opened his door and came around the gleaming black SUV to open the door for her. Tessa met his golden eyes again before taking his outstretched hand.

"Tessa." He seemed to want to say something else, but stopped. "Thanks again. I'll see you tomorrow morning."

She nodded and hurried up the walk to the big, old house. She knew Seth stood there watching until she was inside. Only then did she hear the sound of the engine as the Cadillac pulled away from the curb.

Chapter 4

Seth sat in his office the next morning staring out the windows. He didn't really see what was outside. The beauty of the sunrise over the DC skyline had no impact on him. Without giving it much thought, he snapped one pencil in two, then another and another.

Tessa.

He hadn't been able to get her off his mind. There were so many layers to the woman, he wasn't even sure what was real. Educated at Smith. From a Virginia family with blood bluer than his own. Working as his secretary? The pieces didn't fit. Any way he turned them, they just did not fit. The logical part of his mind searched for some ulterior motive, some reason beyond needing a job for why she was working at Barrett Newspapers. He couldn't buy into the hare-brained thought that she was there at his parents' instigation.

And what about his feelings? She fascinated him. The way she protected her little brother, stepping in as a surrogate parent when she wasn't much more than a kid herself. He looked forward to her arrival every morning. He had spent so many years feeling caged in this office, doing the duty expected of him, he sometimes wondered if he'd ever done anything else. Tessa brought a vibrancy that broke through the bars of his cage despite the obvious restraints she put on herself. He remembered her as she had looked last night, laughing and animated.

She stirred him at so many levels, he couldn't even begin to describe it. But she was so young. His logical mind intruded even here, bringing him back to earth with a thud. What would she want with him? Cool, calm Tessa. Even last night, she had been the realist. Not him. And that was the biggest reason to tread with care. Underneath it all, he was too idealistic for his own good.

"Good morning, Mr. Barrett." She greeted him with a small smile as she set his coffee on the desk.

He glared back at her. As much as his fingers itched to loosen that fiery red hair and feel it slide through his fingers as it fell around her shoulders, he would keep this on a business footing. He was not some kid fresh out of school.

"Bring the laptop and your coffee in here, Tessa. I want to work on more details on the Midwest Papers acquisition, and then you need to make arrangements for me to return to Chicago tomorrow." He paused. "Is there any way you can go along? I know it's short notice, but I have the feeling I could use another set of eyes and ears on the negotiations. We need to leave tomorrow morning, with a return Friday afternoon. I'm hoping this will clinch the deal."

Her lack of an instant response showed he'd caught her off-guard. Yet she must have known travel might be a part of the job.

"It's not a problem." She recovered quickly. "I can have a neighbor watch Zach. She's retired and stays at home most often. Do you want to take a commercial flight or use the corporate jet?"

"The jet," Seth replied. "Brandon's back, so it's available. Pack something dressy for Thursday night. I believe we'll be celebrating."

She nodded.

He was relieved it had been that easy. He was also relieved when they settled down to work. Tessa was so fast at following his train of thought, it made finalizing the acquisition details a snap. She excused herself mid-morning to type up the final copies and finish arrangements for the trip.

Seth watched her go. She was back to being the ice queen again, with a vengeance. He missed the softer, befuddled Tessa who had fallen asleep in his SUV. Perhaps that was for the best. He sighed and snapped yet another pencil in two. Before she left in the afternoon, Seth made arrangements to pick her up the following morning.

* * * *

Tessa was already waiting for him, her laptop and oversized purse in one hand, a hanging bag in the other, when he pulled up to the curb in the darkness of the following morning. He strode up the sidewalk, suit coat open and tie askew, and took the bags from her, stowing them in the back of the SUV before opening the door for her.

"Coffee?" he asked, pointing to a cup from Starbucks.

Tessa glanced at the cup holder with curiosity. Did the entire world revolve around getting Seth Barrett coffee? Even to the point of Starbucks opening at this hour?

"Thanks," she murmured, surprised when the coffee was prepared the way she liked it--plenty of cream and no sugar. She would never have guessed he even noticed how someone else preferred their caffeine. Every time she thought she had him figured out, he showed her some new aspect to his character. The problem, of course, was that what he revealed just made him more appealing.

On the long list of things Tessa had never done, riding in a private jet was definitely one of the entries, so she was amazed when Seth drove right onto the tarmac and up to the waiting aircraft. The pilot was there to help them load their belongings, and a waiting ground crew employee from the private aviation service hopped into the SUV to park it.

The jet looked like a long, narrow metal tube, and sudden trepidation filled her. Even the windows didn't reassure her. Her palms started to sweat and her pulse increased. What if it was like being in an elevator? As she sucked in a deep breath, Seth turned, his foot on the bottom stair.

"Tessa, you have flown before, haven't you?"

"Once or twice," she replied in a tight voice.

He arched one thick brow and gazed steadily from those leonine eyes. "How was it?"

She shrugged. "It was okay."

He smiled and stood aside for her to precede him. "This will be better. I promise."

Tessa wasn't as confident, but she stepped inside the jet and was struck right away by how open it felt in comparison to a commercial airliner. This wasn't designed to pack people in like sardines. It had been designed for the comfort of five or six people at most. She wasn't sure if the windows were larger, but they seemed to be.

Seth put a hand on her shoulder, squeezing. "Well?"

Tessa turned and smiled gratefully at him. It surprised her to see the warmth of concern in his gaze.

"This is fine, Mr. Barrett," she sighed.

Seth chuckled at her obvious relief. "You will need to strap yourself in for takeoff, but after we're up you can move around."

Tessa nodded. This was so much better than the couple of times she had flown to and from school. Most often, she took the train because it didn't feel as confining as an airplane. The whine of the engines increased as they sped down the runway. Tessa watched their ascent make everything on the ground shrink. When they reached cruising altitude, Seth came over and sat in the chair across from her, the Starbucks cup still in his hand.

"I thought we could talk a little bit about what I need you to do during our meetings today."

Seth outlined his plans. He was presenting the final proposal to the Midwest Papers board and hoped to get their vote. She would need to take detailed notes of the meeting and be ready to go with an altered proposal the following morning if the board wasn't satisfied with his initial plan. He wanted this deal clinched before they returned home.

"If we can reach an agreement with Midwest," Seth added, "we'll be a presence in more than a third of the major newspaper markets in the US. As things stand right now, that could be crucial for the future of Barrett Newspapers." He turned his face toward the window and gazed out. Watching his reflection, she saw him close his eyes and heard him sigh.

Tessa startled him a moment later, she could see from his reaction. "You don't really like any of this, do you, Mr. Barrett?"

Seth opened his eyes, staring at her with an intensity that might have unnerved a lot of people, but not her. Not today. She had discovered the thorn that might be making this lion snarl all the time. Although she would never let anyone take Zach from her, she did understand being confined by duty. In her case, it was a duty she loved. But was it for Seth?

"I never wanted this," Seth admitted. "I'm tired of pretending. It's an obligation to me. My love has always been journalism--the research, reporting, writing. The best times of my life were the four years fresh out of college. As plain Seth Barlow, I reported and wrote from all over the world."

"Then why do you do it?" Tessa wondered if she was hoping for some validation for what she herself was going through.

Seth's mouth quirked. "Probably for the same reason you took the job as my secretary. Out of a sense of duty. Yours is to your brother. Mine is to my father. As the eldest son, everyone assumed I would take over. I was earmarked to be the next Barlow-Barrett paper tycoon, whether I wanted it or not. Other than those four years freelancing, my entire existence has been spent trying to please Alexander Barlow-Barrett." He paused and his generous lips stretched into a quick smile. "Perhaps we do have some things in common, hmm?"

Tessa laughed at his odd sense of humor. "An overdeveloped sense of duty is not the basis for a match made in heaven."

Seth's expression turned serious once again. "Maybe more than you think."

She chose to ignore him. She had to focus on Zach. Exploring the possibility of a personal relationship with any man, let alone the scion of another blue-blooded Virginia family, was impossible.

The pilot interrupted their conversation to inform them over the intercom that they were beginning their descent. Per Seth's request, a limousine met them at the airport. The driver took them to Midwest's headquarters in downtown Chicago. Tessa told him she would contact him a half hour before they needed to be picked up.

She turned to follow Seth into the building, and hit the first glitch in her otherwise perfect planning. The conference room they were going to was on the twentieth floor. Tessa began to panic. She couldn't climb that many stairs. Seth took her by the elbow and led her to the back of the elevator. She sighed in relief as she saw it was designed to give her a view of the street as they ascended.

"You all right?" he asked under his breath.

She nodded and even managed to look at him with a small smile. He stared hard at her for a moment and inclined his head. Nevertheless, she found that brief acknowledgement of her fears reassuring.

They entered the conference room exactly on time. It was another quirk of Seth's she had at first found very amusing, as if it had been drummed into him since birth: a Barlow-Barrett was never early or late, but always right on time. As his executive assistant, Tessa found she was all but invisible to the executives of Midwest. That suited her fine. She settled into her seat behind Seth, who was given a seat of honor at one end of the conference table, and set up her laptop.

Tessa knew Barrett was putting an excellent offer on the table. Like papers all across the country, Midwest had undergone a drop in circulation that translated into declining ad revenues, and a drop in the stock value of the company. Seth's proposal would not just buy Midwest, it would pump more money into the firm.

Barrett had done an excellent job with its other holdings in developing alternative revenue sources, like websites and joint ventures with other media, and was prepared to put the investment into Midwest to do the same thing. Tessa could tell from the financial sheets that Midwest couldn't launch a similar undertaking without Barrett's backing.

Tessa observed the players at the table even as she took notes, and the only reluctance she detected was on the part of Midwest's chairman, but that could be enough to nix the deal. He was an older man, older than Alexander Barrett. Unlike the younger executives with their designer suits and slick hair, he was dressed as if his mind were on more important things than the business at hand. In fact, he reminded Tessa of her English Lit professor at Smith.

There was a break in negotiations about mid-morning. Seth excused himself and asked Tessa to join him. He took her arm and led her out to a small terrace at one end of the building.

"What do you think?" He asked once the door shut. This high above the city, the breeze ruffled her tightly confined hair.

"I think you're not selling the chairman."

"Damn!" Seth turned to stare out of the skyline of the city, his jaw clenching in frustration.

"Mr. Barrett… Seth," Tessa said, "I didn't say you can't sell him on your plan. I said you're not."

He turned and studied her without smiling. "And what do you think I need to do?"

Tessa looked him straight in the eye. She might not have his years of experience, but she had learned a lot about human nature, good and bad, through her own childhood and her work with juveniles and their families.

"Play to your strength. You've enumerated all of the sound business reasons for the acquisition, but you haven't mentioned the thing you love, and more to the point, the thing I believe Mr. Golding loves…the journalism."

"What makes you believe he cares more about the papers' journalistic stature?"

Tessa smiled. "Present company excepted, he has the stereotypical look of the reporter or editor who is so focused on other things, they forget their appearance. If you look, I bet the man still has printer's ink under his fingernails."

When she paused, Seth waved his hand for her to keep going.

"Now we're into your area of expertise," she told him. "So think of it from that position. How would this acquisition make Golding's newspapers stronger journalistically? Will a stronger internet presence bring more national and international attention to quality columnists?"

Seth scratched the back of his thick blond hair before grinning at her.

"You are a genius, Tessa!" He grabbed her face in his hands and kissed her on the lips. Heat flooded her cheeks and other areas she didn't even want to think about. Before she could feel any awkwardness, he took her elbow to lead her back inside. "Let's go close this deal."

And Seth proceeded to do just that. By lunchtime, Jacob Golding was smiling and slapping him on the back like they'd known each other for years.

"Let me buy you lunch, Barrett. We'll work out a few more things and get the contracts out."

Seth cast one look over his shoulder at Tessa, who smiled at him and went back to packing her things. She knew the invitation didn't include her and didn't care. It would be easy enough to pick something up at the deli she'd seen down the street, maybe even give her a chance to look around. She'd never been to Chicago before. She was the last one out of the conference room, juggling her laptop case and her oversize bag.

With a heavy sigh, she looked at the stairwell, but there was no way she could carry all of her belongings down twenty flights, and she was reluctant to leave anything behind in the conference room where someone could get access to it. She marched toward the elevator and pressed the down button. She could do this by herself. She was sure of it. After all, she'd ridden up in it, even if it was with Seth, and didn't she ride in Alexander Barrett's elevator every day now? She'd come a long way. It would be a breeze.

The doors opened and Tessa stepped on. After punching the button for the lobby, she retreated to the back of the car and stared out the window. The doors snicked shut and the elevator moved. Tessa didn't even look at the floor numbers; she kept her eyes focused outside. The elevator lurched to a stop, so she expected to hear the sound of the doors and more people getting on. When all that followed was silence, she pivoted to look at the floor indicator. Both nine and ten glowed, and the gold-toned metal doors remained sealed.

Tessa's heart hammered, and she took a slow, deep breath. Stay calm. She pressed the button asking the elevator doors to open, but nothing happened. She then tried pressing the button once more for the lobby, but again nothing happened. Finally, she noticed the phone and picked that up.

"Security."

"I'm in the elevator at the rear of the building. It seems to be stuck between the ninth and tenth floors."

"Sorry, Miss," the guard on the other end said. "There's a problem with it."

"I'm more than aware of that." Tessa breathed in exasperation. "I'm stuck in here."

"There's no need to take that tone, Miss," the guard responded. "We've called the repair company and they should be here within the hour. Is there anybody else in there with you?"

An hour. Her mind barely registered what he'd asked as she closed her eyes and tried to calm herself down.

"Miss? Is there anyone else in there with you?"

"No," Tessa answered him in a voice that had begun to shake.

"Are you okay?" The security guard's tone still held that impersonal politeness saved for strangers. The roaring started in her ears and the guard's voice sounded as if it came from a long way away. It was like when she was a child and she and her cousins would play telephone with empty towel paper rolls.

"I'm claustrophobic," she whispered at long last. "Please, can't you get me out of here?"

"I'm sorry, Miss, not until the repairmen get here." The guard sounded more sympathetic, even apologetic, but not as though he was going to make any additional effort to free her from the shrinking box in which she was trapped. Didn't the man understand what she was going through? Didn't he realize how awful it was to be locked into such a small space with no way out?

Tessa hung up the phone and retreated to the corner of the elevator, where she could keep her eyes on the Chicago skyline. Her bag and the laptop case slipped from her hands. She worked very hard to control her breathing, but the fear closed in on her and she clutched at her chest. She kept remembering that day so many years ago. Everyone had thought it was a big joke. It hadn't been then, and it was not now.

They had gone to Mont Clair. Tessa had been nine that summer, and her mother had left her for the day to play with her cousins. Tessa still remembered how she and the rest of the younger children had always giggled and laughed. The big old house and grounds had been one gigantic playground, filled with all sorts of fascinating things.

They had played hide and seek around the house and barn. Until then, it had been one of her favorite games. As small as Tessa had been at nine, she could squeeze into some pretty tight spots. This time she had managed to wiggle her way into an old trunk out in the barn. Someone had moved it from the tack room to the loft. She had closed the lid, meaning to leave it open a crack, but that wasn't what happened. It had jammed, or felt like it had. Tessa had always suspected someone had a helping hand in that. While it had been open enough she could get air, she couldn't escape. By the time anyone heard her and found her, Tessa had been only half-conscious.

She fought back the suffocating panic and forced herself back to the present. Call Seth. She could call Seth. She grabbed for her oversized purse and rummaged through it. Her hands were sweating so much it took her a while to find the phone. She found his name in her contacts and punched Send.

The phone rang.

"This is Seth Barrett…"

"Seth!" Tessa felt a wave of relief.

"…I'm not available at the moment."

Tessa hit End and sank down the wall of the elevator until she sat on the floor. She tried texting him, but her hands shook too much. Disappointment swirled through her along with the ever-growing gnawing feeling that she was trapped. Her teeth chattered and she trembled to such a degree, she dropped the phone to the floor beside her.

Hang on, one small part of her rational mind urged. Just keep looking outside and hang on. She turned her head away from the solidly shut metal doors to stare at the bright summer day. Cars and people moved about, made smaller by the distance of nine floors. She hated herself for it, but she could not stop the slow tears oozing from the corners of her eyes. She picked up the phone again and hit Redial. She had to leave a message.

"Seth," she said in a shaky whisper, all pretense of formality gone. "It's Tessa. Please call. I…I'm stuck in the elevator. Please, please call." She disconnected and stared once again out the window. It wasn't like all the other times. She could see. It wasn't dark, and it would be an hour, maybe less. They were working to fix the problem. That's what the security guard had told her. She knew she would get out. It would be okay. They wouldn't leave her here, wouldn't forget about her.

It wasn't working. Her breathing turned shallower and faster. Time inched by. Tessa pressed her palm flat against the glass and leaned her forehead against it. The coolness of the thick pane did nothing to soothe her. A small, frightened sob escaped.

Stop it! She hated the feeling of being confined, but she hated even more how the panic made her lose control. Tessa forced herself to take a deep breath, afraid she would hyperventilate. She managed another deep breath. One at a time, she kept reminding herself. One breath at a time. It helped to relax her a little.

The elevator lurched once and she looked with hope at the floor indicator lights, but then there was nothing. No more movement, and the doors remained as shut as always. She was no longer certain how long she'd been stuck. When her phone rang, Tessa scrambled to find it. Her hands trembled so much she had to hold it with both of them.

"H-hello." Her voice was a thin shaky whisper.

"Tessa." Seth's voice was low and calm. "It's Seth. Which elevator are you in?"

Tessa tried to choke back a sob, but didn't quite succeed. "In the elevator with the windows," she muttered.

"Are you by yourself?" His voice stroked her frayed nerves, and she latched onto it like a lifeline.

"Yes."

"I'm getting on another elevator in the lobby. How long have you been in there?"

Tessa sucked in a deep breath and let it out on a shaky sigh. Time didn't have any meaning for her at the moment.

"I--I don't know," she said at last. "I can't remember. Please get me out of here, Seth. Please. I thought I could ride the elevator by myself. I thought it would be okay..." She trailed off as her throat tightened once again with panic.

"It will be. I'm right outside the door now, here on the ninth floor. Okay? Just a few feet away. Can you hang in there for me?"

Tessa glanced at the doors. Why wouldn't they open? "I'll try."

"You can stay on the phone with me. Does that help?"

"Yes." Her voice shook again. Tessa darted a look from the door back to the skyline outside. If she could just get out.

"Where do you like to go best with Zach, sweetheart?"

"What?" She couldn't get her mind around what he was asking.

"Where do you like to take Zach when you want to relax and get away?"

"The beach." Tessa latched onto the soothing timbre of his voice as if it were a lifeline tossed into a stormy sea.

"Okay. I want you to close your eyes and think about walking across the sand. Paint a picture in your imagination. It's early in the morning and the tide is out. The sand is cool against the soles of your feet because the sun hasn't yet warmed it. You and Zach are hunting for shells. In the distance you hear the gentle slap of the waves as they drift into shore. There's no one there besides you two. Just infinite sea, sand, and sky with gulls wheeling overhead."

Tessa began to relax as she pictured the scene he described. Her breathing evened out and her heart started to slow its frantic pace. She smoothed a shaky hand over her skirt, plucking at the fabric out of habit.

"Are you there?" she whispered.

"Sure I am. You're watching me windsurf beyond the breakers. Zach is laughing and pointing because he wants to learn too, but you won't let him yet."

"He's too little," she agreed.

"That's right." Seth kept her going. "But you're not. So this weekend I will take you both to the beach. We can fish and sail. How does that sound?"

"You don't have to do that." Wistfulness colored her voice even as she made the protest.

"Yes, Tessa, I do," he said. "We could all use a break. It will be a celebration."

She stared out the window again, hitched a breath but couldn't seem to get enough air in her lungs. It was stifling and suffocating.

"H-how much longer will it be?" she asked in a small voice.

There was a pause on the other end. "Not much longer, Tessa. You okay?"

"I want out, Seth. Please, please get me out." Tessa's voice dwindled away, and she swallowed another sob. "Please, Seth."

The elevator lurched again, dropping a few feet. A ding sounded and the doors whisked open. Tessa turned her head as Seth pushed past the security guard and the maintenance worker. He bent and picked her up, cradling her against his chest. Tessa had never been so glad to see his dear, scowling face. Over his shoulder he barked at the security guard to get her purse and the laptop. Someone opened an office door for them and Seth took her into a spacious corner office with plenty of windows. He started to set her in a large overstuffed chair near the windows, but she clung to him.

"Please. Hold onto me for a minute. I'll be okay."

He sat down in the chair instead, and brought her with him on his lap, her head tucked under his chin.

"I'm sorry, Tessa," he murmured. "I should never have left you on your own, knowing you would have to take the elevator. I don't know what I was thinking."

The steady beat of his heart beneath her ear was soothing.

She shook her head against him. "It's not your fault."

Her breathing settled back to normal and she became conscious of his large hand where it rested against her thigh. This was her boss. Fear may have left, but now embarrassment flooded in. She should be standing on her own two feet, not leaning on him for support.

"I--I should get up. We need to finish the contracts."

She straightened away from Seth's solid chest, her back ramrod straight. He reached into the inside breast pocket of his suit coat and produced a large white linen handkerchief. As he handed it to her, she noticed his initials were embroidered in the corner of it.

"Wipe your eyes, Tessa." The order was gently spoken. "I've called the limo. I want you to go to the hotel and relax. All we have to do is sign the contracts, thanks to you, and I think I can handle that."

Tessa opened her mouth to protest.

Seth set a finger against her lips. "No arguments. You've been through something that would have rattled anyone, let alone someone who's claustrophobic, and you've still got to get back down to the ground floor. If you don't want to get back in the elevator, I understand. I'll be happy to walk down with you."

Tessa scrambled off his lap and smoothed her skirt. She gulped. This man was her boss, and she had clung to him like some helpless airhead. She detested women who tried to appear weak and helpless. It so went against her grain, just thinking about it made her stomach tie up in knots.

There was a mirror in the far corner. She grabbed her purse from the chair where the security guard had left it and went over to repair her hair and make-up. It gave her something to do, a chance to regain her composure. She needed that now more than ever. She had never begged a man to hold her. How mortifying.

* * * *

Seth watched her, eyes narrowed as his mind worked overtime. He could still hear the fear in her voice as she'd begged him to get her out. He swallowed. There had been much more than simple claustrophobia there. She had sounded traumatized. He had expected her to be worse off than she was. As he watched her, she wiped the tracks of the tears she'd shed and reapplied some of her makeup. After that, long, nimble fingers set about smoothing and pinning the sleek French twist she always wore back into place. He'd never seen her hair down. He wondered again what she would look like with it loose and flowing.

He let his gaze drift down to her narrow waist and her heart-shaped bottom, outlined by the snug suit skirt she wore. He also remembered how that firm little derriere had felt snuggled in his lap. What did she wear beneath it? Something practical or silky? He could almost feel the touch of warm silk on his fingertips.

Seth shook his head in disgust at himself and where his thoughts had gone. She was his secretary--and a damn good one, for a change. So he had better watch his step.

"Are you about ready, Tessa?" he asked, a hint of gruffness back in his voice.

She turned from the mirror, her poise back in place. "Yes, sir. I'm sorry, Mr. Barrett."

"Seth," he corrected her. "Call me Seth. It's about time we dropped some of the formality, don't you think?"

God in heaven! What was he doing? He just finished telling himself he needed to cool it, and in the very next breath he made things less formal between them? He began to wonder which head was doing the thinking for him when it came to Tessa Edwards, and he was afraid he knew the answer already.

Tessa smiled slightly. She picked up her bag, but when she bent to grab the laptop, Seth beat her to it.

"I'll get this. Come on, Tessa, the limo driver can run you to the hotel. Once you're there, take a dip in the Jacuzzi and relax."

Tessa had booked a two-bedroom suite connected with a living room between the two bedrooms. In addition, it featured a terrace with a Jacuzzi, one of the little perks that a man like Seth could not only afford but was accustomed to having.

As they stepped into the hall, Tessa turned away from the stairwell and back toward the elevator. Seth grabbed her hand to stop her.

"Are you sure?"

"Yes." Tessa's blue eyes met his. "If I don't do it now, I'll never get back on one. I can't live like that, Seth."

He took hold of her hand as they stepped in, noting her surprise, but in a moment, her slender fingers relaxed within his grip. Not until the doors opened to the lobby did he relinquish his hold. He didn't make any big deal out of it. In fact, he kept his expression as frowning as ever to ease her discomfort. She smiled at him, fingers trembling.

"Okay?"

Tessa nodded. "Thanks, Seth."

Chapter 5

It didn't take Seth long to finish closing the deal. He and Golding had enjoyed a very productive lunch. Tessa's message had cut things short, but Golding understood. Once the contracts were signed, Seth shook hands with the older man and the board.

"We'll make the announcement in the morning, Barrett, if that suits you. When you get to be my age, you don't always want to field a bunch of questions late in the day."

"Excellent, sir. Tomorrow morning is fine."

"Can I take you and your assistant to dinner tonight?" Golding offered, his expression genial.

Seth shook his head. "I appreciate the offer, but I believe Miss Edwards has had enough excitement for one day."

Golding smiled. "Another time, perhaps. It's always a pleasure to meet a fellow journalist."

The two men shook hands and parted ways in the lobby. Seth sat back in the limo, ran his fingers through his thick hair, and pulled his phone out to call his father. His conversation with Alexander Barlow-Barrett was short and to the point. The deal was closed pending shareholder and government approval. He shoved his phone back into the clip on his belt.

The conversation over his future role at Barrett Newspapers could wait until the ink had dried and he was back home where he could talk to his father face-to-face. What he had to say needed to be handled in person. It was time Alexander Barrett took a hard look at Brandon and realized he was grooming the wrong Barlow-Barrett to step into his shoes. Seth's heart was not in it, Brandon's was.

He turned his thoughts back to Tessa. Hearing the panic and fear in her message, he had felt an instant need to go to her. Getting her to think about the beach had helped. He wondered if she remembered it. Panic sometimes made people blank out about details, but he wanted her to remember. He was serious about taking her and Zach there. They could stay at his beach house, go for a nice easy sail, nothing too adventurous the first time out. He'd take Zach fishing.

Seth snorted at where his thoughts had led him. What was he hoping for? A ready-made family? Or some social life at all that didn't involve elite clubs and the rest of his family? He flicked a speck of lint off his suit slacks. He was tired of meetings, trips, formal dinners, and making meaningless small talk on topics about which he cared nothing at all. He wanted… The limo stopped in front of the hotel and the doorman rushed to open the door for him. Seth tossed him a tip and sprinted up the steps.

He wanted Tessa, but he doubted that was possible or even probable. She gave off more than the usual volume of keep-off signals. Except for an odd moment now and then, he got the feeling she not only didn't like him but secretly laughed at him. It was damned annoying and intriguing at the same time. Seth wasn't sure that anyone had dared to laugh at him, with the possible exceptions of Brandon and Anna. Even their other siblings always seemed to regard him with awe.

He opened the door of the hotel suite, surprised by how quiet it was. A quick glance around the living room showed it was empty. He stepped out on the terrace, but the Jacuzzi was still, and Tessa was nowhere out there. Seth turned toward the smaller of the two bedrooms. The door was open a crack.

"Tessa?" he murmured, but got no response.

He pushed the door farther open, feeling a little like he was intruding but concerned enough about her in the wake of the elevator incident, he went ahead and peered inside. She was wrapped in a white terry cloth robe that swallowed her. Delicate toes painted a soft pink peeked from beneath the hem. She lay on her side, one arm resting on the bed and covering her breasts, the other curled beneath her cheek. Her lips were parted in sleep, and her thick, auburn hair spilled across the pillow and around her shoulders. Seth drank in the sight of her like a man stranded in the desert getting his first sight of an oasis. She looked so tiny…and so damn young. What the hell was he doing?

He had started to withdraw when she sighed and opened her eyes. He couldn't leave now. It would seem like he was snooping. And hadn't he been? A flush warmed his cheeks.

Her eyes opened wider when she spotted him.

"Seth?" she mumbled while she struggled to wake up. "Did everything go okay?"

Relieved she hadn't taken offense at his looking in on her, he allowed himself a slight smile. "Yes. The contracts are signed. I thought I might take you out on the town. Are you up to it?"

Tessa sat up and pulled the bathrobe tighter, but not before he'd gotten a glimpse of one generous, rounded, creamy breast. "Sure. What time is it?"

"A little before five, so there's no rush. I thought I might grab a drink and sit in the Jacuzzi for a few minutes. Care to join me?"

Tessa shook her head. "Not in the Jacuzzi. I tried that and it made me sleepy, but I will come outside with you."

He nodded, pleased she would spend some time with him. She was already curled up in a lounge chair on the terrace when he came out in swim trunks, with a towel slung around his neck and a whisky in one hand. He sipped it and sighed.

"Hmm. I needed that. Would you like anything?"

"No, thanks. I have a bottle of sparkling water."

They talked about work. It seemed to be the safest topic. He liked the way she flushed with pleasure when he praised her for her insight about Golding.

She ran one of her manicured nails along the arm of the lounge. "I'm sorry about the whole elevator thing, Seth."

"Don't be. As long as you're all right, there was no harm done. Let's forget about it, okay?"

Tessa smiled. "Gladly. Where are we going to dinner?"

He arched one brow at her. "Getting hungry?"

"Well," Tessa drawled, "I didn't get any lunch."

* * * *

She watched in amazement as Seth downed the rest of his whisky in a gulp and stood up. Water dripped off his powerful body. It was all Tessa could do not to stare open-mouthed at him. The water accentuated what she had noted in the most abstract of ways before. He was muscled, as if he spent a lot of time outdoors. His golden-brown skin was covered with fine, blond hair arrowing down to the low-slung waist of his swimming trunks, which now clung to his body. Tessa's eyes wandered lower and she averted her gaze. The man was her boss. What on earth was she thinking?

"I have reservations at Charlie Trotter's for seven," Seth was saying. "Did you bring something dressy?"

"Yes."

"Great. Let's head that way then."

It was the proverbial little black dress. It had to be. Operating on a tight budget, Tessa was always careful to keep her wardrobe as classic as possible, so a short while later, she smoothed it over her hips. The material flared just past there into a swingy skirt that ended a few inches above her knees. The bodice was strapless and form-fitting, and her breasts swelled at the top of the heart shaped neckline. She added a strand of pearls and strappy stilletos.

Seth waited for her in the living room. He blinked when she walked in before he smiled at her.

"You look lovely, Tessa. Once again."

So did he. Dressed in a dark dinner suit with a pristine white shirt and a conservative gold-toned tie that brought out his unusual eyes even more, he oozed power and money. He'd brushed his thick, wavy blond hair off his face. As he held out his arm, Tessa took it without hesitation. She stepped into the elevator, which faced a central lobby, with hardly a blink of the eye, though she did keep a firm hold of Seth's arm the whole way down.

The restaurant was amazing, and so was Seth. He put himself out to entertain her. Tessa had never enjoyed such a wonderful time with anyone. For all his taciturn ways in the office, he could be a very amusing dinner companion.

"Would you like some wine to start?"

At her nod, he conferred with the sommelier before choosing a chardonnay. Once he tasted the wine and nodded, the sommelier filled her glass, then Seth's. Tessa hid a smile. She had watched many men over the years botch this part of an evening. It was refreshing to see Seth pay it no more notice than he would putting his napkin on his lap. It was just another part of dining out for him, not an ornate ordeal.

"I know you were a little stressed in the elevator today when I talked about the beach," Seth began, "but do you truly like it?"

"As long as I have a crate of sunscreen for Zach and me, we love to go as often as we can." Tessa laughed. "Zach loves fishing. I'm not that keen on it, but I try to humor him. It gets him away from the video games some."

Seth smiled. "What do you do for fun?"

"Swimming. There's something so peaceful about it, whether I'm in the ocean or working out in a pool. It's quiet, you know?"

"Mmm. That's the way I feel about sailing. Perhaps not always the quiet part, but being able to be alone with my thoughts--that's what I appreciate most." The sparkle in his eyes made it obvious how much it meant to him.

"I've never been sailing. Riding, swimming… Those things I've done, but sailing was never part of the Edwards family hobbies."

"Ah, if you ride," Seth said with a grin, "then you need to meet my sister Anna. She has a real gift with horses. She's a veterinarian in North Carolina. In fact, you remind me of her in some ways." A wicked gleam entered his topaz eyes. "Short, stubborn… Did I say short?"

Tessa arched a brow at him. "Very funny."

When they arrived back at the hotel, she was relaxed. Seth looked that way too. His verbal bantering had put them at ease with each other. She was reluctant to end the evening and return to their roles of boss and assistant. For now they were Tessa and Seth. Two people with more in common than she'd suspected. The lobby was all but deserted as they entered, the clerk at the reception desk giving them a respectful nod before returning to his work.

"There's a piano bar to the left. We could have an after-dinner drink there, if you'd like. A toast to your success."

Tessa smiled. "No, to your success."

Seth ordered cognac for himself and Tessa requested a Bailey's. When the drinks arrived, Seth lifted his glass and touched it to hers with a faint ting of crystal.

"To our first successful business venture."

They sipped in silence for a few minutes, listening to the music. One or two couples danced on the small dance floor. Tessa watched them, but was still surprised when Seth asked her to join him. She nodded, not knowing what to expect, but she should have known. He was smooth and confident, as if it was something he did all the time.

Tessa wished the evening could go on forever. It seemed Seth did too. He pulled her closer to him. One of her palms was splayed over his chest, the other hand held there by his large fingers. Seth's free hand had slipped down below the small of her back to press her hips to his thigh. Tessa soon found that the motion created liquid heat in the pit of her stomach that left her breathless.

"Maybe we should go upstairs," she said, still not at all sure she wanted the night to end, and even less sure what she was suggesting.

Seth searched her face with slumberous eyes and nodded. As they rode upstairs in the elevator, he tucked Tessa against him, keeping her there as they walked down the hall to the suite. The lights were set on dim in the main room when they entered.

"Are you tired?" Seth asked.

"Not really." Tessa's nerves tightened. Sleep would be elusive tonight.

"Join me out on the terrace? I think the lights and the view from there are something you won't want to miss."

He held the door open in invitation, then stood next to her, one arm thrown around her shoulders. There didn't seem to be much to say, but the silence wasn't uncomfortable. They both watched the lights twinkling below them. When Seth turned her toward him and tipped her head up, it was the most natural thing in the world. Then he kissed her.

Tessa's experience with men was limited at best. She'd been sheltered through her teens, and attending an all-women's college hadn't given her the constant male contact many women took for granted. Seth's stroking tongue startled her into opening her mouth to him. Heat spiraled through her body as he held her close.

"Tessa," he murmured before pulling her even closer and plundering her mouth with his tongue. He smelled of shampoo, soap, a citrusy cologne that tickled her nostrils...and Seth. She leaned into him, giving herself over to his teasing, tantalizing kisses.

She heard a moan and realized it came from her. As he continued his toe-curling kisses, Seth kneaded her bottom, pushing the silky material of her skirt higher until he rested one hand above the lace of her stocking on the bare flesh of her thigh, then cupped one round cheek of her ass. With his other hand, he drifted up over her waist until he stroked her nipple through her dress with his thumb. Heat burned her, not just where he touched but everywhere. Arousal made her ache.

Tessa sighed as he lifted her, holding her tightly, and lowered his head to the swelling globe of her breast. "Seth, I..."

"Shh," he soothed as he traced the neckline of her dress with the tip of his tongue. "Ah, Tessa," he mumbled and pushed her breast upward until it spilled onto his waiting lips. "Mmm."

She was alive with feeling and sensations she'd never experienced as he squeezed her butt with his big hands, all the while suckling her breast. Along her thigh, the bulge of his arousal pressed. With a guttural growl, he swung her into his arms and carried her along the terrace to the open French doors to his room. Tessa was dimly aware of him setting her on the bed before following her there. He braced his hands on either side of her as he once again lowered his mouth to hers.

"I've dreamed of this," he murmured. "Dreamed of holding you, of touching you."

Tessa was drowning in a fog of sensation. His voice was a smoky whisper near her ear, his fingers were the stroke of a satin ribbon on her bare arms before he eased back just enough to undress. He stripped off his jacket, his tie, his shirt. With a deft touch, he slid her dress from her, so she lay on the bed clad only in pearls, a silky black wisp of underwear and stockings. He kissed her again, then stood and let his slacks fall to the floor. As he lay down next to her, there was nothing but the silk of his boxers to disguise his erection.

* * * *

"Touch me, Tessa," he whispered, his lips next to hers, but somewhere in the back of his head, warning bells clanged. He wanted to ignore them. He really did, because his body was demanding release, but enough of his conscience prevailed to keep him thinking beyond what his cock wanted. Her touch was too tentative, from her kisses to her caresses. Even as his gaze and lips devoured her, some sane, logical part of himself warned him to stop. Her fingers trembled a hair's breadth from his straining erection. She was no sophisticated, well-heeled woman looking for quick sex.

"Tessa," he whispered against her ear, his conscience pricking him. "Are you sure this is what you want?" Please say yes.

"I…" She stirred and trembled.

The hesitation told him everything. A sudden vision of Anna on the video that had been sent to his office popped into his brain. She and Chris Stevenson had been drugged when they'd ended up in bed together as virtual strangers. What was Seth's excuse? Tessa was obviously inexperienced. He stalked into the bathroom, grabbing the robes hanging from the hooks on the door. After shrugging into one, he brought the other to Tessa.

In his absence, she'd sat up on the bed and now had her arms crossed over her breasts. As he approached, she faced him.

"I'm sorry," she mumbled, her posture one of pure misery. Her blue eyes looked haunted, not at all what he'd hoped to achieve, but it was too late now.

Seth handed her the bathrobe and turned away as she put it on. When he turned again, she sat, staring straight ahead, her fiery hair tangled around her head. Seth gazed at her, his muscles knotting.

"Have you ever been with a man before, Tessa?"

"No," she admitted as if it had been dragged from her.

"Why me?"

She shrugged. What had he hoped for? A sudden declaration of her undying love? Seth turned away and walked to the French doors to stare at the city below. He knew his motives. He'd been lusting after Tessa Edwards since right after she started working for him. Anything beyond lust, though, he refused to even examine. But her? Why would she? His thoughts were interrupted by a small hiccupping breath. Seth knew that sound. He spun around. Tessa still sat on the edge of the bed where he'd left her.

He strode back and knelt down.

"Don't cry, Tessa. Please." Seth reached out to squeeze her shoulder.

"Did I do something wrong?" she asked. "I can't afford to lose this job, Seth."

He jerked his hand back, horrified. She'd done this because she thought he expected it? He took her slender hand in his and stroked his thumb across the back of it. She gazed at him without flinching. There was no shame in her face--instead he saw hurt, confusion, and a wariness that hadn't been there before. He'd done that. And she thought she had to do this to keep her job with him. Seth closed his eyes for a moment. That hurt. It hurt a lot more than he wanted to admit.

"You did nothing wrong," he reassured her, trying to keep his voice even, unemotional. "Nothing. What happened was my fault. And I would never, never tie what happens between us outside of work hours to your job in any way." He paused again and raked a hand through his hair. "Your first time with a man should be something meaningful, Tessa, with someone you love. Not a quick hop in the sack."

If anything, her expression closed more.

"And that's what this was? Boss and assistant engaged in a little celebratory sex. Like the Vikings after a successful conquest?" Her tone was once again the cool, composed voice he'd grown accustomed to at work.

Seth sighed. He was making a mess of this. "Tessa," he began again, but she pulled away from him to bend down and pick up her dress. "I've already told you this had nothing to do with the job."

"I should go to my room. Did you want me to have breakfast sent up tomorrow morning, Mr. Barrett?"

"Yes. Tessa..." He ground his teeth in frustration and reached to stop her, but she slipped--no flinched--from his grasp.

"Good night, sir."

She hurried from the room, and Seth watched her retreating form with frustration and anger. *What an idiot I am!* He'd made a complete mess of things. He reviewed what he'd said and cringed at the way it had sounded. He'd implied he had no feelings for her and viewed what had happened as meaningless sex. Seth smacked the heel of his hand against his forehead. For someone who had made his living as a professional communicator, he had thoroughly screwed up.

* * * *

Tessa hung her dress in the closet and went to the bathroom to remove her makeup and wash her face. Her actions were automatic. All in all it had been one of the worst days of her life. A small sob broke through her control, but she stamped it out as if it were no more than a bug. She would not think about it right now. That would bring more pain, and she couldn't handle anything else. Not tonight.

The last things she did before turning off the light and going to sleep were to call room service to place a breakfast order and the front desk to leave a wake up call. Whatever else, she would never be accused of neglecting her job as Seth's assistant. To keep Zach, she had to keep the job. All she needed to do now was find some way to balance that with her feelings for Seth.

Chapter 6

Seth stared at Tessa for most of the flight home. Maybe it was better if they kept things on a business footing, but not this, not like it had been in the beginning. They were back to Mr. Barrett. She had done everything he had asked her to, but there was no extraneous conversation. She was her usual efficient Tessa, except the mask of cool composure had hardened into one of withdrawn iciness.

Even now, she sat in her seat near the jet's window with the laptop open in front of her while she finalized her notes from the Midwest acquisition. She barely looked up when the pilot came on the intercom to let them know they were beginning their descent. She finished what she was working on and packed everything away in preparation for landing.

Seth offered her a hand to help her down the steps and onto the tarmac, but Tessa ignored it, just as she ignored the hand he offered to help her into the Escalade. When Seth pulled into the curb in front of her apartment, he put the SUV in park and looked at her.

"Tessa, we need to talk."

Her expression impassive, she responded, "About what, Mr. Barrett?"

Seth slammed his fist against the dashboard. "Damn it! I'm sorry. Is that what you want to hear? I'm not used to groveling, but if that's what it takes, then I will."

At last he got a reaction. The detachment disappeared. Her eyes shot sparks of blue fire. "Tell me one thing, Mr. Barrett. Last night, did any of it mean anything to you? Anything at all? Or was it just a merger you decided not to complete?"

Seth looked into those ice blue eyes. A touch of wariness and hurt like he'd seen last night peeked through the tight control she had on herself.

"It meant enough to me that I stopped," he admitted and continued to meet her gaze. She blinked rapidly, and for a second her lower lip trembled. "Tessa…"

"Don't!" Before he could stop her, she threw open the door, grabbed her oversize purse and ran into the house.

Seth uncoiled from the driver's seat, snatched the laptop and her hanging bag from the back and carried them up to the door. Zach met him there with a mutinous look on his freckled face.

"You made my sister cry," he accused. "Tessa never cries! What did you do to her?"

Seth's chest ached as he studied the boy. His little hands were knotted into fists and his small chest rose and fell with indignation.

"It's a grown up thing, Zach, but if it means anything, I didn't intend to hurt her." He held the bags out to the boy. "Can you manage to carry these for me? I think Tessa has seen enough of me for today."

Zach glared at him again and then snatched the bags from Seth before slamming the door in his face. Seth stared at the closed door and sighed. Yes, all in all, he had screwed things up. He walked back to the SUV and stared at the house for a moment longer before climbing in and driving off. He'd wanted to take her and Zach to the beach this weekend to say thanks, but right now that seemed like the lousiest idea in the world--and the one thing he kept thinking about.

* * * *

Tessa tried to be upbeat over the weekend for Zach. She knew seeing her cry had upset him. She had hoped to get in the apartment before he left the neighbor's and saw her. It would have given her at least a few minutes to calm down, but Zach had been watching for her and had run out into the hallway to greet her. She'd wiped her eyes, but it was too late, he had seen and his excited grin had faded. She spent most of the evening in her room, apologizing to Zach, but telling him she was tired and did not feel well. The look on his face was enough to let her know he didn't believe her.

She played video games with him over the weekend and they watched movies together. She even took him to the theater to see an animated movie he'd been wheedling to go to. By Sunday evening, she thought her head would burst if she had to listen to one more note of arcade game music.

It was almost a relief to enter the relative quiet of Barrett Newspapers Monday morning. She still didn't care for all the chrome and glass, but this morning the thick carpeting of the upper floors was comforting in a way, as though there might be a softer side to something at Barrett. Tessa would go on as if the trip to Chicago had never happened. She needed this job, and she was not going to let embarrassment over what had happened--or almost happened--get in the way. What on earth had she been thinking? The man was her boss and he was at least ten years older than her. She'd never wanted to sleep with anyone before. So why him? And bringing the incident up again, even if it was to apologize and assure him she would never bother him again, was not a good idea.

She sprinted up the stairs, pausing at the top to slip on her pumps before opening the door. The first thing she noticed was the huge bouquet of summer flowers sitting on her desk. It was not a formal florist's arrangement; instead it looked like someone had cut as many flowers as they could stuff into a lead crystal vase. Her lips twitched. There was a card leaning against the vase. Inside was a picture of Seth holding the flowers in front of an almost denuded flowerbed, and scrawled on top of it, "Please forgive me?"

This time she smiled, but she sure wouldn't let him know it. She made his coffee as she always did and took it into his office.

"Hmmph," he grunted from behind the pages of one of the innumerable newspapers he read each morning. The day continued as it always did, with Seth working nonstop and barking orders at her. It made her wonder if the flowers and the picture with the hastily scrawled note were figments of her imagination, but no, every time she stopped by her desk, there they were. She took the flowers home with her at the end of the day. They were too much of a distraction sitting beside her while she tried to work.

The next morning when she arrived, a large coffee from Starbucks and a cinnamon scone awaited her...along with another card. Tessa flipped it open to find a single question scrawled on a thick note card, "Would it help if I were sweeter?"

Tessa glanced at Seth's office door and smothered a giggle. Seth? Sweet? But she smiled at the thought, and somehow many of the objections she kept raising to Seth Barlow-Barrett as a man began to disappear.

He grunted when she took in his coffee and then drove her like a workhorse until late morning when he stopped and looked up. And then she wondered why she had ever thought him at all appealing.

"I'm supposed to meet my mother for lunch at the club," he stated. "It's this Habitat thing again. Would you come with me?"

Tessa tilted her head. "Do I have a choice?"

"Would you still come if I said yes?" he countered.

"Yes. I happen to have a lot of experience with Habitat."

"Then you have a choice."

"I'd be happy to go with you."

By the end of lunch, Seth was scowling, his mother was beaming and Tessa was smiling wickedly at her boss. She could almost feel the steam rolling from him as he helped her into his SUV. He'd raked his hands through his wavy, golden hair so many times it stood on end.

"Did you have to volunteer me to work with a bunch of Women's Club do-gooders who have some insane idea about building a house?" he bit out as he slid behind the wheel and slammed his door. He glared at her with eyes that shot angry sparks at her.

Tessa smiled at him with as much innocence as she could muster. "I'm sure you can handle it, Mr. Barrett. You do know how to hammer a nail, or does the butler see to that?"

Seth dropped an F-bomb before putting the car in gear and driving in stony silence back to Barrett. Tessa kept her expression blank, but congratulated herself on setting him up. It would do him good to learn a little patience on a volunteer work crew.

The next morning when she arrived, there was a construction apron and a hammer on her desk with a note that said, "Mother was so happy when I told her you loved working on Habitat houses and would be joining us this weekend."

This time when she set his coffee down, he lowered his paper and stared at her.

"You know what they say about payback," he said in a silky voice.

Tessa arched one brow at him. "Bring it on, big boy. I can hammer a nail. Can you?"

Thursday morning she arrived to find a short piece of rope tied in an intricate knot. With it was a card. Tessa found herself looking forward to Seth's morning messages. The card read, "It's called a fisherman's loop. If we work all day Saturday, may I take you and Zach fishing on the bay Sunday?"

Tessa's hand trembled as she read the note. Two thoughts raced through her mind at the same time. He'd remembered what she had told him about Zach's love of fishing. More to the point, he wanted to see her again, not just mend a working relationship.

Friday, a single red rose in full bloom in a delicate bud vase awaited her with no note. Tessa touched the velvety petals with trembling fingers and leaned over to inhale its rich fragrance. She glanced at the closed door to his office. She would not read anything into it. Seth fascinated her more and more, however wrong she knew that might be.

She arranged for Zach to stay at her neighbor's Saturday since the house under construction was just getting started, so there wasn't much he could do. She told him Seth was taking them fishing Sunday.

"He's not going to make you cry again, is he?" Zach demanded in a tone that said he would take care of Seth, if need be.

Tessa smiled at her little brother. "No, he's not going to make me cry again."

He couldn't hide his obvious relief. Tessa grinned at him, wondering if he was relieved she wasn't going to cry or relieved because now he wouldn't be disloyal if he showed how excited he was about the fishing trip.

Tessa was one of the first volunteers to show up at the work site Saturday morning. She checked in with the site foreman, described her previous experience, and discovered why he seemed so happy to see her.

"We're looking at putting up exterior walls today and one of our crew leaders has called in sick. Can you take over that spot?"

"Sure." She was comfortable with any phase of the construction, and today's work would not be that complicated, at least if the crew could swing a hammer.

Seth arrived a few minutes later. Tessa almost groaned when she saw he was on her crew list, but the practical side of her knew his physical size and strength would come in handy when they were setting the walls.

"You're my crew leader?" Seth asked with an odd note in his deep voice. His eyes glinted, but Tessa couldn't tell whether it was with humor, respect, or a bit of both.

She grinned at him. "Someone called in sick. When they heard what my experience was, they asked me to fill in."

Seth studied her. "And what is your experience?"

"I helped with my first house in Jamaica and then another one in Bolivia. I worked on two more as a crew leader while I was in graduate school." Tessa paused. "Did you want to know anything else?"

Seth shook his head. "Tell me what you need me to do, Boss."

By lunchtime, Tessa was glad she had Seth there. True to his word, he did what she asked him to do, proving that he was no stranger to building things. Between the two of them, they more than made up for what he had accurately described as a bunch of 'Women's Club do-gooders.' She wasn't sure how many more times she could stand to explain why it would be easier to drive the nail if they learned not to choke up on the hammer. When they raised the exterior walls and set them in place in the afternoon, Seth grinned at Tessa. She'd never seen him look so relaxed and had never realized he had dimples in both lean cheeks. He worked without complaint, pulling nails and re-driving them with amazing patience behind a couple of their volunteers.

At the end of the day, Tessa produced a big water jug from the trunk of her car. She offered it to Seth, who popped open the spout and poured it straight down his throat. When he handed it back to Tessa, she took a long swig, then poured water on the bandana in her hand. After setting down the jug, she wiped her face and throat down to the V of her shirt. She looked up to find Seth watching her movements, his stare intense.

He shifted his gaze and cleared his throat. "Are we still on to go fishing tomorrow?"

"Yes," she replied a little breathlessly. "Zach is very excited."

"I'll pick you up around seven, if that's okay? Oh, bring your swimming suits in case we decide to cool off in the water."

Tessa nodded and closed the trunk of her car. "Okay."

He started to say something else and stopped. She'd never seen him hesitate before. After clearing his throat, he said, "I didn't expect it, but I had a good time today."

Tessa grinned. "Me too."

He grinned back. "I'll see you tomorrow, then."

She watched as he walked over to his SUV. He was dusty and sweaty, his faded polo shirt wet with perspiration and the worn jeans molding his long legs streaked with dirt. His hair was damp with sweat where he'd removed the baseball cap he'd worn most of the day, and despite his blond beard, she saw the glint of a thick five o'clock shadow. He'd never looked better.

* * * *

When he got home that evening, Seth soaked for a long time in the hot tub on his deck. He had a whole new respect for Tessa and the aching muscles to prove it. She'd drawn the most out of their crew, patiently directing women who'd probably never held a hammer or nails in their lives, but the brunt of the work had fallen on Tessa and him. He'd watched her several times during the day. She didn't hesitate, measuring angles and hammering with an efficiency that would put a lot of men to shame. For all her small size, she possessed amazing strength.

Her hair had been pulled back into a ponytail that stuck out the back of her ball cap. A t-shirt had hugged her upper body and snug jeans had fit her hips and thighs like a second skin. Seth grinned. He had almost hit himself in the thumb a couple times, watching as she bent over to help someone pull a nail or finish hammering one home. She was a lot more relaxed working on the house than he could ever remember her. Seeing the way her smile made her eyes sparkle, he felt himself sliding closer and closer to the edge. Of what? Love? He was thirty-five years old and had neither expected nor looked for a serious relationship. Yet every time he looked at Tessa, he felt a catch in his chest somewhere awfully close to his heart.

He hoped she would like sailing. He hadn't told her about that part of the fishing expedition, but it was something he wanted to share with her. He'd never taken another woman sailing, other than his sisters, and they didn't count.

* * * *

Zach was somewhat subdued when Seth arrived the following morning. When he arched a questioning brow at Tessa, she explained, "He's not awake yet. Give him a few minutes. Then you'll find out."

As they pulled into the Marina, Zach piped up. "Wow, Tessa! Look at all the boats."

And there were hundreds of them, everything from huge houseboats to sleek speedboats. In the distance, the masts of various sailboats weaved and bobbed with the motion of the bay.

"Seth?" was all Tessa said.

"I thought we could go out on the bay in my boat, if that's okay?"

"Sure," she replied, as if it was something she did all the time. She'd told him she'd never been sailing. He must have remembered. She was touched. It was something she had longed to try, but never expected to have the chance.

Zach bounced all the way down the dock. "Which one is it?" he trilled.

"Her name is Wistful," Seth told him. "Try to find that."

Tessa opened her mouth to say something and then decided to let it go. She watched as Zach studied each boat. He looked back and forth between two boats before pointing to a dark-hulled sailboat.

"Is that it?" he asked at last, a note of uncertainty clouding his voice.

Seth grinned at him. "Good job, Zach."

As they cast off, Seth explained to Zach that they would use the motor until they were out of the marina. Then they would switch to sails. As Seth continued to explain how to sail the boat, Tessa watched how he related to Zach. He was patient with all her brother's questions and even promised to show him how to handle Wistful once they were under sail. The boat was designed so it could be sailed by one person, despite being about forty feet long.

The breeze on the bay ruffled Seth's blond hair. Dressed in shorts, a t-shirt and deck shoes, he was more casual than she'd ever seen him-- well, almost. She had seen him far less clothed. Tessa turned away as heat rose in her cheeks at the memory of his aroused body, clad only in his boxers, pressing close against her. Watching him work, it was obvious he was at ease with the boat and being on the water, but then, she'd read somewhere that sailing was a family pastime.

"I thought we'd go to a cove south of here," Seth told her. "There's usually some pretty good fishing there, and if the fish aren't biting, we can always go swimming."

Tessa nodded and leaned her head back to stare up at the billowing sails. It was as wonderful as she had imagined, made more so by seeing how happy Zach was.

* * * *

Seth studied Tessa as Wistful skimmed over the water. She looked relaxed today, even more than yesterday. The wind was already sucking loose tendrils of her fiery hair. Dark sunglasses hid her eyes from view, but a smile curved her generous lips.

He wanted to know more about her. He already knew her mind was faster than many business tycoons', and he could appeal to that part of her, but he wanted to know how to make her laugh, how to pleasure her in bed or out. And that was saying a lot. Seth couldn't remember the last time he'd met a woman he'd looked at as anything more than either an office irritation or a convenient way to relieve sexual tension. He wasn't getting much relief now. Tessa had already starred in a couple shower fantasies, and it looked like today's excursion would end the same way.

She wore a cropped t-shirt and low-slung khaki shorts that left her midriff and most of her slender thighs bare. As she leaned back to look up at the sails again, he noticed something he hadn't seen before--a small diamond sparkled below her navel. Seth had never been into the body-piercing or tattooing fad, but seeing it on her sparked images of his tongue swirling around it and his teeth tugging on it. He'd let his tongue slide lower then... As his body responded to the image, he turned to adjust himself.

Presenting her with the evidence of his arousal while her little brother was with them was not smooth. After giving himself a firm down boy, Seth went back to thinking about her. The diamond was also surprising, given the cool personality she conveyed in the office. He wondered if there was another side of her she kept under wraps. But even so, he knew from what had occurred in Chicago, she was not like the experienced women he'd dated in the past. Far from it, and God, that was its own turn-on.

They reached the isolated cove in a little over an hour. Seth dropped anchor and set up a rod and reel for Zach.

"You going to fish, Tessa?" he asked as he handed Zach the baited rod.

"No. Not right now. I think I might stretch out on these cushions if you don't mind?"

"Not at all." Seth could fish and enjoy the view of long, bare legs and the sweet curve of her waist and hips. So even if the fish were not biting, he'd still have a great morning. The time sped by. Zach caught several fish with Seth's help before everything slowed down around midday.

"They're not biting any more, Seth." Zach stared overboard. The disappointment was evident in his voice. Seth hid a grin as he watched the boy trying to see any fish in the opaque surface of the water.

"What do you say we take a break, eat some lunch, and then we can take a swim before we move to another spot?" Seth suggested.

"Yeah!" Zach cheered.

"Give me a hand with the cooler, Tessa," Seth called, enjoying the view of her stretched on her stomach, reading a book.

She rolled to her feet and came aft, her sea legs already a given. He thought of his poor sister, Anna, who stumbled around and spent half her time on any boat with her head over the side, vomiting. It was something that made her feel alienated from her seafaring siblings. In some ways Tessa reminded him of Anna, prickly and stubborn--not to mention petite--but Tessa was already a lot tougher than Anna had ever learned to be.

Seth wondered sometimes why someone with the family background Tessa had would be so tough. He almost said streetwise, but then there was one major area where she didn't fit that picture.

"I want a cheese sandwich," Zach said, "and pickles."

"Coming right up," Tessa said with a laugh. While she made Zach's sandwich and one with ham and cheese for herself, Seth layered at least one of everything onto his bread, slathered on the spicy mustard and topped it off with some lettuce and tomato.

"Yuck!" Zach pronounced, taking one look at Seth's creation. "That looks disgusting."

Seth grinned and took a big bite out of it. As tomato juice dripped down his chin, he used the back of one hand to wipe his mouth. Zach's eyes rounded in amazement.

"Wow! You have a big mouth!"

"Zach!" Tessa scolded, but Seth threw back his head and let loose a roar of laughter that shook his big frame.

* * * *

Tessa's eyes widened. Where was the gruff man who barked orders at her all day long during the week? When he caught her staring at him, he cocked one eyebrow at her. Tessa's cheeks heated, but she smiled back at him. Seth in this mood was hard to resist.

He stretched his arms along the gunwale after he polished off his sandwich. "So tell me about this new school Zach's going to."

"It's Chesterfield Academy. It's not far from where we live." Tessa gathered up the lunch leftovers.

"I've heard the name, but I don't know much about it."

"It specializes in working with children with attention and learning disorders. They have a small student-to-teacher ratio, so Zach will get lots of personal attention, something he hasn't received in the public schools. I know that's a matter of funding, but…"

"You have to do what's best for your brother."

She nodded, pleased he understood.

"I'm going to camp before I go to school," Zach offered. "Two whole weeks!"

"I had a great time at camp when I was your age," Seth told him. "It was a chance to get away from all my brothers and sisters for a while."

"How many brothers and sisters do you have?"

"Two younger brothers and three younger sisters. Scary, huh?"

"That's a lot. Can we go swimming?" Zach asked, changing the subject again.

"Do you know how?" Seth asked.

"Yes. Tessa taught me when I was real little. She swims a lot. Well she used to when Mom and Dad were still alive." Zach's smile dimmed for a second.

"Why don't you get your trunks on?" Tessa suggested, to divert him from thinking about their parents. The last thing she wanted was for him to have sad thoughts on a day designed for fun.

"Do you want to go below to change?" Seth asked her.

Thinking about the small confines of the cabin made her skin crawl. He looked around and gave her an understanding look. The area where they'd dropped anchor was deserted. "Change up here. No one's around, and Zach and I will go below."

"Thank you." As soon as they were gone, she scrambled into her bikini.

A few minutes later, Seth and Zach reappeared, dressed in their swimming trunks. Seth's eyes widened when he saw her, but he said nothing and turned his attention back to Zach.

"I know you're a good swimmer, buddy, but one of the rules of my boat is everyone under the age of eighteen must have on a lifejacket when they swim, and I can't go against the rules."

Tessa was surprised when her brother nodded as if that made perfect sense. Seth handed him the lifejacket and helped him adjust the straps so it fit. With a casual helping hand, Zach was up and over the edge, his giggles echoing across the water. In a matter of seconds, the boat rocked as Seth dived in after him. That left Tessa. She stood on the edge of the boat and executed a perfect cannonball, hoping it sent water everywhere.

She came up laughing. Seth dunked her, so Tessa decided to give him a little payback. Staying under, she waited until she saw his legs shift. He must be looking for her. Tessa popped out of the water behind him and started to push him under as he continued his search, but Seth twisted and wrapped one arm around her waist.

"If I go, you go," he threatened.

Their legs tangled as they trod water, and they started to sink. His eyes locked with hers for a moment, and time stopped. The sounds of Zach laughing nearby faded. Tessa's own laughter stopped as she saw something in the depths of Seth's eyes. Stillness surrounded them, and Tessa knew without a doubt there was more going on between them than she was ready to admit, and she doubted that he was any different.

"Get her, Seth!" Zach splashed them both, and the moment was gone.

They swam and played until Zach began to tire. Tessa didn't want the day to end.

"What do you say we look for another fishing spot for the afternoon before we return to the marina?" Seth suggested. It seemed he felt the same.

"Okay. I need to put more sunscreen on Zach and me before we turn into lobsters."

Seth climbed the ladder first and then reached down to pull Zach up and into the boat. Tessa jokingly held her arm up, squealing as he pulled her out of the water and clear of the hull with just one arm.

"You must be strong if you can pick Tessa up with one hand!" Zach said in awe.

Tessa made a face at her little brother. "Thanks a lot."

"She's a tiny thing," Seth said, watching her. "No trouble at all."

"Did you want to change clothes, Zach?" She had to do something to relieve the sudden tension between Seth and her.

"No. Can I stay in my swimming trunks, please?"

Tessa nodded. "As long as you put a t-shirt back on."

"And shoes," Seth added. "I don't want anyone slipping."

Tessa let the sun dry her bikini and then slipped her shorts and shoes back on. She slathered Zach with sunscreen and rubbed her arms, legs, and stomach, but still needed help with her back.

"May I?" Seth asked from behind her.

Tessa pulled her hair to the side. "Thanks."

His even breathing brushed her skin as he spread the lotion across her shoulders, being extra careful, it seemed to her, to rub it in. As his hand slid lower, that coil of nervousness twirled deep in her belly. Seth took an uneven breath and continued, still without a word.

As his fingers massaged lotion around the top of her low-slung shorts, Tessa inched away. "I think that's good."

She turned to catch an expression of such unbridled heat on his face that she took a half step away. Seth reached out and yanked her to him.

"What are you doing?" Panic surged and she pushed against him.

"Stopping you from a very painful fall below deck."

Tessa looked over her shoulder. "Oh, sorry."

"What did you think I was going to do? Ravish you in front of a ten-year-old?" He frowned.

Tessa closed her eyes for a heartbeat and took a deep breath. "No. I...I'm sorry. You startled me. That's all."

Seth released her, but the doubt on his face was apparent. It spoiled the mood. Tessa went forward again as he pulled anchor and then got them under sail. Zach stayed with him and Seth let the boy help him, explaining each step of what he was doing. Her brother soaked it all up like a sponge.

Tessa slipped her sunglasses back on her nose and observed the two of them together. Seth's manner was easygoing, as if he spent every day in the company of kids, and it was obvious Zach enjoyed the attention.

She bit her bottom lip, fighting back a sudden feeling of envy. Why hadn't there been someone like a Seth in her life when she was Zach's age? All Tessa remembered were endless summers with cousins, who did their best to make her life miserable.

As the sails filled and Wistful gained speed, Tessa stretched out on her back, propped on her elbows, and looked out across the bay, but she saw very little. Instead of the pristine sky and the turn of a gull as it swept down to pick up some morsel from the water, Tessa's mind filled with memories.

Finding herself mysteriously jammed in the tack trunk was just the first of many incidents. Once her cousins had discovered her fear of confined places, they'd done their best to torment her. The next incident had occurred when someone locked her in the storm cellar of the old mansion, but Tessa had found something to break the door open. She had been the one punished for "damaging" Mont Clair. *What about the damage to me?* Tessa had wanted to scream at her father's family, but in the end she had shut down.

Tessa hadn't wanted to tell her mother what was happening while she was struggling so hard to support them. But that last summer, she'd had to speak up. Her mother had just begun seeing Zach's father, Jack Mallory. Tessa had fought going to Mont Clair for the summer, but her mother had laid a guilt trip on her about the importance of nurturing family connections. Tessa had closed her mouth and packed her bags.

At twelve, she'd begun to mature. Her baby fat had disappeared and in its wake she was developing a woman's figure, not full by any means, but enough to draw some very unwelcome notice. Her cousin, Peter, was four years older and the primary instigator to making her life a torment every summer. But that year the torment had changed. Instead of trying to lock her up somewhere by herself, he was always trying to be alone with her, touching her and making comments about her body, his body, and what he would like to do to her.

Tessa had quit eating and had begun to lose weight. She had worried so much that Peter would come in her room at night that she'd had trouble sleeping. Then, the night he did come to her room and Tessa had screamed over and over for him to get out, somehow it had been her fault. She must have done something to lure him there.

Tessa closed her eyes, goose bumps prickling her skin despite the warmth of the day. Blue-blooded families with their proud pedigrees could hide a whole wealth of family faults. She shivered. She'd never gone back after that, not after she'd told her mother what had happened, what had gone on for years. They'd cut ties with her father's family at that point, and Tessa had been glad.

She shook herself out of the past. She had put it behind her, but every once in a while, when someone grabbed her, it all came back. Peter hadn't even done the most damage. The worst part was, no one had believed her. It had destroyed her trust and taught her to rely only on herself.

"Tessa!" Zach shouted, "Look! I'm sailing Wistful."

She rolled over and looked at her little brother, controlling the boat under Seth's close supervision. She smiled at both of them and waved. She'd never seen Zach have such a great time since before Jack and their mother died. Her brother's freckled cheeks glowed and his eyes sparkled. She didn't know what she'd do without him in her life.

He would go to camp in another two weeks. Tessa had wondered if she was making the right decision, but now she saw it would be a good thing. Sponsored by his new school, the camp was based at the bay, where he would learn skills that included sailing and hands-on work with sea life and eco-systems. She looked at it as a way to get him outside and away from computers and video games for a while, but perhaps it would spark some new interests. Without academics as the main focus, Zach would have a chance to meet kids in an atmosphere where the pressure was eased.

Seth took over as they reached another sheltered cove. This must be the new fishing hole. Tessa watched as boy and man worked to get poles baited and set up, and then Seth told Zach he was in charge.

He turned to Tessa with a thoughtful look on his face and headed her way. She had already thought about her reaction earlier and spoke up as he approached.

"I'm sorry, Seth."

"For what?" he asked as he sat down next to her.

Tessa waved her hand toward Zach. "For spoiling the mood back there. You've done a wonderful job with Zach, and I...well, I'm sorry."

Seth tipped her chin up. "Are you having a wonderful day?"

"Oh yes! I can't even think when I've had such a blast. I love the sailboat. And Zach... It's been so long since I've seen him this happy, and it's not just because of our parents' accident." At Seth's look, Tessa continued, "It's hard to get him to interact with people. Zach is brilliant when it comes to computers and video games. Light years ahead of me."

"That's scary," Seth commented.

Tessa nodded. "The problem is, he struggles to read and write. Kids make fun of him. They also tease him because of the hair and the freckles. He's had a lot of problems in school and he doesn't have many friends."

Seth glanced at where Zach kept a careful eye on each rod and reel. Tessa knew it was hard to imagine him having problems, let alone not having friends. Yet sometimes character traits that made a child easy to get along with for an adult made the same child unpopular with kids his own age.

"Kids can be cruel," he murmured. "I ran interference for years for my sister, Anna, and not just from kids. Adults can be just as cruel." His glance shifted back to her. "I'm glad you're both having a good time."

Their eyes met and there it was again, that feeling everything else faded away. Tessa's guard slipped, but she didn't care if he saw what she was feeling. He leaned toward her, his expression tense as though he wanted to gauge her reaction before doing anything. Her lips parted and a flush of desire suffused her entire body. It stole her breath for a moment. He was going to kiss her, and she was more than willing for that to happen. She needed to feel that.

"Seth," Zach shouted. "Come quick! I think I've got a fish on the line."

Seth's laugh was rueful as he pulled away. "I'll be right there, buddy!" He turned back to her, his smile lopsided. "Were we having a moment?"

"I think we were."

"Can we try that again some time when we don't have an audience?"

"I think we could."

"Excellent."

Chapter 7

The atmosphere had shifted between them. Tessa sensed it as the day drew to a close. She was glad of it. She still had no idea where they were headed, but an easy camaraderie now existed. Zach fell asleep within five minutes of climbing into the back seat of the big black Escalade. Seth reached over, grabbed Tessa's hand, and held it, stroking the backs of her fingers with his thumb. She had noticed that about him, a need to touch what was in his world. It seemed so at odds with the cool concentration he demonstrated at work.

"I have a house at the beach," Seth began as he drove. "Would you spend a weekend with me while Zach is at camp?"

As Tessa opened her mouth to reply, Seth continued, "Don't answer right now. Think about it. No strings attached. I want to get to know you better. I want you to know me better. I don't think Barrett is the place for that."

He trailed off as if uncertain where he was going with his thoughts. Tessa found that rather endearing.

"I'll think about it," she promised.

He smiled at her and squeezed her hand before returning his attention to the road.

If Tessa had expected the weekend to change their working relationship, it didn't. When she brought Seth his coffee the following morning, she received the usual grunt from behind a wall of newspaper. He had spent some time with Barrett Senior on Friday in the afternoon, but hadn't shared anything with her about what the meeting concerned. Since he hadn't, Tessa had to assume it was personal, particularly as he hadn't looked pleased when he came back. Brandon had gone up after Seth. He, too, hadn't looked happy when he returned. Tessa could understand that. Alexander seemed cold and aloof to her, definitely a man she didn't want to be on the wrong side of.

Seth's mother called midweek to see if she and Seth could help out again with the Habitat project. With a wicked smile, Tessa assured her it would be no trouble at all. She hoped to get some sort of rise out of Seth, but he nodded and smiled as if she'd suggested they go to lunch.

* * * *

This time around, Seth picked her up. They worked on the same crew, but as equals, since the crew chief was back on the job. The roof trusses were already in place, but they would be putting the plywood on the trusses, then adding the felt and shingles. When the crew chief realized Tessa had experience at that, he assigned her to go up. Seth was left doing a lot of the heavy lifting and moving supplies while he watched her with one eye. She scurried around the roof as if she did this kind of work every day.

It amazed him to watch her. She was so different than any of the women of his previous experience, not to mention younger. There was nothing of the country club debutante about her, nor the bored sophisticate. The biggest thing that set her apart was the dichotomy she presented between the blueblood pedigree and education, and the tough, reserved young woman who also possessed pretty amazing business insights. Which one was the real Tessa?

He knew her need to care for her little brother was what drove her. She enjoyed sailing and swimming, but she tolerated the fishing because Zach loved it so much. There had been that one moment, though, when she'd pulled away from him almost in fear. A reaction that again did not seem to fit with a privileged, pedigreed upbringing. Altogether, those paradoxes made her a puzzle, and his need to solve it grew more intense.

Around mid-afternoon, Seth's cellphone rang. He was right in the middle of carrying a hundred pounds of shingles from the truck to where they were lifting them up to the roof, and he almost didn't answer it in time. His sister, Anna, shared news that she was getting married. She and Chris Stevenson had worked out their problems after all. He was happy for her. His gaze drifted to Tessa as he listened to Anna. When it penetrated his brain that she wanted to get married the following Wednesday and wanted him to be there to give her away, he paused.

"Hey, Tessa," he yelled. "My sister in North Carolina's getting married Wednesday. Can I be there?"

He saw her mind working and grinned. Who needed a planner with her around?

"I can move everything on that day to either Tuesday or Thursday without a problem," she called down.

"She'll clear my calendar," Seth told his sister. "Make it right before lunch and I'll take everyone out somewhere."

* * * *

Tessa watched him work below her. A couple times she banged her thumb as he hefted the heavy packs of shingles. There was an interesting play of muscles in his arms and under the snug fitting material of his shirt. For someone who spent so much time behind a desk, he managed to stay in shape. He bent over to attach the shingles to the pulley system they were using to haul them to the roof. The powerful muscles in his long thighs flexed and bunched inside the taut material of his jeans. She gulped, then flinched as she smacked herself with the hammer once again and had to stick her thumb into her mouth to suck the pain away.

At the end of the day, Tessa scrambled across the roof. Seth held the ladder while she climbed down, caught her around the waist near the last step, and swung her in a wide arc before setting her on her feet.

"Come on, Spiderwoman, let's go grab a burger and some fries on the way home." He threw a casual arm around her shoulders and fitted her next to him as they walked back to his SUV.

"Mmm," Tessa sighed. "That sounds wonderful."

As they headed back into town, Seth glanced over. "You want to swing by and pick up Zach? I'm sure he'd enjoy a burger and some fries too."

"That would be wonderful, Seth. Thanks for thinking of him. You know he's got a case of hero worship going anyway."

He surprised her by flushing and clearing his throat. "He's a great kid."

And you're a surprising man. The few times she'd dated, she couldn't imagine any of those guys thinking about including her little brother in anything. She watched the way Seth made an effort to draw Zach out then listened to him as if he were the most important person in the world. It touched her to the point where she had to blink back the sudden moisture in her eyes.

"So when do you head off to camp?" Seth asked the little boy as they stuffed themselves on greasy burgers and crisp, crunchy fries smothered in ketchup.

"Friday," Zach got out between bites. "Tessa drops me off Friday afternoon and we take a bus to the camp. I can't wait. We're even going to learn how to sail, Seth."

He smiled at Zach. "You'll be a step ahead, buddy, since you've already had your first sailing lesson on board Wistful."

When they returned to her apartment, Tessa invited him in. She had enjoyed the day and was reluctant to see it end so soon.

"I've got a cold beer in the fridge, if you'd like something a little stronger than a milk shake," she coaxed.

He smiled as he pulled his shirt away from his body. "If you can stand the smell, I could stand a beer."

Tessa laughed. "Like I'm any less filthy than you?"

They sat out on the front stoop. Zach disappeared inside, back to his PlayStation and the latest game he was whipping his way through. Seth held up his bottle and clinked it against hers.

"To a successful day of house-building and a beautiful lady to make the time fly by." He held her gaze as he tilted the long neck for a deep drink.

Tessa blinked, pleased by the compliment. "Thank you."

They drank in companionable silence, watching a few couples, mostly older, pass on their evening strolls. Tessa thought it amazing that here was the COO of Barrett Newspapers sitting next to her on the stoop of an old converted house in a working class neighborhood, slugging back a beer as if he lived here. She couldn't begin to imagine any of the Loudoun Edwards slumming enough to do something similar, and most of them didn't have a pot to piss in compared to Seth. Good grief, she remembered her grandmother's maid having to pop the caps on bottles of Coke before she left for the day because her grandmother didn't know how to use a bottle opener!

Seth finished the beer and set it down on the porch. With his hands dangling from the knees of his spread legs, he spun his baseball cap like a wheel. She was mesmerized by the muscles that rippled in his forearms. A scent of clean male sweat drifted to her nostrils. It was an incredible turn-on.

"I should go," he murmured, as if it was pulled from him because that was what good manners dictated.

Tessa didn't want him to leave yet. He was easy to be around, accepting and not grilling her all the time about her past and why she no longer associated with her prominent family.

"You don't have to. Go, that is." Tessa's hand trembled on the leg of her jeans, stroking the material until he covered her fingers with his own. "I could get us another beer. If you want one."

He shook his head.

"Do you want me to stay for a while?" Seth seemed a little unsure, nervous even, and that surprised her.

"Yes. It gets lonely sometimes with just Zach for company. I know he's my brother, but he is ten, and sometimes I feel more like his mother than his sister."

Seth turned and leaned a shoulder up against the porch pillar. He reached out with one long finger and stroked a stray piece of hair from her face.

"It's tough to always feel like you're the responsible one."

"I never felt that way until I got the call at school about the accident."

"How did it happen?"

"One of those freak things," Tessa said as she stared into space. "They were coming home from a business dinner. A trucker was passing them when his tire blew and slammed into their car. My stepfather lost control. He died at the scene."

"What about your mother?"

Tessa bit her bottom lip. "I was able to say goodbye. It was almost as if she waited, you know? Once she said goodbye and asked me to watch out for Zach, she kind of let go."

Seth squeezed her shoulder. "You miss them."

"Both of them. Jack was more a dad to me than my father ever was, and I watched the way he was with Zach. He was a great parent, and he loved my mom so much." Her voice trailed away toward the end and she swallowed. "I'm sorry. I don't usually dump that on people."

Seth pulled her into his shoulder and pressed her against his side. His voice was a deep rumble as he said, "I don't want to be just 'people', Tessa. You do know that, don't you?"

His gaze was sincere, intense.

"I know," she whispered.

He tilted her chin and kissed her then. Rather than an attempt to start anything, his kiss was gentle and undemanding, more of a benediction. He released her and stood up, a half smile tugging at his firm mouth.

"I'm leaving now, while I still can. I'm leaving because you do have that little brother inside, and I won't have him think less of you if I stayed."

She nodded and watched his easy stride as he walked to the Escalade. Warmth flooded her. She'd dated a few times since Zach came to live with her, but had never before felt respected because a guy left. She smiled and shook her head. It was still difficult to realize he was the same man who growled at her from behind newspapers and barked orders left and right when he was at work. Which man was the real one, or were they both parts of the whole?

Seth sprang the wedding preparations on her Monday, right after he grunted his way through his morning coffee. As he outlined what he wanted her to do, Tessa stared at him. No problem, she thought. In forty-eight hours they would fly to North Carolina for his sister's wedding, where Seth would give her away, then Tessa would somehow have managed to cater a luncheon reception, complete with a wedding cake for about twenty people at the groom's parents' home. Of course, all he knew was their last name and that they had a horse farm.

Tessa nodded through all of his instructions.

"Will that be a problem?"

"Not at all," Tessa assured him and turned on her heel. She would not give him the satisfaction of letting him see what she really wanted to do was drop her mouth open, stare at him and ask, "Are you crazy?"

She made a few well-chosen phone calls and came back before lunch to set the travel itinerary, the menu and the choices for wedding gifts in front of him. She refrained from giving voice to the na-na-na-na-na-na.

"If you'll select one of these gifts, I'll have it ready to leave with us Wednesday morning. I assumed you might want me to come along with you and Brandon, since I moved your meeting with the West Coast division to Thursday, and you could use the travel time and any downtime to complete your meeting prep."

Seth gaped. "You're done already?"

"Piece of cake. No pun intended."

Now and then, through the rest of the day, she caught him staring at her, which was so rewarding, as if he couldn't quite believe she had managed to carry out his orders.

The trip went without a hitch. Tessa stepped in to organize getting everyone to the church on time, enjoying being able to watch Anna's baby girl, Becca. After Seth sat next to her during the ceremony, she couldn't stop a little wishful thinking. What would he be like as a father? In her heart of hearts, she already knew the answer. She saw how he was with her brother, how he put Zach at his ease and explained things to the boy with a patience that would have surprised anyone who knew him from Barrett. Yes, Seth would make someone a wonderful husband, but it would not be her. Pedigree or no pedigree, money married money, and that was one thing she didn't have.

Unless she counted the cash that had appeared in her bank account. The problem nagged at the back of her mind all day. She'd hoped for a moment to call the bank, but so far that hadn't happened. She'd discovered the snafu as she'd done her monthly bills and balanced her checkbook before logging online to verify that it jived with her actual balance. She'd sent the bank an email, but that late at night, all she'd gotten in response was the standard form reply that someone would look into it.

Now, with Seth's sister getting married and both he and Brandon in high spirits, Tessa didn't want to think about it, let alone mention it. Some way, somehow, a very large amount of cash had appeared in her checking account. Money that should not be there, was there, and she would have to figure out where it had come from. She didn't play the lottery, and her luck had been pretty spotty, so it was doubtful the money belonged there. It made her nervous, but until she could get the bank on the line, there was little she could do.

By the end of the day, as they got ready to return to DC, Tessa began to feel some of the fatigue that plagued her most often in the evenings. She hadn't been sleeping well since the elevator incident, but she suspected the stress of all the recent upheavals with a job change, the custody hearing and a nagging uncertainty over what was going on with Seth were threatening to overwhelm her. The foul up in her bank account was one more stressor she could do without.

Tessa stumbled as she prepared to get on the jet, and Brandon caught her arm.

"You okay?" He glared at his older brother. "Are you trying to work this girl to death, bro? She looks beat."

Seth helped her into the jet and to a seat near the window, his brow furrowed with concern.

"Tessa, are you feeling okay?"

"Just tired." As he took the seat across from her, he continued to frown at her, until Tessa felt like she needed to add something. "I haven't been sleeping well, and I've been busy trying to get Zach ready for camp. It's nothing. Really."

"Take tomorrow and Friday off."

"There's no need--"

Seth cut her off. "It will give you a chance to get Zach set for camp and, Tessa?"

She looked at him, weariness dragging at her.

"I'll come by and pick you and Zach up Friday, and then I want to take you to the beach house for the weekend. Will you come?"

It was on the tip of her tongue to pour everything into his lap, but she held back and pushed the matter of her bank account out of her mind, along with any of the doubts she still had. Seth, the man she found incredibly attractive, was inviting her to spend a weekend in a beach house with him. What was wrong in that? He'd already told her there were no strings attached. She knew he meant it. If there was one thing she knew about him since coming to work at Barrett, it was that Seth was honest. He demanded it of himself and those who surrounded him.

Tessa nodded and his frown disappeared. It was amazing what a sense of relief she felt. As the whine of the jet's engines intensified before they started down the runway, Tessa leaned her head back and stared out the window. After the initial pressure of taking off, the jet climbed to its cruising altitude. Tessa's eyes drooped and she quit fighting her need for sleep.

* * * *

As Tessa dozed on the way home, Seth frowned. She did look washed out and faint circles even makeup could no longer disguise lay under her eyes. He felt like a heel. She was always so efficient, it was easy to keep driving her at the same pace he drove himself. But on top of work, she also had the care of her little brother, and he suspected that could be draining more often than not. He knew firsthand how high-energy Zach was. It would take a lot out of a mother and a father, but here she was at twenty-four playing both roles. Difficult enough with a regular kid, but Zach's special needs would make it even tougher.

Seth rubbed his hand over the center of his chest. She was too young and too fragile to be taking on so much by herself. And he could imagine how well that idea would go over if he ever mentioned it to her.

They landed less than an hour later. Tessa had slept the whole time, only stirring as they touched the ground, but she was still not quite awake. Seth loved the way her cheeks flushed in sleep, and the slight confusion in her expression when she awoke, then dozed off again.

Brandon glanced at the two of them with a faint grin, and Seth frowned at him.

"I'll see you later," his brother called as he ducked out the doorway.

"Hmm." Seth acknowledged him, his attention still on Tessa. He wished he could let her sleep. "Tessa," he murmured. "Sweetheart, wake up." The endearment slipped out so he was barely aware he'd even used it, but it felt right.

Her eyes fluttered open once more, and she turned her head. Awareness returned, this time all the way. She smoothed her hair back and unbuckled her seatbelt.

"I'm sorry. You should have awakened me sooner."

"We've just arrived. Don't worry about it." Seth held out his hand. "Come on, I'll run you home, and I meant what I said. Take tomorrow and Friday off."

Tessa smiled. "Thanks. I guess I could use a break."

As they pulled up in front of her apartment, Seth turned his head and caught her watching him. The expression on her face made his cock stir. God, he wanted her, but he'd screwed it up so much in Chicago. She swallowed and blushed, sending his desire that much higher knowing she also felt something.

"What time do I need to come get you and Zach Friday?" His voice was a little hoarse.

"Noon. They leave from his new school by bus at one."

"If you'll have your things packed, we can go on to the beach house after his bus leaves."

"All right."

He came around to help her out of the SUV. When he'd handed her down, he caught hold of her wrist, ducked his head and brushed her lips with his. He wanted so much more than that, but didn't dare. Not yet.

"What was that for?" she whispered, her eyes wide.

Seth stroked her cheek. "Thanks. For your help. It meant a lot to Anna...and me."

She nodded. "I'll see you Friday."

Seth leaned against the SUV as she hurried up the sidewalk and through the door. A weekend. It was more than he'd dare hope. Now all he needed to do was convince her he was interested in more than a romp in bed. As he walked back around the Escalade, he asked himself what he was interested in--a relationship for sure, but more permanent than that he couldn't wrap his mind around yet. Moreover, he wasn't sure Tessa would be able to either.

Chapter 8

As impatient as she was to have Zach's last minute camp list out of the way, Tessa waited to do anything until she could get hold of someone from her bank. She could find no actual deposit to her account, just a balance that read ten thousand dollars more than it should. She was past the initial heart failure stage, now she was anxious to get it straightened out, but the bank was little help.

"I'm sorry, Miss Edwards. We're doing what we can, but so far we haven't been able to track where the money came from...or where it should be."

"Can't you move it out of my account?"

"Until we can locate the exact source of the money, no. If it turned out to be a computer glitch of some sort, then your account would be overdrawn to the tune of ten thousand dollars."

Tessa pressed her lips together in irritation. "Fine, but I need some reassurance that this will be taken care of as quickly as possible."

"We are working on it. I can assure you of that."

She hung up to see Zach standing right behind her.

"Get your clothes on, bud." She gave him a bright smile. This was her problem. Not his. "Let's go get your stuff for camp."

Thursday passed faster than Tessa would have thought. After rushing around all morning, the afternoon was spent packing. Tessa made sure everything was labeled and stowed so it would be easy for him to find without having to tear his whole trunk apart--though that would happen anyway. She included some snacks and a double amount of sunscreen, knowing how Zach needed to keep from getting fried to a freckled crisp.

Friday morning she took him out to breakfast. He loaded up on his favorite, pancakes smothered in butter and syrup. It was almost enough to make Tessa, who was not a big breakfast-eater, gag. She sipped coffee and munched buttered toast as she ran back down the list of things he was supposed to have.

"Don't forget to turn over your medication to the camp counselor," Tessa reminded him. "I put it in a plastic bag, along with written instructions."

"Tess," Zach said around a mouthful of food, "I'm not a little kid anymore. I can remember that."

Tessa smiled at him. "Sorry. Oh, and Zach?"

"What?" he asked in exasperation.

"Have fun." Tessa grinned at him.

He beamed, his tension gone. "I will. I can't wait to show Seth how well I can sail when I get back."

The man in question showed up promptly at noon. As Tessa double-checked that the windows were locked, the Escalade eased up to the curb. Her bag was already sitting at the top of the steps, and Zach was pulling his trunk onto the porch.

"Seth!" Zach shouted.

After locking the door, she hovered in the dimness of the hall. What was she doing? This was her boss she was getting ready to join for the weekend. Seth was still dressed in the suit he'd worn to work that morning, a deep charcoal gray with a thin burgundy pinstripe. Knowing he would still be dressed for the office, she had worn a slim-fitting sundress and sandals rather than the hip-hugger shorts and t-shirt she would have donned had she been running Zach to camp and then coming back home. There was still time to back out. But as she watched the sun glint off his hair and the grin he shared with Zach, her nervousness decreased, and she stepped outside. Boss or not, this man liked her brother, and how cool was that?

He opened up the back of the Escalade before coming up the sidewalk.

"Tessa." He nodded at her and glanced at Zach. "Hey, buddy, ready for camp?"

"Oh yeah!"

"Grab one end of your trunk, then. I'll get the other and we can get it out to the car." Once the trunk was loaded, Seth gave Zach instructions to get in and buckle his seatbelt while he grabbed Tessa's bag with his free hand. Zach adjusted the belt as Seth came back to the passenger side to open the door for Tessa.

"You look beautiful," he murmured for her ears alone as he held out his hand to help her in.

Tessa smiled at him. "You don't look bad yourself."

His gaze held hers for a moment. "Is your bag a sign that you haven't changed your mind about the weekend?"

"I haven't changed my mind, Seth."

His lean face relaxed, and this time his smile was wide enough to show his dimples. His eyes twinkled, the faint creases at the corners adding character rather than age. Her heart beat a little heavier. Like this, he was hard to resist. And did she even want to?

"I'm glad." His quiet murmur caressed her nerve endings. Had there been an edge of uncertainty in his look?

Before getting in this time, he took off his jacket and laid it on the back seat. They arrived at the school in plenty of time. It was a hub of activity, with parents pulled up willy-nilly in the parking lot. Interspersed with the Volvo station wagons and BMWs were a couple chauffeurs and even some embassy cars. Tessa hid a grimace. The downside to paying for a school like Chesterfield was Zach landing in a more elitist atmosphere, but if it helped overcome his learning differences, she would live with it.

A couple teenagers approached to help with his trunk while Tessa supplied emergency information to a camp counselor. Seth added his cellphone number as an emergency contact in case Tessa couldn't be reached. She smiled her gratitude.

Seth held out his hand to Zach, who took it with an air of grave formality and gave it a firm handshake. When her little brother turned to her, Tessa smiled at him, mortified to find her vision was starting to cloud.

"Oh snap! You're not gonna cry are you, Tess? That would be sooo embarrassing," Zach informed her.

Tessa pulled herself together and tugged the hair at the back of his neck. "No. I'm not going to cry. I've been counting the days until I could ship you off, twerp. Give me a hug."

She watched him get on the bus, and to her chagrin found her eyes were getting blurry again. She blinked several times to dispel the tears, smiled big, and waved.

When the bus pulled away, Seth held out his crisp white linen handkerchief. "Need this?"

"No," Tessa said with a sigh. "I'm fine. I just hope he will be. These are the kids he'll be going to school with after he gets back. It's kind of a team-building trip, so I hope everything goes okay."

Seth put his arm around her shoulders as they walked back to the SUV. "He'll do fine."

It seemed he was about to say something else when a man's voice interrupted.

"Seth Barrett? I didn't realize dropping kids off for summer camp was exactly your cup of tea."

Seth turned, a polite but cool smile on his face. "Good afternoon, Trip. We were dropping Tessa's brother off."

Tessa had already sized the man up. Medium brown close-cut hair, hazel eyes and a tan that showed he didn't spend all his time in an office. The fact he was already dressed in tennis whites also indicated leisure was more his style. A lot of women might find him handsome, but her keen eyes caught the beginning of the paunch and an overall lack of the muscular hardness that was so much a part of Seth. She'd met a hundred of his type before. As he started to size her up, Tessa felt Seth's body tense.

"Allow me to introduce you. Trip, this is Tessa Edwards. Tessa, this is Trenton Thompson the Third, better known as Trip. His family's also from Loudoun." There was a tone in Seth's voice as he mentioned family that could almost have been laughter.

Trip's eyes widened. "The Edwards of Mont Clair?"

Tessa decided right then and there she was going to kill Seth, or at the very least get even. She smiled. "Yes, though I'm afraid I don't keep in close touch with them. I assume you're the Thompsons who bought Medfield Park?"

If possible the man's eyes widened even more, and it was all Tessa could do to keep from laughing. Seth had done this on purpose, knowing the man was a social climber who would be as impressed if he trotted out Tessa's bloodlines as though she were a prize Thoroughbred up for sale.

"My parents bought it, although Bitsy and I live there now."

"It was a real pleasure to meet you, Trip." Tessa smiled at him, drawing on all her charm, and saw him swallow. She snuggled closer to Seth's lean frame. "Seth and I were on our way out…to lunch."

She inserted enough pause to make Trip Thompson think they were going to do quite a bit of eating, just not food. She batted her lashes at him and he swallowed once more.

"Oh. Well. Nice to meet you." Trip turned tail and hurried back to his hulking, black Mercedes. Tessa pursed her lips, trying hard to keep from laughing out loud.

"You are an evil young woman," Seth rumbled with soft laughter.

"Me? You were the one who started pulling out the Edwards's pedigree like you were showing off a prize mare."

"I couldn't help it," Seth said as they turned to walk back to his car. "He's such a schmuck! How about some lunch before we leave town?"

Tessa nodded. "Only if you don't take me anywhere we can run into more of the Trip Thompsons of the world. It's bad enough Zach will go to school with all their little clones."

Seth drove to a deli not far from Tessa's home. It was a place she'd been to a time or two, but didn't figure Seth would know. Her surprise must have shown on her face.

"I don't live that far from here, Tessa, so I do know the area pretty well."

While she settled for a salad, Seth ordered a sandwich with everything but the kitchen sink on it. As he squashed one half of it together, getting ready to bite into it, her amazement must have shown.

"What?" He looked at her salad and then back at his sandwich. "Look. You're what--five-two, five-three?"

Tessa nodded.

"I'm six-five and probably at least double your weight. I need food, not rabbit nibbles."

Tessa laughed. Seth raised both brows at her and took a big bite out of his sandwich. He demolished his lunch and was already loosening his tie before Tessa had even half-finished. She was glad to see he didn't start fidgeting like a lot of men but was content to people-watch while she finished eating.

"Where is your beach house?" Tessa asked once they were on the road and Seth was headed east.

"Crosswick Island. It will take us a couple hours to get there." He glanced over at her. "If you don't want to travel that far, we can always stay at the bay house."

Tessa laughed. "No. The beach is fine. Just how many houses do you have?"

"Only two. The Crosswick Island house and my townhouse. The bay house is an old family home. The Crosswick house is one I bought several years ago. It's my escape."

"From your family?" Tessa asked, already having an excellent idea what his answer would be.

"Yes. Since Anna left…" Seth didn't finish what he was going to say, but there was a brooding quality to his expression as he drove.

"Zach is the only family I really have anymore," Tessa said. "But I can understand the need to get away every once in a while."

Seth glanced at her before returning his gaze to the highway. "What about all those Loudoun Edwards? Don't you get some support from them?"

The mention of them brought up bad memories. Tessa didn't answer for so long Seth glanced at her again.

"I haven't seen them since I was twelve."

"Did they toss you out the family door when your mother remarried?"

"No."

When Tessa didn't say anything else, Seth reached over and took her hand where it was clenched in a fist on the console between them. She relaxed her fingers and let her hand rest in the curve of Seth's big palm.

"I sense a whole lot more to this story than what you want to talk about, but that's okay. This isn't some true confessions weekend. If you want to tell me…fine. If not, that's fine too. I want us to relax and have some fun, okay?"

His gaze was still on the road, but she saw the tension in the line of his jaw. She studied his profile and swallowed hard. The fact that he was nervous warmed her and made him seem more human.

"Okay."

"And Tessa?" His fingers shifted on the steering wheel.

"Yes?"

"Let's go ahead and get the sex thing out in the open." Now she couldn't mistake the tightness in his voice.

She jumped, she was so startled by what he said.

"Seth…" she began, feeling awkward again and wondering if she had somehow made her attraction to him obvious, embarrassing them both.

He glanced at her, his smile a little lop-sided. "I don't want you to do anything that doesn't feel right for you. I am not some hormone-crazed adolescent, but I won't deny I want to make love to you."

Thank you, God. He felt the same way--well, except for the hormone-crazed adolescent part because she did feel just about like that. Tessa laughed a little shakily. If they were going to get things out on the table, then she had a confession of her own. "Then I must be, the hormone-crazed part, because I've done almost nothing but think about making love to you."

A tremor shivered through his hand. He fidgeted in the seat. "Jesus, Tessa. You pick some time to make that announcement."

"Well, you said you wanted to get the whole issue of sex out in the open," she responded logically.

"Well it is now," he groaned. "Since I now look like a hormone-crazed adolescent."

Tessa's eyes dropped to his lap. She saw the way his dress slacks were tented and glanced back up at his face. She sucked in a shaky breath and wondered if he'd laugh if she fanned herself.

"Exactly!" He chuckled ruefully. He squeezed her hand and released it, putting both his on the steering wheel. He cleared his throat. "I-I want you to know, this isn't something I do…taking women to my beach house for the weekend."

"Seth? I'm not sure…well, what I'm doing."

He took a deep, breath and blew it out. "Don't worry about it, Tessa. I'm a big boy."

It was on the tip of her tongue to agree with him on that score, but she decided to keep her mouth shut for a change. He was a very big boy. Instead, she watched the scenery as they headed to Crosswick and tried to calm the jittery, aching heat suffusing her. She and Zach went to the beach farther north on the Delaware shore where they could camp, but that also meant beaches and beach communities that could get a little rowdy.

As Seth used a remote control to open the gated drive nestled between windswept pines, Tessa took in the house. It was tall, but not as large as she'd feared.

Seth pulled the Escalade into the carport underneath and said, "I had the cleaning service come open the house yesterday and stock the fridge for us, so if you'd like to change into your swimming suit, we can go right out on the beach."

Tessa nodded and smiled. "That sounds great. I can't think of anything I'd rather do."

Seth led the way, carrying their bags with him up the steps and into the large, airy combination kitchen and great room. Tessa's eyes widened as she stepped around him. The house was as informal as his office was the epitome of corporate elegance. Overstuffed, overlarge furniture and tile floors with scattered throw rugs. Several photographs of the ocean and sailing ships decorated the walls. It was a masculine atmosphere without being overpowering.

"This is wonderful, Seth," Tessa breathed in genuine pleasure. "I can't imagine a better place to relax."

He grinned, those dimples of his once more making an appearance. She looked around again. Perhaps this house was a truer reflection of the real Seth, not the chrome and glass version he reserved for Barrett Newspapers.

"I'll put your bags in the oceanfront guest bedroom. The master bedroom is to your left. If you want to change first, you can meet me on the deck in a few minutes. We'll have a drink and go down to the beach. That sound okay?"

"Wonderful." She sighed in complete contentment. His home was beautiful. The view was gorgeous and the weather equally so.

Tessa shut the door behind her and looked around her room. The tile floors continued in here, but the rugs on either side of the queen-sized bed were large and thick enough to sink her toes into. Sliding glass doors led onto the deck. To the right was an airy bathroom with a garden tub and a separate shower cubicle roomy enough for two. Tessa blushed at the thought, but she was also relieved he'd given her a room of her own. It underscored the fact he was trying to keep the pressure to a minimum.

After hanging up the one other dress she'd brought with her and putting away the rest of her clothes, she changed into a turquoise bikini cut high in the legs but low enough to show off her flat stomach. The halter-top was sturdy so it would stay on in the ocean, a lesson she'd learned a long time ago. She twisted her hair up under a neon pink baseball cap and slipped her feet into her Crocs. While nothing was ideal for walking through deep sand, these at least let the sand out as well as in.

She slipped through the sliding glass doors and stepped out on the deck. Seth was already there, a beer dangling in one hand as he leaned on the deck rail and looked out to sea. His smoothly muscled back was bare and brown. Tessa admired the way it tapered down to narrow hips. The faint indentations at the top of his butt were visible right above the low-slung waistband of his board shorts. Two dimples just begging for the touch of her fingers. She swallowed, once again a little breathless. The breeze lifted and ruffled his golden hair, which glinted in the glare of the summer sun. She must have made some noise because he turned his head to look at her, his gaze taking her in from head to toe as he smiled with a slow laziness that made her stomach flutter. He held his beer bottle aloft.

"Can I get you one?"

"Sure."

Tessa took a long swig, closing her eyes and savoring the cold, malty taste of it.

Seth laughed. "If you look any more ecstatic over that beer, I'm going to find myself jealous of a drink." He extended his bottle and clinked it against hers as he had done on her front stoop. "Here's to a weekend where we can forget for a while who we are and just be Tessa and Seth."

"Sounds good."

It set the tone for the rest of the afternoon. Seth rubbed sunscreen down her back, and if his hands lingered in a couple of spots, Tessa chose to ignore it--at least her mind did, even if her body instantly stirred, pulsing in places she wasn't used to.

The part of the beach where Seth's house was located was not crowded, giving them a feeling of isolation. Aside from the cry of the gulls and the sound of the surf, it was peaceful, without the overwhelming screeching and laughter always present at the places where she'd taken Zach. Seth took her hand to steady her across the loose sand beyond the dunes, and then didn't release it as they walked along the water's edge. Tessa noticed little things that endeared him to her even more. As tall as he was, he shortened his long strides to make it easier for her to keep up. When a couple of kids with boogie boards almost crashed into her. Seth moved between her and the boys to keep them from running her over.

They had tossed their towels and shoes farther up the beach. When they returned to them, Seth spread out the king-sized blanket he'd brought. Tessa lay down on her stomach and sighed. He stretched out next to her, his head propped on one elbow. As she watched him through her dark sunglasses, she saw his gaze travel down the length of her with a hungry expression in his golden eyes that sent a tingle of awareness through her.

"Do you want more sunscreen?" Seth asked in a gruff tone. "Or would you like to go swimming first?"

"You're looking for an excuse to put your hands on my butt again, aren't you, Mr. Barrett?"

Seth threw back his head with a full-throated laugh. "Sweetheart, it's not just your butt I'd like to get my hands on."

Tessa rolled onto her side and pulled off her glasses and hat. "Then maybe we should go swimming first to cool you off. This is, after all, a family beach."

Seth jumped up before extending his hand to pull her to her feet. The feel of the salt water against her skin and the sound of the surf rolling in were experiences Tessa could never get enough of. If she could, she would live near the ocean.

As the water reached her waist, she dived forward and came up with a big smile. It felt good to get back in, to feel the motion of the tangy seawater. She always felt a sense of peace moving through it, being gently rocked and rolled. She struck out, slicing the surface with arms and legs accustomed to swimming. As she turned her head for a breath of air, Seth swam beside her, his motions as fluid and graceful as if he'd spent most of his life around the water. She supposed he had. She'd seen how comfortable he was aboard his boat and in the waters of the bay, and he spoke as if sailing was an integral part of his life.

* * * *

Seth stopped when he saw Tessa had rolled onto her back and was floating with the rolling swell beyond the breakers. The expression of utter, carefree joy on her face was entrancing and arresting. She fit here, so much so it frightened him.

"I love the ocean," she said on a deep, contented breath.

I love you, he almost blurted, and was somewhat shocked that the thought had even occurred. He'd engaged in few serious relationships and never told a woman he loved her. It had always been business first. Sure, he'd escorted plenty of women to different social functions, even engaged in some casual flings, but never had he felt like this. Even the age difference between them seemed meaningless. Tessa was mature for her age, no doubt in part from having responsibility for her younger brother. Yet the fact he felt as he did made him a little uneasy. Tessa was comfortable in any social milieu. Beautiful, intelligent, kind--and too good to be true? For God's sake, even his mother liked her.

"I feel so at peace when I get away from DC," Tessa continued. "Life here on the ocean seems to move more in tune with the rhythm of the seasons and the sea."

"You can feel that even more out in the open ocean on a sailboat," Seth commented. That was his true love when it came to sailing, not the competitive hustle and bustle most of his family loved. Seth enjoyed the sound of the wind. The aloneness. The sometimes aimless drifting without the noise of a motor or even a crew, if he could get by without one. "It gives you a perspective on how small and insignificant we are compared to the vastness of the sea."

Tessa smiled at him, her eyes as clear as the ocean he loved. "Too bad your sailboat is moored on the bay."

Seth grinned. "I keep one here too--a little larger than Wistful, but she's designed so I can still sail her without a crew if I want to."

He felt an odd tug again as her eyes lit up.

"Seth! Can we…."

"I'd like nothing better than to spend the day with you on the ocean," he murmured as he reached out and brushed her lips with his.

He intended the kiss to be light, but as her mouth softened beneath his, Seth caught his breath. Hunger crashed through him, making it difficult to restrain the desire to take her right then and there. He broke away, taking in her startled expression.

"Perhaps we should go back," he suggested, his tone harsher than he intended, as he wondered how he could leave the water with the raging hard-on he sported.

* * * *

Tessa didn't like Seth's closed expression. The lean planes of his face were once again set in austere angles that gave no hint of the sudden flair of passion they'd shared. She started to say something, but Seth turned away, his long arms and legs cutting through the water. She followed him, wondering what had happened and if she'd somehow done something wrong. His moods were mercurial--certainly more than hers--and she was the redhead!

He waited for her at a spot where the ocean still hit him about waist deep. Tessa swam up to his side and stood up. The swim had given her a chance to think and get a little angry. He had invited her down here to get to know her better, so why was he going all moody?

"Just what was that?" Tessa demanded.

"What?" Seth's casual tone made her wonder if he was keeping his feelings hidden on purpose.

"Back there? You kiss me and then act like I've done something wrong. What was that?"

He looked down at her, raked a hand through his wet hair and sighed. "It's not you. It's me, Tessa. Every time I get around you, I revert to a hormone-driven idiot. Exactly what I said I wouldn't be." At her raised eyebrow he continued, "I don't want to start something in the middle of the beach that we can't finish. I don't want to start anything at all if it's not what you want."

"It was one kiss," she protested, still confused by his sudden and complete mood reversal.

Seth laughed self-deprecatingly. "For you, maybe, but I now find myself in an embarrassing dilemma. I can't even get out of the water at the moment."

He glanced down. Tessa followed the direction of his gaze and felt herself blush. "Oh!"

"Oh, indeed. Why don't you get your things and go on up to the house. I'll join you as soon as I can. Maybe reciting the Bill of Rights or doing multiplication tables in my head might help."

Tessa wished they were alone. If the beach were indeed deserted, there would be no need to stop. What would it be like to make love out in the open, under the sun with the sound of the water and the birds?

"I-I'll see you at the house."

Chapter 9

He heard her in the shower in her room when he returned. He hung the blanket and towels on the deck railing and slipped through the sliding doors into the master suite. If he'd hoped to impress Tessa Edwards this weekend, so far he was a miserable failure. Seth stalked into the master bath and stripped off his trunks. He adjusted the shower to a cooler temperature, hoping it would help him regain some control. Shrinkage would be a bonus at this point.

For God's sake. He was thirty-five years old, not some callow college kid, but something about Tessa ignited his senses. It took him another ten minutes to lose the hard-on he'd gotten from one kiss.

He washed away the film of salt and sand and shaved to rid himself of an all-too-obvious five-o'clock shadow. As he stared at himself in the mirror, he admitted it was in hopes he'd have his face nestled in tight against Tessa's milky skin. Most weekends he came here, he didn't even pick up a razor. After towel-drying his hair, he found a clean pair of boxers and a baggy pair of khaki cargo shorts.

He'd just slipped on a lightweight cotton shirt when the door opened. He turned in surprise as Tessa stepped into the room. She wore a silky wraparound robe that ended right below mid-thigh and her blown-dry hair fell thick and straight below her shoulders. Seth's heated gaze took in the fact she wore nothing else.

"Tessa?" he questioned tightly, his body already reawakening.

She smiled with some uncertainty, but her voice was steady. "It occurs to me that 'the sex thing' is starting to be kind of an eight-hundred pound gorilla between us. I thought," she continued as her hand went to the belt of her robe and slipped it loose, "perhaps we could get to know each other better, if we went ahead and…"

Seth's gaze locked on the loosening belt, and his breathing hitched. "Are you sure?"

Beneath the parted edges of the robe, he saw the shadowy valley between her breasts, the sparkle of the diamond at her belly button and lower still, the dark red curls that hid her femininity. His glance traveled back up to meet her wide blue gaze. Her lips parted and trembled, but she did not drop her eyes from the lust he knew must be plain in his face. He'd never experienced such heat. Slowly, Tessa shrugged out of the robe. It slithered to the floor with a whisper of silk, leaving her bare to Seth's alert, hungry perusal. He felt like a starving man presented with a feast. And, oh God, did he have every intention of gorging himself.

"Tessa." It was a low, throaty growl.

In two strides he pulled her into his arms, cupping her bottom and lifting her against him. Her slender arms twined around his neck and her head tipped back. Seth groaned. His lips slanted across her soft mouth, tasting, touching and exploring.

"Wrap your legs around me, sweetheart," he urged her, groaning again with desire as she pressed against his cock. The feel of her nestled against him made his balls ache. With one arm balancing her, he pulled back the covers on the master bed and lowered her onto the cool Egyptian cotton sheets.

He stood up, hands at his waist, to strip off the shorts and boxers he'd put on, then paused and looked down at her beautiful, creamy body. "Are you sure this is what you want?"

"Yes, Seth. I'm very sure."

* * * *

Her gaze slid down his body as he stripped off his clothes. He was an intimidating figure in his expensive, tailored suits, but even more so standing before her nude. Muscles, well-defined but not exaggeratedly so, rippled beneath golden brown skin. She'd noticed it earlier on the beach, but now the complete picture took her breath away. He looked like one of those Greek statues.

Something must have shown in her face, for Seth said, "Tessa? Doubts?"

She shook her head. It was all the invitation he needed. He came down next to her and pulled her against him, the bed sagging beneath his weight. His long fingers tangled in her hair before he touched his mouth to hers in a deep, drugging kiss. Heat spiraled through her, but that wasn't all. When his free hand caressed her hip and his tongue tangled with hers, his warmth reached out to her. She felt loved. He might not have said the words, but she felt it in his every move, his every touch. For a man so large, he was amazingly gentle.

His lips trailed from her mouth to her neck, and lower, until he sucked the bud of her breast into his mouth. With so much tenderness she thought she would cry out from the pleasure of it, he rolled her nipple with his tongue. Even as he did, his hand traveled from her hip to the nest of curls at the base of her belly. A soft, seeking touch stroked her, parting her swollen flesh to slip along the warm wetness of her. A moan escaped Tessa. The heat was so intense it was almost painful, yet she wanted more. She wanted him never to stop.

She clutched his thick hair and brought his lips back to her own. This time she was the aggressor. While his fingers continued to caress her and bring her to a fever pitch, it was her lips and her tongue that ravaged his mouth. When he slipped a long finger inside her and glided it back and forth, Tessa tumbled over the edge. She arched against him. Her lips parted on a long, low moan. Never had she felt anything this earth-shattering.

"That's it," Seth urged. "Go with it, sweetheart."

That moment of pure, sweet pleasure lasted forever and ended too soon. Her eyes met his hot, golden gaze, but more than heat met her. She saw a tender warmth that sent her climbing once more up that slope of ecstasy. As she surrendered once again, Seth covered her mouth, his tongue mimicking the movements of his finger inside her.

"God, Tessa," he groaned. "I want you so much I'm afraid I won't be able to make our first time together good for you." He paused, his fingers brushing her cheek.

She wrapped her arms around his shoulders. "You already have."

Tessa lay back, watching him lazily as he rolled to his side and slid open the nightstand drawer. Her eyes widened as he retrieved a foil condom package and ripped it open. As he put it on, her gaze fell to his cock. His finger had felt snug in her, but his erection was so much bigger, and she felt so swollen she couldn't imagine how he might fit. As Seth turned back to her, her doubts must have been there for him to see.

"Don't, sweetheart," he soothed her. "We'll go slowly. I won't lie, it might sting a bit the first time. I'll make it as good as I can. Trust me, Tessa. I'll make sure you're ready for me."

Tessa, who trusted no one, did trust Seth. The warmth in his eyes told her without words he would do what he promised. This was not a weekend of bedroom Olympics, not for her and not for him. This was the culmination of the closeness they'd experienced at other odd moments, a shared laugh, a soft touch, a vase full of summer flowers he'd cut himself.

He kissed her again and she answered him, wanting him to feel all the passion that was overflowing so much it made her groan. While his hands caressed her, she touched him with her slender fingers, teasing his flat nipples and over his hard belly. That ache built between her thighs yet again, made even greater by the trembling of his big frame as he held himself under firm control. Seth nudged her legs apart and positioned the blunt tip of his penis at the hot, wet core of her. His gaze held hers as he pushed forward.

So full. She felt so full, and then he stopped.

"Tessa," he whispered and their gazes locked. "I don't want to cause you pain. If you say stop, I will...even now."

She shook her head. "I want you, Seth. All of you."

He thrust forward, breaking that final barrier. At Tessa's small hiss, Seth stilled. "Are you all right, sweetheart?"

"Yes. I just need a moment to adjust."

His weight was on his knees and forearms. He watched her, moving a hand to smooth a strand of hair off her face.

"So beautiful, Tessa," he whispered. His words made her tremble and tighten on him. Seth closed his eyes and groaned. "Easy, or this will be over before it starts."

He moved within her, setting a languid rhythm that rocked her, reminding her of the ocean as she allowed herself to be carried on a wave. Only this time the wave was one of sensual pleasure. The momentary pain of his penetration passed and the heat of desire bubbled deep inside her. Seth's movements quickened. His breathing grew ragged. She clenched around him in spasms as another climax crashed over her. Seth sat up, holding and guiding her hips as he drove into her and threw back his head, his control shattered. He groaned in release. They were both frozen there for an instant, bodies glistening with sweat, breathing harsh and uneven.

Seth rolled onto his back and pulled her close to his side, her head nestled on his chest. He stroked her hair off her face and Tessa felt the faint trembling in his fingers.

"Are you all right?" he asked, his voice husky.

"Mmm."

He kissed her hair and her forehead as their breathing returned to normal.

"Is it always like that?" Tessa asked a few minutes later as she rubbed her palm over his chest muscles.

"Only with you," he answered and tilted her head to kiss her on the lips. "Stay there, baby. I'll be right back."

Tessa watched as he levered himself out of the bed and disappeared into the bathroom. He returned in a minute, carrying a washcloth and towel. He sat next to her and began to wash her thighs.

"Seth?" she questioned, shyness making her want to clamp her legs together. "What are you doing?"

"Washing away the blood," he explained. "It's not much, but I thought the warm cloth might ease any discomfort." He flashed a smile at her before turning his attention back to his task.

Tears gathered in her eyes. How could this man be so thoughtful? He was so different away from Barrett.

When he finished, he leaned over to kiss her. "Take a nap if you'd like. I'll get dinner going. I thought we could eat here tonight."

Tessa smiled, her eyelids already drooping. He was amazing, like the prince in a fairy tale.

                                        * * * *

Seth whistled as he worked in the open kitchen area. He was once again in well-worn cargo shorts and a short-sleeved cotton shirt that he'd left unbuttoned. Flip-flops cushioned his feet. More relaxed than he could remember in a long time, he ran his hands over his messy hair.

Tessa.

She'd surprised him, although he didn't know why. He'd known since Chicago that she was inexperienced, but as cynical as he was about the world, maybe there had been a part of him that hadn't quite believed it. He did now. Ever practical Tessa Edwards. How had such a beautiful young woman remained a virgin? He smiled to himself. Well, she wasn't any longer. Just thinking about how she'd responded to him made his cock start to swell. He couldn't remember an occasion when he'd been so relaxed and so turned on at the same time. His body hungered to get back in bed with her, get back inside her, but heaven knew it was far too soon. In fact, he wasn't sure how soon she could handle him again.

It was a half hour later before she emerged from the bedroom. She had slipped her robe back on and it clung to the swell of her breasts and the curve of her hips. Seth's gaze traveled the length of her. He shook his head to clear his thoughts. Down, boy. She needed time to recover, and he was hungry for some real food.

"There's beer in the fridge if you'd like one," he offered. "Or wine."

She shook her head. "Can I help you with anything?"

"You could make a salad. I thought we'd have pasta with steamed shrimp and vegetables in an alfredo sauce."

Tessa looked at him with one arched brow, found what she needed in the refrigerator, and went to work on the salad. "Where did you learn to cook?" she asked as she finished the salad and contented herself with watching him. He grinned at her, not minding at all that she appeared to find him so interesting.

"I had to learn while I was freelancing. I can't cook a lot of things, but I can manage pasta." He glanced at her and grinned. "I'm pretty good at roasting almost anything over an open fire too--also courtesy of freelancing in less than ideal circumstances."

Tessa laughed, as he'd intended.

They took everything out to the table on the deck. The sun had just set, and the sky still had a glow of pinks and yellows and oranges to the west. Over the ocean, the first stars were beginning to come out. The sound of the surf was quieter, the waves lapping against the sand.

"The food's delicious, Seth," she complimented him. "I'm ashamed to admit I assumed you had hired help like your parents."

"After life at their place, I like my privacy." Seth told her about growing up in his big family, how little privacy there was and how everything had always been a competition for all his siblings, all of them except Anna. "What about you? I know you didn't have a large family like mine, but you mentioned spending time at Mont Clair. Was that during the summers?"

"Yes. When I was small. We didn't go anymore after I was twelve." Her voice had gone high, strained.

"Because your mother met Mallory?"

Tessa looked down at the food remaining on her plate. "Partly."

Seth touched her cheek. "Tessa? You tensed before when this came up. Did something happen?"

As she met his steady gaze, he saw the hurt she had buried behind so many layers.

"I hated those summers," she admitted. "My cousins picked on me without mercy. Unlike the rest of them, I had no older brothers or sisters to come to my rescue. When my mother began dating and leaving me there more, things got even worse."

Seth covered her hand with his and squeezed. He wanted to offer her more in the way of comfort, but had the feeling it would be rejected.

"The summer I was nine, I got shut up in a tack trunk while playing hide and seek."

"Was it an accident?"

Tessa looked at Seth. "Everyone said so, but I've always wondered. They told me later a pitchfork fell in such a way it prevented me from pushing the lid open, but I never heard anything fall."

God, she could have smothered in that trunk. Seth arched a brow, showing his own doubts about that explanation. "That would explain your claustrophobia."

Tessa looked beyond Seth out to sea. "That was the beginning. There was an older cousin--Peter--he would say things and do…things." Tessa paused and grimaced. "The summer I was twelve, it all came to a head. I tried to stay away from him, but he came to my room late one night and tried to touch me. I screamed for help, but when my aunt and uncle got there, it wasn't Peter who got in trouble, it was me."

Seth lifted her hand to his lips and kissed her palm. The pain and rejection she'd felt were obvious, and he wished he could have been there for her. Maybe he should just be grateful that he had been able to help his own sister.

"I hated those summers," Tessa continued. "Momma came and got me. There was a big fight and as we left, she told me I would never have to see any of them again. I was so relieved, I started crying. I thought my aunt and uncle would protect me, but had I not been able to get in touch with my mother, I believe they would have turned a blind eye to Peter actually raping me, instead of…" Tessa stopped and stared out at the ocean again.

"Molesting you?" Seth finished. He stroked his thumb over the back of her hand, drawing her back to the present. "It's over, sweetheart. No one will ever treat you that way again."

She smiled. "I know that, with you."

His breath caught for an instant. There it was again, that tug pulling him closer and closer to the edge of falling completely in love. There was a pause and he opened his mouth to say some of what he was feeling, but the moment broke when Tessa stood up and collected the dishes. Seth closed his mouth and helped her. Together they cleaned the kitchen and made coffee, which they took onto the deck. The sky was black now and a full moon peeked above the horizon. Its reflection stretched in a silvery beam across the smooth, glassy surface of the ocean. The waves sounded somehow muted in the darkness.

Tessa sucked in a deep breath and closed her eyes. "Thank you so much for inviting me here. I think I could stay here forever."

"That's how I feel." Seth stepped behind her and cradled her with his arms and chest. He bent his head to touch the top of hers.

While one hand wrapped around her waist, his free hand cupped the curve of her breast. The feel of the warm silk-covered weight made him hard. He wanted her again with a raw, aching need he'd never before felt. She was like a drug in his blood.

"How do you feel?" he rumbled. God, he was such a cad. "If you're sore…"

Tessa turned in his arms and pressed against him. "I'm fine, Seth."

He lifted her with a growl and surprised her by setting her down on the edge of the table. He kissed her, tongue diving and tangling with hers while he untied her robe and pushed it from her shoulders. Moonlight bathed her creamy breasts. Tessa sighed with pleasure. His lips traveled downward, and she leaned back, her arms braced on the table. His teeth nipped her belly before he moved lower. He wanted to taste her, the perfect dessert.

"Seth?" It was a whisper that ended on a soft purr of pleasure when he reached her sex.

He teased her with his fingers, parting her and fondling her with his lips and tongue. He found the sweet bud of flesh at her very center and nuzzled it. This time Tessa gasped and arched. He chuckled. There was something to be said about being first, especially with this woman.

"You're so responsive."

When she cried out, he lifted his gaze to watch her, amazed at how lost she was in the wonder of it, the almost mindless pleasure that washed over her again. He was able to do this for her, his woman. His cock throbbed in response. Not about to take her in the middle of a table on the deck of his beach house, Seth stood and lifted her, carrying her through the sliding glass doors and into the master bedroom. The pace of their loving slowed as they each took time to explore the other's body, learning what touch or taste teased or pleased. They dozed, only to wake and turn to each other again.

Seth awoke before dawn. Tessa slept next to him, curved along his side. He slipped off the edge of the bed and pulled on his boxers before stepping out on the deck so he could watch as the sun lightened the eastern sky, turning it from a midnight blue to an ever-burgeoning and brightening array of colors. As gorgeous as that was, the woman now sleeping in his bed fascinated him even more. He turned and leaned against the railing, devouring her sleeping curves. Thinking of the passion he'd awakened in her was enough to have him hardening once more in desire.

Over the years, plenty of women had set their sights on him. As the eldest Barlow-Barrett, he was a matrimonial catch, but Seth had avoided those entanglements. It had made him cynical, leaving him with the feeling that no woman would ever be able to see beyond the name and the empire to Seth, the man. Even the women he chose to date had understood from the start he was looking for sex, not commitment. If they had a problem with that, he had always walked away.

Tessa was different. He'd thought about an affair with her, but had thrown that idea out the window in Chicago. As jaded as he had become over the years, even he couldn't take what she wasn't sure she even wanted to surrender. But it was more than that. At last he had admitted to himself it wasn't just sex he wanted with her. Although that was fantastic, he wanted more. He wanted all of her, every day and every night.

The problem was he didn't know if she felt that same way. There was the age difference between them, and her own stiff-necked independence. Even her revelations about her family appeared to him to be more of a wedge than a bridge between them. While she might come from the same type of background he did, she had no fond memories to go along with it. And as far as seeing him as a man? She had seen him at his worst in the office, yet she was not only still working with him, but had allowed their relationship to become more than business.

He would take her sailing. Out on the ocean, maybe he could talk about feelings so powerful he felt awed when he touched her.

* * * *

Tessa awoke to the gentle brush of lips against her cheek and a whisper in her ear. A smile curved her full lips as she turned toward Seth. He knelt next to the bed.

Rich coffee with just the right amount of cream. The aroma teased her senses awake.

"Come on, sleepyhead," he coaxed. "I have breakfast waiting outside. Get dressed and we'll spend the day sailing."

An hour later, Tessa was seated at the rear of the sailboat with the wind already teasing tendrils of hair loose from the ponytail she had tucked through a baseball cap. Her dark glasses were back in place, the better to watch Seth unobserved. He was so at home out here, his motions second nature to him. As the wind filled the sails, he tacked, taking them along the coastline. He was far enough off shore they could enjoy privacy, but close enough the water was still not so deep they couldn't anchor when it came time to make sandwiches. The sole tense moment for Tessa was when she had to use the head, but Seth told her to leave the door open so she wouldn't feel so confined.

After clearing up lunch, he pulled off his shirt, leaving him clad in his trunks. Tessa slid off her shorts to reveal her bikini bottom and was getting ready to pull off her shirt when Seth's quiet voice interrupted her.

"You don't have to leave your suit on if you don't want to." His eyes twinkled as he said it. "We appear to have the ocean to ourselves today."

Tessa smiled at him and then pulled her shirt over her head. Her bikini top followed, and she stood before him with her creamy breasts bared to the sun. Still holding his gaze, she took the bottle of sunscreen and massaged lotion over them, her motions slow and seductive. She watched his Adam's apple bob and his gaze lower to the movement of her hands, and she laughed. If he'd been teasing, she'd called his bluff.

"May I help?" he purred, stepping closer to her.

"By all means." Tessa let him take over. In just minutes, she gasped with pleasure, her breathing ragged and uneven.

"Sit down," he commanded, and gently pushed her to the cushioned seats along the edge of the boat. He poured more sunscreen into his broad palms and massaged the warm lotion into her skin, starting at her feet and working his way up over her delicate ankles to her calves and then the sensitive area behind her knee. Tessa sucked in a breath and Seth smiled, his teeth gleaming against his tan. His hands moved higher, rubbing the sunscreen along the length of her thighs before parting them to touch the sensitive skin along the inside.

"Seth?" Her voice wasn't much more than a moan.

"Why not take it all off, Tessa?" he coaxed. "I will too. Would you like that? Only the two of us are here to see."

She nodded, his gentle stroking hands again making the heat spiral through her and leaving her wanting so much more. His fingers hooked in the top of her briefs and Tessa lifted her hips so he could slide her bottoms down her thighs and toss them to the side. He stood up and slid his own trunks down so he was as naked as she. Tessa's heated gaze traveled from his intense stare down over his furry chest to the thrust of his cock.

He was so close. She leaned forward and clasped him in her hand, enjoying his low moan as she massaged him from base to tip, and cradled his sac in her other hand.

"Tessa!" It came out on an agonized groan after she leaned forward and let her lips trace the path of her hands.

Tangling his fingers in her hair, he moaned in pleasure, and she teased him again and again. He pulled her up and sat on the seat, with her straddling him. Their hands continued to caress each other until he grasped her wrist to still her movements.

"Condom. In my shorts," he gasped.

She found the packet and ripped it open before sliding it over his hard length. He lowered her onto his erection as though he wanted their coming together to last all day. Then he was buried inside her.

"Is it too much? You're so tiny, I'm always afraid I'll hurt you."

"Never," she whispered against his mouth. "We fit together just right."

Bracing her feet on the seat and wrapping her arms around his neck, she began to ride him. Seth's head lolled backward in complete abandonment as she brought him to a shivering, groaning orgasm. Still deep inside her, he caressed her with his fingers until she collapsed against him and found her own sweet release.

They swam, the ocean cool against their nude bodies, and then Seth once again massaged her with sunscreen before they dozed on a thick blanket atop the boat he'd named Wanton. She felt that way with him. She woke up to find him studying her, his golden eyes soft and serious.

"I'm falling in love with you, Tessa," he admitted, his voice gruff.

She wanted to believe. Every instinct cried out to her that she could trust this man. He would not tell her what he thought she wanted to hear. If Seth said it, he meant it. She wanted to believe, but the part of her that had seen her trust destroyed so many years ago still held itself aloof, refusing to believe it was anything more than the afterglow of some really great sex.

"Seth…"

She knew wariness lingered in her eyes. Rather than hear her put a voice to it, he put his fingers over her lips. "Shh. You don't have to say anything, Tess. I promised no strings and I meant it. I just wanted you to know you mean more to me than just an amazing lover." He leaned over and kissed her. "Let's go home."

They went out to dinner that night, traveling north along the coast to enjoy some of the rowdier night life. Some of the bars they visited shocked Tessa, but Seth laughed and whisked her onto a dance floor crowded with couples not always of the opposite sex. They made love on the beach that night. Seth brought a thick blanket out with him. He undressed her by the light of the moon and then as the surf rolled in a few yards away, he rocked her in perfect time with the crashing waves until desire overtook both of them, making their movements hurried and intense. Their eyes locked just moments before Tessa arched underneath him. He caught her scream of pleasure with his open mouth and plundering tongue and rode her until he too slipped over that edge of ecstasy.

They agreed to head home around lunchtime. Neither one of them wanted the weekend to end, but reality had a way of intruding. Seth reached for her hand as they traveled and held it to his lips for a brief kiss. She accepted it as a benediction of sorts, a sign they were back to the real world where he was Seth Barrett of Barrett Newspapers, and she was the ever-capable Tessa.

Chapter 10

Monday morning Tessa called her bank again since she'd heard nothing back. The representative on the line insisted the mystery deposit was supposed to be in her account. Tessa insisted it wasn't, and no one yet seemed to know the source of the unexplained money.

"Every time we try to pull up the transaction record, we're getting an error message, Miss Edwards."

"That's because it is an error." Tessa ground her teeth in frustration. "It's not supposed to be in my account. Well, I'm sure someone will come looking for it. I can't imagine ten grand would disappear from an account without someone, somewhere taking notice."

"We'll continue to try to correct the problem, Miss Edwards."

She hung up in disgust. She'd certainly want to know what had happened to ten thousand dollars if it were hers. At this point, though, she felt it was the bank's problem to resolve. She'd told them and would just pretend the money wasn't there. Anything else would be foolish in the extreme. She understood their reluctance to remove the money when they couldn't yet pinpoint if it was even there, but her unease over it lingered. She supposed most of that was due to her innate desire to have everything in order.

In the meantime, she had other tasks to complete, so she went back to work on Seth's trip to the West Coast papers. He would leave mid-week to visit northern California and Oregon before returning home late Friday. Brandon had the jet on a trip to Dallas, so Seth would have to take a commercial flight. Tessa took care of booking and paying for the flight with the travel account, and returned to the itineraries and meeting schedules for each of the papers he would visit. Seth had insisted he fly back late Friday because he would be making a turnaround to be at his niece's christening in North Carolina.

Tuesday, Tessa reviewed the final itinerary and meeting agendas and made last minute adjustments before faxing everything to the papers on the West Coast. Seth was back in a brooding mood again. Tessa knew it had to do with the subject of the meetings. The papers weren't performing up to expectations, and Seth was going in to troubleshoot and, if necessary, fire managers who weren't cutting it.

She called the bank once again after lunch, but they had still not resolved the problem. As she hung up, Seth captured her hand. "May I take you to dinner tonight?"

She swallowed at the hot look in his eyes, everything else going right out of her head, and nodded. She floated through the rest of the afternoon, feeling somewhat reassured. With the way Seth's mood had been, she had begun to wonder if their weekend together had been a fantasy she had dreamed up because it was what she wished would happen. He picked her up at seven and took her to one of the most exclusive restaurants in the area. They sat in a back corner, where they had some privacy, and talked about their weekend at the beach.

"I'd like you to come with me to North Carolina this weekend," Seth said.

Tessa looked at him with uncertainty. "But it's a family event, Seth."

"All the more reason for me to want you there."

Tessa's temperature climbed at the look on his face. His words of love on the Wanton hung there, seducing her. As he drove back to her house, he caressed her hand. He switched the ignition off when they arrived.

"Would you like to come in for some coffee?" Tessa asked, hoping he wanted more than that.

He nodded and came around to open the door for her. He escorted her up the sidewalk and opened the door that led into her small two-bedroom apartment. She'd furnished it with quality pieces that would withstand the wear and tear of a small boy.

"Have a seat," Tessa said over her shoulder. "I'll go get the coffee started."

Seth grabbed her and twirled her back in his arms. "Forget the coffee." He smiled. "I'd much rather sip this."

His lips tasted hers with a gentle demand that soon grew to ravenous proportions. She sighed against his lips, and his hands dropped to caress her bottom through her skirt. He dragged his mouth from hers and pressed her face against his broad chest.

"Lord, I've wanted to do that for the past forty-eight hours. I nearly bent you over my desk a couple times. The fantasy was so strong I swore

I could feel my hands rubbing your ass, pushing your panties out of the way so I could plunge my tongue deep inside and taste your sweetness."

He bent now and swung her into his arms. "Where's your bedroom, Tessa? I think dessert is definitely on the menu, and I am a starving man."

Tessa giggled and pointed down the hall.

He dwarfed the room with his size. As soon as they entered, he let her slide to her feet, so she could feel every aroused inch of him before he began to undress her. It was erotic to watch him as he removed her clothing piece by piece while he was still clothed in his dinner suit. When she stood before him nude, he let his eyes roam over her.

If he was a man ready for dessert, then she was a woman also starving. Tessa stepped forward and grabbed his tie. "My turn." She kissed and caressed each part of him she bared, leaving him gasping when she knelt and wrapped her mouth around him, pleasuring him with her lips and tongue.

He pulled her up with a muffled groan and their lovemaking intensified, soon plummeting them both over the edge. As she lay on the silky sheets, he slid the head of his cock along her opening and pushed forward, filling her so they could think of nothing else while he rocked his hips. Seth arched his back and drove into her with a guttural growl of the most intense pleasure. His seed spilled into her and it was only then they remembered the condom still lying on the bedside table.

Seth stroked the hair back from her face. "I'm sorry, sweetheart," he murmured. "I'm afraid we got a little carried away."

"It's okay," Tessa dismissed. "The timing probably isn't a factor anyway." They dozed for a little while in each other's arms and the next time, Seth made sure the condom was in place. Tessa had no idea what time it was when he woke her up with a kiss on the cheek.

"I've got to go, sweetheart, but I'll call you as soon as I get back."

Tessa smiled, her brain still fogged with sleep. "Bye, Seth."

He kissed her one last lingering time on the lips and then he was gone.

* * * *

It seemed strange to be in the office the next day without Seth barking orders from the next room. Everything was so quiet and deserted, as if his mere absence had sucked the very life from the building. In a way it had. Brandon was seldom in town for long, spending a lot of time on the road in both business and pleasure. From the amount of work Seth handled, Tessa suspected Brandon's share was mostly pleasure, and neither brother seemed happy with that. Of the elder Barlow-Barrett, there was seldom any sign, and she thanked heaven. Seth and Brandon were both strong-

Laura Browning

willed men, but they stepped around their father like they were walking on eggshells.

Tessa tried her bank again to see if they'd gotten any further in figuring out how the extra money had landed in her account, but they were still reading an error message and no one had filed any complaints yet that any money had been incorrectly credited.

"Can't you put it in escrow or something since I've explained it doesn't belong to me?" Tessa asked, her patience wearing thin.

"We'll see what we can do," the employee handling the discrepancy told her.

Right after Tessa returned from lunch, her extension rang. "Miss Edwards," the young woman from her bank greeted her, "we located where the deposit came from and the date."

Tessa listened to the girl and a cold knot formed in her stomach before she said, "That's not possible. I was returning from Chicago that day, and I would never have authorized a deposit to my personal bank account from Barrett's travel account. Transfer the funds back to Barrett's account immediately, and I'll try to figure out where the error occurred."

Tessa hung up the phone, perplexed. She didn't even like to think about the Chicago trip between being stuck in the elevator and the disastrous scene with Seth at the hotel. She was still trying to recall all the details from the trip when her phone rang again with an interoffice call. Tessa checked the caller ID and saw it was Miss Tallmadge, the senior Barrett's secretary.

"Tessa Edwards here. How may I help you, Miss Tallmadge?"

The older woman's voice sounded even colder than normal. "Mr. Barrett would like to see you in his office, Miss Edwards."

"What time?" Tessa inquired as she started to check her schedule on the computer.

"Now."

Tessa was left with the click of the phone disconnecting. She sat for a moment, wondering at the abrupt summons to Barrett senior's office. Was he going to dress her down for spending most of the weekend undressing his son? But hot on the heels of that irreverent thought, something else occurred to her, and cold seeped through her. Could it have something to do with the money that had ended up in her account? Was it possible that at the same time she'd been trying to figure out where it had come from, they had also been trying to figure out where it had gone? As she racked her brain about how it could have happened, she walked up to the next floor and down the long hallway carpeted in a sound-deadening pile.

She had been so upset when she came home from Chicago that evening and had rushed in the house. She'd wanted to hide her tears from Zach... Tessa paused outside the door to Alexander Barlow-Barrett's suite of offices. Her computer and bag... Zach had brought them in. Had he... She shook her head. No way. He couldn't have known the account number, could he? She went over and over possible scenarios as to how he might have accessed the account as she turned the knob. Although she didn't want to pin it on Zach, she couldn't fathom how it could be anyone else.

If at all possible, Tallmadge looked even icier than usual. She punched the intercom as soon as Tessa walked through the door.

"Miss Edwards is here, Mr. Barrett." Tallmadge examined her with cold, colorless eyes. "Come with me."

Tessa made a face behind the older woman's back at her imperious tone, but worry haunted her. She knew Zach had been angry at Seth, but surely he wouldn't... She didn't even want to go there, and she knew no matter what happened, she would never admit it might have been her little brother who had fiddled with the Barrett account. She would do anything to protect him. He was a kid.

"Miss Edwards." Alexander Barrett's tone was as cold as a nor'easter blowing in as he turned toward her. He did not invite her to sit. "The accounting department has been researching an irregularity with one of our accounts, and it was brought to my attention you might know something about it."

"Which account would that be, sir?" Tessa inquired, trying to stall for time. Sweat trickled down her spine. If any of this came back to Zach, her aunt and uncle would return to court seeking custody again.

"The travel account Seth and Brandon use," Barrett said.

"What seems to be the problem?" Tessa asked, but inside she quaked.

"A matter of some missing funds, ten thousand dollars worth. I spoke to Seth, who said you are the only one who's accessed the account in the last month." Alexander Barrett paused. "Now, Miss Edwards, let's stop playing games. Perhaps you should tell me what's going on."

Tessa raised her chin. She hated lying, but Zach had to come first. "I know nothing at all about it."

"Then perhaps you would care to explain the note I have from your own bank saying you authorized a deposit this morning from your account to replace the money."

Tessa could do nothing to hide her involuntary start.

"Ah, I see we're jogging your memory."

"I have no idea how the money ended up in my account to begin with," Tessa protested, but she knew it sounded weak. He'd caught her in a lie, so her credibility was shot.

Alexander Barlow-Barrett eyed her with all the warmth of a pit viper. "For the sake of my son, who seems to value your...services, I am not handing you over to the police. However, as of right now, your employment with Barrett is terminated."

"Seth..." Tessa started to protest, but if anything Barrett's gaze became even more glacial.

"Knows what I am doing and agrees it is the only course. Since he's out of town and can't do it himself, he's left your departure in my hands." With one last look that dismissed her as being no more important than a speck of lint, he went back to the papers he'd been scanning. "Tallmadge will escort you out."

Tessa was in shock. Seth knew? He had agreed--without even talking to her? She barely heard Tallmadge as she returned to her desk. She grabbed a picture of Zach and the fisherman's loop Seth had tied and followed Tallmadge into the elevator. Tessa closed her eyes the whole way down, refusing to let the older woman see her fear at being in that confined space. She ignored the strange glances they received as Tallmadge walked with her all the way to the sidewalk, where a cab waited.

She sat in the back seat, her hands shaking so much she tucked them between her knees. It had to have been Zach, but she would not, could not throw him to the wolves to save herself. They had just a few months to go until she turned twenty-five and could access his trust. Their aunt and uncle would no longer be a threat to them then. She would have to find some other job in the meantime and try to keep this under wraps. No way did she want her aunt and uncle finding out.

All the mistrust she thought she had put behind her surged back tenfold. How could Seth have gone along with his father without even speaking to her? She knew he did what he felt was his duty to Barrett Newspapers, but didn't what they'd shared give her some claim on a portion of that loyalty? Was this what his words of love were worth? Tessa pushed Seth from her mind. She had to, for her own sanity. She couldn't afford to think about him. He was like everyone else. When it was all said and done, the only person she could trust was herself. Hadn't she learned that lesson the hard way?

Tessa called her old employer as soon as she got back to her apartment, but hung up the phone with a dispirited shrug. They had filled her position and things were tight right now. They couldn't even take her on a temporary basis. She had to find a job, fast. If Aunt Kathleen and Uncle Edwin got any inkling her and Zach's circumstances had changed... Tessa didn't even want to go there.

The real problem was going to be replacing the income she'd lost. Zach would start school in two weeks, and she still had uniforms to buy, plus other items on the long list of supplies he needed, not to mention the remaining tuition payments. Tessa poured herself a glass of wine and curled up on the window seat. When the phone rang late that evening, she checked the caller ID and recognized Seth's cell number. She turned away and let the answering machine pick it up.

Thursday morning she took a hard look at what skills she had. Her degree in social work wasn't getting her anywhere. She had computer and organizational skills, but she now also had no reference from Barrett. She had waited tables in college to help with some extra spending money and had done pretty well, but again, what reputable restaurant was going to hire her, much less pay her what she'd made at Barrett? Tessa tossed the newspaper onto the coffee table and grabbed her gym bag. She would go to the Y and swim. Maybe she could think of something while doing laps.

Another young woman joined her, asking if they could share lanes since the pool was crowded.

"No problem."

The woman towered above Tessa and looked like a Nordic goddess in her suit. They kept an even pace, and when they finished working out, they headed back to the locker room together.

"I wish I could just swim every day," the woman confided. "But I have to throw some running in there too in order to keep my figure or I'll lose my job."

"Are you a model?" Tessa asked.

"Lord, no." The lissome blond laughed. "I'm a dancer."

"Ballet?" Tessa asked at the same time she was thinking the woman was a little tall for that.

This time the blonde almost doubled over with laughter. "No, I dance at Flamingo Road."

Tessa had heard of it. It was a 'gentlemen's' club, although it did have a reputation for being high class.

"My name's Lucy, but at work I'm known as Jasmine Le Fleur. Fancy, huh?" She laughed as if it was all a huge joke. "What's your name?"

"Tessa Edwards. And my name's the same no matter where I am."

The two women shook hands and grinned at each other. Lucy invited Tessa out for coffee. It was while they were sipping away on lattes that Lucy asked, "So what do you do?"

"Nothing at the moment. I just got fired from my last job, so I'm looking."

"Any luck?"

"Not so far. My job before the one I got fired from was filled and they're not hiring anyone else right now."

"My boss is."

Tessa stared at Lucy and almost spit her coffee out as she started to laugh. "No offense, Lucy, but I can't picture me doing exotic dancing. I mean, let's be realistic. You're almost six feet, I'm barely five-foot-two. You are built and I'm..."

"Built," Lucy finished for her. "Look, Roberto's not looking for dancers right now. He's looking for a waitress. The pay is good and the tips can be even better." Lucy named a figure that at last caught Tessa's attention.

"What do I have to wear?" she asked the taller woman, unable to keep the skepticism from her voice.

"It has a top." Lucy laughed. "And a bottom. Not much of either, that's for sure, but the important parts are covered. You'd be a knockout with that red hair of yours. Most of the wait staff works six to three. You should come with me and talk to Roberto. I can vouch for the fact that he's an excellent boss--and a great guy. The shoes are tricky--high, high heels-- but you get used to them."

And somehow, Tessa Edwards, from one of the bluest-blooded first families of Virginia, found herself talking to Roberto at one of the finest strip clubs in the area. Even more amusing, she left with a job she would start the following evening.

Tessa explained what had happened at Barrett to her neighbor. The older woman shook her head. "I'm so sorry to hear that, honey. That Seth seemed like such a nice man, taking you and your brother sailing and all. I guess you just don't know."

"Well, it's in the past. I'm starting a new job and I'll need your help because of the hours." Although she was reluctant, Tessa explained where and what her new job was, and the older woman nodded.

"I had to work where I could when I was bringing up my two, so I understand. There's no shame in honest work. Don't you worry about a thing. I'll keep an eye on Zach for you."

Tessa checked her messages when she walked back in and saw Seth had called two more times. She listened to the messages, steeling herself against him.

"Tessa, pick up the phone!" he demanded in the last message. "Talk to me, damn it, and tell me what's going on!" She heard him swear. "I'll come by when I get back tomorrow. We need to talk."

Tessa's finger shook as she pressed the button to erase the message. There was nothing to talk about, and she wouldn't be here when he came by. She lifted her chin and pressed her lips together. She would be working at her new job, taking orders from a new boss. It was just as well. It would be a clean break.

* * * *

He'd moved heaven and earth to get everything on the West Coast settled so he could fly back home. As the limo ferried him from the airport to Barrett headquarters, Seth tapped his fingers against the doorframe.

He needed to know what the hell was going on before he talked to Tessa. He didn't want to believe what appeared to be damning evidence. He'd seen the transfer of the money himself. Ten grand that had left the travel account and then been replaced--out of Tessa's personal checking account. It was a classic scheme that a lot of people got away with, for a while--"borrowing" money to cover a temporary shortfall and then paying it back. Sooner or later, it caught up with them. Seth knew she had her brother's tuition and other school expenses and was still waiting on access to the trust fund, but he didn't want to believe it. His father already had the business office checking to see if there'd been any other suspicious transfers from that account or any of the others Tessa would have had access to.

His head pounded and his stomach knotted with tension.

As soon as the limo pulled up in front of the glass doors, Seth was out of the car and stalking up to the building. The security guard started to greet him, but then apparently thought better of it and went back to work.

Great.

Seth had only one person he wanted to see right now. Alexander Barlow-Barrett.

Even Tallmadge got out of Seth's way as he swept past her and entered his father's office with barely a knock. His father looked over the rim of his reading glasses and eased back in his big leather chair, steepling his fingers in front of his face.

"It's customary to knock."

Seth ignored him. "I want to know what the fuck happened around here."

His father's eyes narrowed. "No matter what you might think, Seth, I am still the head of this company, and you will not barge into my office and use that type of language. If you're referring to your former assistant--she admitted to my face that she authorized the bank to put the money back, but that was only after I caught her in a lie."

"Tessa wouldn't..."

His father leaned forward. "She did, Seth, and she admitted it. I know you were infatuated with the girl, so I'm not pressing charges..."

He felt as though someone had reached inside his chest and crushed his heart. All at once, weariness crashed in on him. For a while, a short while, he'd dared to think things could be different. He still didn't want to believe. Not until he talked to Tessa, not until she looked him in the face and told him.

He drew himself up, his mouth tight. "It was more than infatuation. I wanted to marry her."

His father stood up. "Well, I hope you hadn't done anything so foolish as propose. I hardly need to tell you that any such relationship would be out of the question."

Seth slapped his palm down on his father's desk. "That is not your decision to make!"

"You have a position to uphold in this community, this industry. How could you even contemplate such a ridiculous thing? Stop thinking with your penis, Seth."

He shook his head. "I have to talk to her..."

Alexander sighed as though he were giving up on trying to make any rational arguments.

"Do it. I know what happened in this office, what she admitted. But if you have to hear it from her, then do so, and let's move on."

Seth inclined his head.

* * * *

Tessa arrived a half-hour ahead of her shift so she had time to change. Roberto had explained all the girls changed into their uniforms in the dressing area at Flamingo Road. Lucy grinned at her and called her name. Tessa gaped as she saw the postage stamp-sized sequins that passed for a costume for Jasmine Le Fleur and the exotic makeup Lucy applied.

"Wow." Tessa laughed. "I would never have known you if you hadn't called my name."

Lucy smiled at her in the mirror. Gone was the freshly scrubbed look she sported at the gym. In its place were thick, false eyelashes topping off darkly rimmed and shadowed eyes. She pointed a mascara wand at the black woman next to her. "This is Tiffany, your shift supervisor. She can get you squared away. I've got to go limber up some more before I go on."

Tessa watched Lucy disappear through a door into a room where she spotted mirrored walls and a ballet barre before the door closed behind her. She turned her gaze to the black woman regarding her with the faintest smirk on her full lips. "First time in a strip club, honey?"

Tiffany turned out to be one of the most down-to-earth, practical women Tessa had ever met. She was supporting three kids on her own after her husband left her, so she could relate to Tessa's situation. Tiffany helped her adjust her uniform. She pushed Tessa's breasts a little higher and pulled her top a little lower.

At Tessa's blush, Tiffany stared at her hard. "Honey, you want all the tips you can get, and that means showing these things off. I'm not saying you let anyone touch you, but the more you smile and flaunt what God gave you, the more money you'll find in your pocketbook at the end of the evening. You got it?"

Tessa nodded, shocked by how frank the woman was. "It's just kind of a switch from silk and suits to spandex and spikes."

Tiffany laughed. "You'll get used to it. It's a job, baby girl, like any other."

By three-thirty in the morning, Tessa had no doubts it was a job, but she was not sure she could agree it was like any other. Her feet ached from running back and forth in high heels with drink orders and munchies. She did her best to follow Tiffany's advice, and had found either Roberto or Tiffany close at hand whenever one of the customers tried to get a little too friendly. Tessa changed back into her street clothes and washed off the makeup, but she still needed a shower to get rid of the smell of cigarette smoke and alcohol, and she would feel better about showering at her own home.

She was bone weary when she pulled up in front of her house. As she walked up the sidewalk, Seth stepped out of the shadows. His size alone was enough to take her breath away and make her heart beat in fear for a fraction of a second before she realized who it was. Then anger and hurt replaced the fear.

"Where the hell have you been?" he barked.

"None of your business!" she snapped back, too tired to want to talk about anything. He wasn't her boss any longer, and he sure as hell wasn't a man who loved her.

"Like hell it's not!" Seth snarled and spun her around and into his arms. He recoiled as the smell of the smoke and booze that clung to her assailed him. "Jesus. You smell like a bar. Is that where you've been? I've waited hours for you to get home and you've been at a bar?"

His face was a mask of fury that almost, but not quite, concealed the hurt and confusion he felt. Tessa was too mad and hurt to let herself see much of anything other than his anger.

"So what if I have? Do you think my life has stopped because I don't work for you? Do you think you're the only man wanting to touch me?" She said it to hurt him. She wanted him to hurt like she did. Tessa jerked her arm away from him. "Go away, Seth," she whispered, hoping the ache in her heart wasn't noticeable in her voice. "Go back to your family duty and your fortress of glass and steel. Find someone else to mouth your meaningless words of love to, and leave me the hell alone."

She ran then, but he didn't come after her. As she shut the door, she saw him stalk off down the block. Tessa leaned against the hall door and let the hot tears spill down her cheeks.

* * * *

Seth sat in his SUV, staring at the front of the house and watching as the light went on in Tessa's apartment. He sucked in a harsh breath, a sob really, and blinked his eyes to clear them. He hadn't wanted to believe his father, hadn't wanted to believe that Tessa was nothing more than an opportunist, but even her own words seemed to back that up. The jewelry box in his pocket felt like a hot poker burning a brand into his thigh. Seth's jaw hardened, and he started the Escalade and drove away. He would not make the mistake of being so gullible again. She had stomped on his love, but he would be the one to kill it.

Bitterness welled, flooding through him. As long as he stayed the heir apparent, this was what his life would be. He'd thought she was different, thought she'd been able to see him, but it was the Barlow-Barrett empire she'd had her eye on, not him. She'd just been careless and gotten caught.

Chapter 11

A week later, Tessa waited at Zach's new school for her brother's bus to return from camp. She had her hair stuffed under a baseball cap and dark glasses on to shield her eyes from the glare. She'd come from a run in the park, so she was wearing a sports bra with a sleeveless crop top and running shorts. Trip Thompson was there again and, without Seth's protective presence, he made no bones about ogling her from her breasts on down to her slender thighs. Tessa raised a haughty brow at him and turned away. She wanted nothing more to do with spoiled, rich, fickle men.

She waved as the bus rolled in, and watched for Zach's bright red head. As soon as he saw her, he grinned and ran over to give her a big hug. "Tessa! I had such a great time, but I am sooo glad to be home. Can I play my PlayStation when we get there? I have so much to tell you. I learned how to sail. I can't wait to show Seth."

Tessa let him go on while she helped him collect his trunk and load it in the car. She stiffened at the mention of his name, but said nothing. Zach, however, was not going to let it go.

"Did Seth give you the day off?" he asked as they climbed in the car, as if it had just occurred to him that Tessa was not in the business suits she always wore to Barrett.

She busied herself with pulling out into traffic before she responded. "I don't work there anymore, Zach."

Her brother blinked a couple of times. "Will Seth be over tonight then?"

Tessa's mouth thinned. "No, honey. Seth won't be over."

"Tessa!" Zach wailed. "What happened? Did you have a fight or something? Can't you tell him you're sorry?"

"No." Tessa bit her bottom lip and exhaled as she waited for a traffic light to change. "I'm sorry, Zach. I know this is a shock. Things happen.

You have to accept that. I've found another job and moved on. It's as simple as that."

"Are you working with those kids again?" he asked in a sulky voice.

"No. I'm working at a restaurant." It wasn't strictly true, but they did serve some food, if nachos and peanuts counted. "I work Tuesday through Saturday from six at night to three in the morning."

Zach stared at her with his mouth hanging open. "But what about me?" he wailed. "I'm going to be alone every night?"

"No, honey. Mrs. Flores will keep an eye on you." Tessa tried to sound reassuring. "I know it's not ideal, but I make good money, so I'll still be able to keep you in Chesterfield, and I'll have all day Sunday with you and Monday nights too. It'll be okay, Zach. You'll see."

He didn't look convinced, but he didn't say anything else about it. He was subdued Sunday when they went out to finish buying his uniforms and school supplies. A laptop was one of the things on his list. Tessa had saved enough cash to buy him a nice computer. She would do anything to help him be more positive about school and find his niche.

* * * *

Classes started Monday. Tessa was able to take him in the morning and pick him up in the afternoon. She kept up that routine in spite of her schedule, trying to catch up on some of her sleep during the day while he was in class. She was relieved to see his attitude about school change as day followed day. Smaller classes gave him more one-on-one attention to help him with his reading. His grades picked up and he seemed to settle into their new routine. Fall had cooled the weather before he mentioned Seth again. Zach was working on a science project that involved constructing his own working model of a sailboat.

"I wish Seth was here." Zach sighed as he tried to fix his main mast again. "He could help with this."

Tessa turned away with a frown. She refused to feel guilty for cutting Seth out of Zach's life. It would have been simpler all around if she'd kept their working relationship just that. It was Thursday afternoon and she was getting ready to leave for work. Her uniform was in her duffel bag, and she was clothed in a bulky knit sweater and leggings.

"I have to go, honey," Tessa said from the door. "Don't forget, Mrs. Flores will be down to help you get squared away for bed, and I'll see you in the morning."

"Bye, Tess," he said, then looked up at her. "Do you feel okay? You look kind of pale."

Tessa smiled. "I'm fine, but thanks for asking."

She got hung up in traffic and arrived at the club with fifteen minutes to spare before her shift started. With a practiced hand, she put her hair up in a ponytail, then used hot rollers to make it curl. She peeled off her clothes and pulled on the slinky uniform and thigh-high stockings that went with it. Without giving it a second thought, she did what Tiffany taught her, pushed her breasts up and pulled the top down until everything threatened to--but never quite did--spill over the top. Tessa grimaced. It did seem to help the tips.

Right before midnight a new group of men came into the club. It was obvious this was not their first stop at a place that served alcohol. Tessa hoped they would head in the opposite direction, and then sighed when they ended up at one of her tables.

"Would you gentlemen prefer beer or wine?" she asked in her sweetest voice, smiling at all of them without looking at any of them.

"Well if it isn't my dear little cousin," a man next to her said in a drawl she had hoped never to hear again. "All grown up and showing it all off as usual. Some things never change."

Tessa felt the blood drain from her face and hoped it didn't show beneath her makeup. Peter was here? She inched away from him, but he seemed content to run his gaze insolently up her legs, pausing at her bare midriff before staring at her chest. Tessa told them which beers they had and what was on tap before taking their drink orders, never acknowledging what he'd said for her ears alone. When she returned to the end of the bar, Tiffany was there.

"Anything wrong, honey?"

Tessa nodded. "A relative, a real slimeball, came in with that last group. He tried to rape me when I was a kid."

Tiffany stood a little straighter and looked that way, frowning thoughtfully.

"We're not that busy tonight, baby. I'll take that table. You worry about the rest of your customers."

Tessa smiled in gratitude. She felt Peter's eyes on her several times as she worked. It took all her willpower not to let him unnerve her. She sighed in relief when he left about an hour before closing. After the lights came up and the last customer left, she removed her makeup and scrubbed her face before changing back into her sweater and leggings. Grabbing her oversize bag, she headed for the door.

The temperature had dropped since she'd arrived at work and she shivered in the night air. Lucy walked with her. The two women said goodnight and headed for their separate cars. Few vehicles were on the road at four in the morning, so it didn't take Tessa long to realize someone was following her. She was two blocks away from home, but turned away and headed in the opposite direction to a police substation. No way did she want whoever it was to know where she and Zach lived.

As she pulled into the parking lot, she saw the car that was following her speed up and disappear down the block. Tessa wasted no time. She pulled back out and hurried home, checking her rearview mirror more often to make sure the car was no longer behind her.

She could think of only one person who might follow her. Peter. Tessa shivered. She sat in her car as she pulled herself together. It reminded her of the way he had always maneuvered to get her alone at Mont Clair. Now, though, she had more to worry about than herself. There was Zach. The feeling someone was watching her persisted over the next few weeks, and Tessa found herself altering her route each night to be sure no one was following her before she would at last head home.

October gave way to November and Zach's eleventh birthday. He asked for the usual video games, but he also wanted to go fishing. Tessa splurged and made arrangements to take him out on a charter fishing trip on the bay. They got up early Sunday morning, giving her just a couple hours sleep after getting home from work. The day was overcast with a brisk wind coming off the ocean.

"It's going to be a little choppy," the guide told them as the captain headed out into the bay, "but we're headed for a cove that should provide some shelter and some good fishing for your brother."

Tessa smiled, a little unnerved by how shaky she felt. The movement of the boat cutting through the waves made her queasy. She wrote it off to a lack of sleep and a lack of breakfast, and tried to ignore the feeling, but it persisted. If anything, it was worse once they anchored in the cove.

Taking pity on her, the captain handed her some crackers. "Try this and see if it helps, Miss Edwards. I'm afraid a lot of the motion sickness remedies have to be taken before you start showing symptoms, but this might settle your stomach."

Tessa nodded, nibbling the crackers while keeping her eyes on the horizon. The crackers did seem to help get rid of her nausea, but only sleep would help her fatigue. She leaned her head back against the side of the ship and watched as the guide helped Zach. He was having such a great time, Tessa had to smile. It was money well spent to see his freckled face light up and split into a huge grin. She hadn't seen him enjoy himself this much since their sailing trip with Seth. Her mouth pulled down at the corners and she bit her lower lip to keep it from wobbling as she stared off to the side and out on the bay. She was just tired and overemotional. She was not missing Seth.

When Zach landed a channel cat around midday, Tessa cheered. The nausea had gone, and even though she was still tired, the rocking of the boat no longer bothered her. Tessa took a picture as the guide helped Zach hold up his fish.

Zach laughed at something Tessa said as they walked back along the dock. His laughter cut off. Curious about what had distracted him, she looked up to see Seth walking toward them, a tall blonde chatting companionably with him. A barrage of emotions struck Tessa all at once. She was amazed how much hurt still flowed through her at seeing him with someone else. On the heels of that was embarrassment at how she knew she must look. After two hours' sleep and a day in the wind, she felt like her eyes had sand in them, she wore no makeup and had crammed her hair up under a baseball cap.

"Seth!" Zach piped up, so much excitement in his voice Tessa couldn't bring herself to make him stop.

She hung back while Zach raced the few feet that separated them, bubbling over about his fishing trip and learning to sail at camp. While Seth listened attentively to her brother, Tessa felt the other woman's gaze sizing her up. She wanted to care, to be able to say it mattered to her, but a wave of tiredness washed over her again, along with another bout of nausea. What did it matter what this woman thought of her? What she'd had with Seth was over.

She attempted to smile and stepped forward. She had to have enough self-respect to show him she didn't care. It didn't matter.

"Come on, Zach," she stated, meeting Seth's gaze with her chin raised. "We need to go. Please tell Mr. Barrett goodbye."

Seth's gaze shifted from Zach to her and his expression hardened. "You look beat, Tessa."

It was one thing to feel it. It was another to have it put into words. The awkwardness stretched as Tessa bit back the acid reply that first sprang to mind.

"Aren't you going to introduce us, darling?" the blonde at Seth's side asked as she put a proprietary hand on his arm.

Something flickered in Seth's eyes. He barely glanced at his companion as he said, "Stacey, Tessa Edwards. Tessa, this is Stacey Winchester, my...fiancee."

The final two words hit Tessa like a splash of cold water. Drawing upon manners drilled into her from the time she was old enough to walk,

Tessa smiled. "Congratulations to you both." Her glance flicked between them, both tall and blessed with Nordic good looks. He'd found a clone, someone to fit right in with his family. "You appear well-suited. If you'll excuse us, we need to go."

"That's right," Zach said. "Tessa needs sleep. She doesn't get home from work until four, but she still got me up at six to come fishing, so she's tired. I guess that's why she got sick on this boat even though she never got sick on your boat, did she Seth?"

Oh, Lord! Sometimes she wished Zach would be a little less forthcoming with information. Tessa wanted to jump off the dock, anything to avoid those golden eyes once again staring at her.

"No," Seth agreed. "She never did."

Tessa avoided his gaze, focusing instead on his beautiful, sophisticated-looking companion. "It was a pleasure to meet you." This time she grabbed her brother by the hand and dragged him after her. "Zach. Let's go."

She made it almost to the parking lot before she stopped and threw up over a trash can. As she gagged, Zach hovered next to her.

"Tessa? Are you all right? Should I go get Seth? He could help."

"No!" Tessa wiped her mouth. "Let's just go home. Please, Zach. I don't want to talk about Seth anymore."

She got into the driver's seat and started the car, but tears clouded her eyes to the point she couldn't drive. She swallowed several times, but it was no use. At last a small sob escaped her.

"Tessa?" Zach asked again, his tone filled with worry. "Are you sad about Seth?"

She nodded and looked out the window on the driver's side door.

"Why did you really leave Barrett?" Zach asked. "I thought you loved your job."

Tessa was too tired to pretend anymore. "I didn't leave, Zach, I was fired."

"Seth fired you?" Zach demanded in an incredulous tone. She could already see him stiffening with indignation, ready to leap to her defense.

"His father, but Seth knew."

"Why did they fire you? Did you do something wrong?" Zach's voice was quiet, almost subdued.

Tessa sighed in defeat. "Zach. I have to ask you a question, and I want you to be honest with me. You aren't going to get into any trouble."

She looked at him and he nodded.

"The night I came back from Chicago, did you get on my laptop computer?"

"Yes."

He was so subdued now, she almost didn't continue, but she wanted it out in the open. "Did you somehow get into one of the accounts at Barrett?"

"Yes." Zach clenched his hands on his jeans. "I was mad. Seth made you cry, and I wanted to pay him back. I found a number written on an envelope you brought home one day, and I started playing with it. You always use the same username and password, and once I got into Barrett's system, it was easy then to find the account. I didn't mean anything by it. I didn't think it had worked. I kept getting an error message…"

"And you didn't realize you'd transferred ten thousand dollars from that bank account into mine?"

"No." Tears welled in his blue eyes. "I'm sorry."

Tessa nodded and put the car in gear. "It doesn't matter anymore, Zach. But in the future, don't do anything like that again. It's a crime. What you did was a crime. It could have gotten you put in jail. We were lucky. All that happened was I lost a job."

"But you lost Seth too," Zach said with more truth than he could even imagine.

"Yes," Tessa agreed. "I lost Seth too."

Zach wanted to play his new video game when they returned home, so Tessa went back to her bedroom to take a nap. She woke up late in the afternoon, once again feeling a wave of nausea overcome her. She should know better than to go to bed on an empty stomach, she thought as she staggered into the kitchen and found some crackers.

* * * *

"Seth Barlow-Barrett!" Stacey said as she watched Tessa and Zach disappear down the dock. "Why on earth did you tell that poor girl I was your fiancee? That's not the same 'Tessa Edwards of the Loudoun Edwards' that mother was going on about a couple of months ago, is it?"

"Yes." Seth stared at the pair until they turned a corner out of sight. He dragged his gaze back to his sister. "Come on, Stacey, humor me."

"That's what I've been trying to do! You've been an absolute bastard, darling, for the past three months, ever since you got back from that West Coast trip." Stacey pulled Seth along with her down the dock. "Bran says he won't even go near you at the office. You've turned down every single one of Mother's invitations to dinner, and you know they're not invitations. They're command performances."

"Hmph," Seth snorted and looked back over his shoulder, hoping for one more glimpse of Tessa. She had looked exhausted, her eyes red-rimmed from lack of sleep. Where was she working that she didn't get home until four in the morning? Was that where she had been that night just a couple days after she left Barrett?

Had he made a colossal mistake?

Seth followed his sister to the sailboat her fiance had bought her. She was as nuts about sailing as the rest of the family. He made all the appropriate noises. It was a boat with beautiful lines, but his mind was still on Tessa.

He missed her with an empty, gnawing ache that had surprised him with its force. He'd come to rely on her cool level-headedness in response to his moods while they worked, and the number of secretaries he'd been through since she had left had grown to the point where personnel threatened to install a revolving door and send him up a different temp each week.

He no longer spoke to his father unless he could not avoid it. In the last month, he had made it clear to the elder Barrett that Brandon needed to be brought up to scratch because at the end of the year, Seth was leaving for good. His father had accused him of allowing his dick to do his thinking for him. It was at that point that Seth left the office without another word.

*   *   *   *

He continued to think of Tessa at odd moments during the next week. Each time, he kept coming back to one thing that troubled him. He just couldn't believe his father's story that Tessa had admitted moving money from Seth's travel account into her own personal account. It didn't make sense. If she had done it, they would most likely still be in ignorance. She knew her way around Barrett's computer system almost better than its programmers. If they could talk, maybe he could clear everything up.

Friday, he sat in his office drinking his third cup of bad coffee that morning, when the latest no-name assistant buzzed him on the intercom.

"M-Mr. Barrett? There's a Mr. Mallory here to see you."

"Who?" Seth barked back, irritated by the woman's tentative manner.

"A Mr. Z-Zachary Mallory. He's a-a boy."

"I'm well aware he's a boy," he snapped. "Send him in." Seth sat back for a moment and looked at his watch. Shouldn't Zach be in school at this hour? Was something wrong? Had something happened to Tessa? He punched the intercom again. "Send him in, for God's sake!"

Seth was getting up from behind his desk when the door opened and Zach sidled into his office. The boy was dressed in his school uniform and carrying his backpack with him.

"Aren't you supposed to be in school, Zach?" Seth asked, keeping his voice gentle in the face of the boy's obvious nervousness.

Zach looked down at his shoes. "Yes, sir, but I needed to talk to you about something. It's been bothering me."

Seth pointed to a pair of chairs near the big windows. "Come on over here, buddy, and have a seat. You want a soft drink or something?"

Zach set his book bag down and stared at Seth with somber blue eyes. "No, sir."

Seth sat and the boy followed suit, perching on the edge of his chair as though he were intent on being able to make a quick getaway.

"It's about the money," Zach said.

Seth stared at the boy, a sudden coldness slinking through his veins. "Do you and Tessa need money? Is that why you're here, Zach?" His tone was harsher than he'd intended, and he grimaced as the boy flinched. Surely she wouldn't have sent her brother to ask for money. Seth felt his last illusions crumbling, and he knew when they were gone there would be nothing left inside him anymore. For once he'd taken a chance and put his feelings on the line, then Tessa had thrown them back at his feet.

"No! No, sir. That's not it. I mean about the money that was missing. You know, the reason your dad fired Tessa."

Seth gazed at Zach. A sudden memory flashed of Tessa saying Zach was even better with computers than she was. "What would you know about that, Zach?"

To Seth's consternation, the boy's brave expression started to crack, his lower lip trembled, and he looked down for a moment. Zach's hands clenched and unclenched on his pantlegs. At last, he looked back up and stared Seth square in the eye.

"I'm the one who transferred the money, not Tessa."

Seth couldn't help the look of disbelief that must have crossed his face.

"It's true," Zach protested. "It was the night you came back from Chicago. You made Tessa cry, and I was mad at you. I carried the laptop inside the apartment. Tessa was in her room. I opened it up and logged on."

"It's password protected," Seth said.

Zach gave him a supercilious look and said dismissively, "She only ever uses a couple different passwords and usernames, so that was no problem."

"How did you access the account?" Seth inquired, still not quite believing what he was hearing.

"I was going through the mail while you and Tessa were gone and came across a number she'd scribbled on an envelope. It reminded me of my savings account number."

"And you just happened to remember it?" Seth asked, unable to keep the doubt from his voice. Could Tessa have put him up to this? He didn't want to believe that. She loved her brother and had appeared to be doing everything she could to make sure he had the best home life she could provide. Was that it? Had she needed more money...

"Yes," Zach replied as if it was the most logical thing in the world. "I remember a lot of numbers. I like numbers."

"Go on," Seth prompted the boy.

Zach was beginning to warm to his task. "I clicked on stuff and looked for places to try the number...you know the number, 023021318991... until it opened something up."

Seth sat stunned as Zach rattled off the travel account number as if he used it every day.

"After I got the account opened up, then it was simple to work the transfer, but I kept getting error messages from Tessa's bank, so I figured nothing had happened, and besides that I'd kinda cooled down by then. And Tessa seemed to be fine in a few days and I forgot all about it."

"So why are you here now?"

Zach looked down at his feet and back up at Seth. "That day at the dock. Tessa started crying again, and she finally asked me if I had fiddled with the account." Zach's blue eyes filled with tears. "I didn't know that was why she got fired. She never said anything about it. Not anything at all. I got back from camp, and she just said she didn't work for you anymore.

"I wanted to tell you about learning to sail an' everything an' Tessa said I couldn't 'cause we wouldn't see you anymore. I was kind of mad at her for a while. She had this new job already, and she's gone in the evenings. I never see her. I mean really see her. And she's tired all the time, Seth, and she's been sick a whole lot. She thinks I don't know, but I hear her, and I'm afraid she might die or something."

"Where does she work, Zach?" Seth asked.

Zach shrugged. "Some restaurant. She won't tell me where. She says Mrs. Flores knows how to reach her if there's a problem. She's the lady who stays with me."

Zach trailed off and stared out the window. Seth watched the boy, his own emotions confused. At last Zach turned toward him.

"I know what I did was a crime, and if you want to put me in jail, that's okay. Only could you please have Tessa work for you again so she won't be so tired and sick all the time? She was really happy with you, Seth. I'd even go to Aunt Kathleen and Uncle Edwin if it would make her okay."

As Seth watched, the little boy could hold it together no longer. Zach's expression crumbled and the tears he'd managed to hold off trickled down his freckled cheeks.

"Ah, Zach," Seth said. "Come here, buddy. It's okay."

The boy came over and curled up on Seth's lap, his red head resting against Seth's broad chest--right where the ache was that hadn't eased since his father's phone call about Tessa.

He had to clear his throat so he could reassure the kid. "It'll be okay. We'll find a way to make it okay, and I promise you won't have to go to jail."

He pulled out a large linen handkerchief and gave it to Zach so the boy could wipe his face and blow his nose. As Zach started to give it back to him, Seth said with a slight smile, "Keep it, bud. Now, can you explain to me how you got here and why you're not in school?"

Zach blushed. "I waited 'til Tess left after dropping me off and then I hopped the train into town."

"Well how about if I take you to school?"

"They won't tell her, will they? She'd be mad if she knew I skipped school and came here."

"I'll make sure it's not a problem this time, but don't do it again," Seth warned. "You're way too smart to be missing school."

Chapter 12

Tessa stared off into space, so stunned she wasn't even really seeing the sage green walls of the doctor's office. She had come in because she feared she'd picked up some sort of flu she couldn't shake. But the reality was so much more shocking.

"Are you sure?" she asked at last. "Couldn't there be some mistake?"

The physician shook her head, a slight smile on her lips. "We get some false negatives now and then, but a false positive is rare. I take it this was not planned?"

Still trying to grasp the reality of what the doctor had told her, Tessa said, "No, not at all."

She leaned back in her chair. "You still have some options open if you don't want to carry this pregnancy to term."

Tessa's eyes jerked up to meet the doctor's steady gaze. "I would never consider an abortion."

Dr. Michaels nodded. "Well, then we need to make sure you do everything you can to help this baby along. Let's get you started on some vitamins. I've included information in here on nutrition, physical activity, and some of the symptoms you will experience. I know you've had some problems with nausea. That should pass, but if it doesn't or it gets worse, you'll need to contact the office."

The middle-aged physician looked at the chart again. "You've lost some weight since your check up last year. That's not something I'd like to see continue. You need to pick up a few pounds, but not too much. Make sure you're eating quality food…not junk."

Tessa nodded, still trying to take in everything Dr. Michaels told her. She gathered up the bag full of vitamins and product coupons and samples, paid her bill and headed out to her car. As she drove home, some of the reality of her situation began to sink in. She looked down at her flat

stomach in the sudden realization that it wouldn't be flat much longer…
and she had no idea what it might mean for her job.

It was after noon when she arrived at the house. Tessa entered her
apartment and took the bag of supplies from the doctor back to her
bedroom where Zach wouldn't see them. Zach! Oh my God! How was
she going to tell him? How could she explain? On the heels of that thought
came another. How could she tell Seth? Would he even believe her?

It didn't matter. With her hand resting on her belly, she entered the
kitchen and pulled open the refrigerator. There must be something she
could tolerate. She settled on a choice that would have left her gagging a
few months ago.

Tessa was lost in thought, munching on the jar of pimento-stuffed olives
she'd unearthed when a firm knock sounded on her door. She opened it,
figuring it was Mrs. Flores, and almost dropped the olives when she saw
Seth standing on her doorstep.

"Tessa," he greeted her. "We need to talk. May I come in?"

She wasn't ready for this. A sudden vision of the blond woman he'd
introduced as his fiancee intruded and Tessa started to shut the door in
his face. Seth stuck his foot in and curled his hand around the edge of the
heavy wood.

"Go away. Please! Now is not a good time for this," she finished very
nearly on a hysterical sob. My God, she was still trying to comprehend
the fact she was pregnant, she didn't need the cause of it confronting her.

"Tessa," he growled, keeping his voice low. "Talk to me."

She looked over his shoulder, searching for the tall blonde from the
marina. "Did you want to have your fiancee here for our conversation?
Tell me, were you giving her a workout in bed at the same time you were
breaking me in?"

"Stacey is not my fiancee," Seth bit out. "It was a bad coverup. I was
shocked to see you and I said it to hurt you."

Tessa glared at him, "Well she sure as hell wore a big, flashy ring."

Seth looked around and hissed, "Come on, Tessa, let me in so we can
talk. I just finished taking Zach to school."

Tessa's hold on the door relaxed and she stepped back in confusion.
"What do you mean? I dropped him off at school this morning."

Seth took advantage of her lapse and slipped inside the apartment before
closing the door behind him. His size dwarfed everything, including her.
Tessa pictured the bag sitting back in her bedroom and knew she had to
get him out of there fast.

Seth took the jar of olives from Tessa's shaking hands and gave them an odd look before he set them down. He tried to lead her to the couch, but Tessa shook off his arm and sat in the window seat. Seth continued standing, his hands dug into the pockets of his dress slacks.

"He showed up at my office this morning with some very interesting things to say."

She should have anticipated he'd do something. Zach would want to make things right. It would have been so simple in his mind. He could tell Seth what had happened, and his hero would make it right. But there was so much more to it now. The lack of trust, the betrayal. Her pregnancy.

"He's just a boy, Seth. He would say anything if he thought it would fix things between us."

"Including that he was the one who transferred that money from the travel account into your account?"

Tessa lifted her chin and stared at him before she laughed without any humor. "Yes," she lied. "Including that. How could you believe that? He's an eleven-year-old, for heaven's sake."

Seth stared at her, his gaze hard and sharp. "I do believe him, Tessa. What I want to know is why you allowed my father to think you took that money, and why you feel you have to lie to me about it now."

It would be so easy to tell him everything. Seth would take control. He would do what was right. He'd proven that over and over again with his devotion to his family, but it was that very quality that stood in their way. He had chosen to believe she would take money from his account. He had agreed with his father's firing her. If she told him she was pregnant, that their one forgetful moment had resulted in a reminder, he would do the right thing, but how could she ever have any faith in him when he'd proven he had no faith in her?

Tessa looked down at her stomach, feeling that sudden churning there. She dragged a hand through her hair. She longed for a nap so much, just standing was a chore, let alone thinking straight.

"Go away, Seth. If we ever had anything besides sex, it's gone. It's dead. You've moved on and so have I. Just leave."

"I want to know what's wrong with you," Seth ground out. "Zach tells me you're sick all the time. Damn it, Tessa, he's worried about you, and so am I!"

Tessa's eyes narrowed. If they looked half as cold as she felt right now, then Seth was getting stabbed by icicles. "I can tell. Get out, Seth. Get out of my house, out of my life. We did fine before you, and we'll do fine after the…"

Tessa stopped and turned her face to stare out the window. Christ. She needed to shut her mouth.

* * * *

"After what, Tessa?" Seth's deep voice was low and concerned. "After what? What is wrong? What's making you sick?" He knelt down next to her and took her icy hands. "Whatever it is, I can help if you'll let me."

Tessa turned a face to him that was once again the cool, composed mask she'd first presented to him so many months ago, before he realized a vital, passionate woman lived beneath it. He knew he would get nothing else out of her. She'd put up the walls and locked him out. In frustration, Seth cupped her face in his palms and kissed her. For a moment, her soft lips yielded to the pressure from his and then she pushed at him.

"Go away. I don't need you. I don't want you. Go back to your girlfriend or whatever she is. You were a wonderful teacher, Seth," she admitted, "really talented in bed, but I've moved on, and so should you."

Seth felt like she'd slapped him. As his jaw tightened and it felt like ice filled his veins, he saw her cringe from him. There was nothing else to be said. "I'm sorry I disturbed you, Tessa."

Without another word, he walked out the door.

The ice didn't melt as he got in the Escalade and drove away. The only realization pounding into him was that he was done. He'd reached the end of what he could take, in his personal and professional lives.

* * * *

Tessa buried her face in her hands, waiting until she heard the sound of his car before the first hoarse sob escaped her.

She had composed herself by the time she picked Zach up from school. She said nothing about having seen Seth or knowing her brother had gone to see him. She appreciated what he had tried to do. Tessa ate dinner with him then went in to shower.

She still had another hurdle to face, and that was at work. She remembered Lucy's comment about needing to keep her figure in order to keep her job, and Tessa worried what might happen to her job once her pregnancy began to show. She arrived early enough to seek Roberto out in his office.

As she told him her situation, he shook his head and her heart sank.

"I can't have you on the floor waiting tables once your pregnancy shows. How far along are you?"

"About three months," Tessa admitted.

Roberto scratched his head. "You say you were an executive assistant before you came here?"

"Yes."

"You won't make as much money as you do waiting tables, but I can use you as a secretary and a receptionist. The girl I have in that position right now would rather be waitressing anyway. Can you keep books?"

Tessa grinned. "If you have a computer program, I can do anything."

Roberto nodded at her and gave her one of his rare smiles. "Good deal. Meagan doesn't have much of a knack with money or math. I figure you got another couple of weeks if you want to keep waiting tables until then to get the tips."

"Thanks, Roberto," Tessa said. "You don't know how much I appreciate this."

"Well, it's not something I can do for most of these girls, nina, but then you are a lot smarter. Get changed."

Tessa joined the rest of the girls in the dressing room. Lucy cocked one heavily made-up eyebrow at her. "How'd it go?"

Tessa smiled. "He says I can work as a secretary-receptionist and help with the books once my pregnancy shows."

"You go, girl!" Tiffany said, joining in.

Tessa was beginning to have trouble getting into her uniform top. It seemed to have gotten a whole lot tighter. She tugged and pushed until she had everything in so she felt it would stay that way. She put everything else out of her mind as she did her best to smile and evade wandering hands. The tips were best on Friday and Saturday nights. Just as he predicted, by the second weekend after she'd told Roberto, Tessa knew it would be her last. While no one else might notice, she saw the tiniest rounding of her belly.

There was an upside. Maybe once she left waiting tables and was behind the scenes, she would lose that feeling of being followed. It had stopped for a little while, but in the last few nights she had the feeling someone was watching her again. Each time, she drove to the nearest police substation until she was sure the car had moved on.

It happened twice during the week after Seth's visit, and this Friday was no exception, but this time she failed to shake the car following her the first time and made several more stops in hope of losing whoever her stalker might be. It didn't seem Peter's style. She didn't think it would be Seth, but she was reluctant to go to the police, reluctant to do anything that might draw the attention of her aunt and uncle. She would continue to play this game of tag, but she would take no chances on someone finding out where she lived.

It was well after five before she arrived home. She knew she would be lucky to get about three hours sleep before Zach would be up wanting to do something. She managed to grab a nap in the afternoon. Still, she was more tired than she thought possible as she got ready for work the next evening. It would be her last on the floor. While one part of her hoped it would be a full house with plenty of tips, another part of her was so exhausted all she could think about was rest.

"We have a bachelor's party coming in tonight," Tiffany told her as she was getting ready. "I know you can use all the extra money you can get, with it being your last weekend. You want me to seat them in your area?"

Tessa shook her head. "Even though the money would be nice, I don't think I could handle a large party tonight, Tiffany. I'm so tired."

Tiffany smiled in commiseration. "Pregnancy has a way of doing that to you. Don't worry. I'll put them in the VIP section."

Tessa didn't correct her that it was more than the pregnancy affecting her.

The club was crowded, and Tessa wasn't lacking for customers willing to give her generous tips. She was putting in another drink order for a table of out-of-town businessmen when the bachelor's party arrived. Tessa gave them a cursory glance and went back to serving her customers. Tiffany seated the party on the other side of the club, which suited Tessa fine. She turned toward the bartender and grimaced as she adjusted her top, afraid she was going to spill out of it.

He winked at her. "You moving to the office soon?"

Tessa made another face. "Tuesday. Good thing too. I don't think I could get everything in this top by then at the rate things are going."

James glanced at her belly, "If it weren't for everybody looking at your cleavage, darling, Roberto would have already moved you off the floor."

Tessa glanced down. "Am I showing that much? I didn't think it was noticeable."

James laughed. "Just a bit, but I know you." He waved to the customers. "They have nothing to compare you to."

Tessa grinned in relief. "I guess you're right. Thanks."

She picked up her tray and wound her way through the tables to the customers near the stage where Lucy danced. As she set the drinks down, one of the men patted her on the bottom.

"Look all you want, honey, but don't touch," Tessa said and smiled at the man to take some of the sting out of her words.

He laughed. "In other words, no lap dances at this club?"

"No, sir. Not here." Tessa picked up the tray again, smiling at the twenty the man had deposited there, and began to check on her other customers.

As she moved through the tables, she had the uncomfortable feeling someone was watching her. Trying not to make it obvious, she looked around, suspecting Peter was somewhere in the club. Instead, she encountered a glittering gaze from near the bar. Seth leaned against the gleaming wood and brass, a wine glass in one hand and an expression of controlled fury on his face. She had to walk past him to give James her drink order.

"What the hell are you doing, Tessa?" he snarled as she stood near him waiting on James to get the drinks. "Is this some kind of joke?"

Tessa did look at him then, lifting her chin in challenge. "It's no joke. It's how I make my living. What are you doing here?"

Seth nodded toward the bachelor party. "My sister Stacey's fiance, Jason Winchester, is having his bachelor party. I'm the designated driver, but Bran is sober, so maybe he can drive and you and I can talk."

"I don't think we have anything else to say," she replied. With deliberation, she picked up the twenty sitting on the tray and shoved it in between her breasts. She never did that. James kept a tip jar for her behind the bar and held her money until the end of the evening. But it achieved the desired effect.

Seth's face flushed with anger and he spun on his heel. She kept her face toward the bar, her hands trembling as she tried to force herself to calm down.

"You okay?" James asked sotto voce as he set two mugs of beer on the tray.

"Yes."

"Someone you know?"

She nodded.

James wiped the bar down with a towel. As a bartender who doubled as a bouncer when necessary, he was almost as big as Seth, with one major difference--James was gay, so Tessa knew he was no threat to her. "If he bothers you, Tessa, let me know."

She smiled gratefully. "Thanks."

She was conscious of Seth's gaze following her as she worked. She tried to ignore it, but it added to her stress. It also made her less cautious about who else was in the club. An hour from closing time, she felt a hand trail up her thigh as she took a drink order. She moved and started to smile down at the offender, but it died on her lips. Peter stared, his insolence plain, and his lips curled in a sneer.

"What will you do for the right tip, baby?" he asked, drawing laughter from the crowd he was with. "I've got something you can sit on. It will get you a big tip, and I'm not talking cash."

All of the men in the group guffawed. Tessa turned away and marched over to the bar.

"James," she murmured just loud enough for him to hear, "let Tiffany know my slimeball cousin is back. I need someone to take table ten."

The next hour crawled. Between Seth's hostile glare and Peter's insolent, leering stare, Tessa felt like she was being stabbed over and over. She sighed with relief when the lights came up. After collecting her tips, she headed straight to the back. Hoping to lose both Seth and Peter, she lingered in the dressing room.

Lucy waited and walked out with her. Tessa looked around. She didn't see Seth's Escalade, nor did she see any other cars beside hers and Lucy's. The two women said good night as usual. Tessa unlocked her door with the remote and slid into the driver's seat. She bit her bottom lip as she sat there for a moment. If she would just tell Seth... He would stand by her. But that was like getting a crumb when she craved the whole loaf. She heard Lucy's car start and the crunch of gravel as she left the parking lot.

Someone grabbed her from behind, slapping a hand over her mouth before she could scream.

"Give me the keys, cousin," Peter taunted. When she froze and didn't respond, he yanked her hair with his other hand. "Give me the keys, bitch!"

Tessa darted a frightened look around the parking lot. Everyone else had gone. The only cars left were the clean-up crew and it would be at least an hour before they were through. If Seth had just cared enough to stay. Now, more than ever before, she needed the comforting presence of his sheer size. But he wasn't there, and she would have to deal with this on her own.

She knew in a flash Peter had been the one following her, and she was terrified of what he might do. They were no longer children, and as sick as he had been then, there was no telling how the intervening years had changed him. She held up the keys. He grabbed them, then tied a gag around her mouth.

He dragged her from the car and popped open the trunk. Tessa struggled. For all she was small, she was very fit. Peter might be bigger, but one look at him told her he was soft. If she could loosen his hold, she had no doubt she could run from him.

As she tried to pull away, he swung his fist and struck her in the jaw. Tessa reeled, fighting the dizzy roaring in her ears and the sudden nausea. And that reminded her she had more than herself to think of. There was her baby. She went instantly still, uncertain where the next blow might land should she continue to fight.

"That's better. Let's go for a ride." He laughed. "You always were rather fond of small, dark places, weren't you, cousin? I'll let you ride back here so it doesn't look suspicious."

Tessa stared at the trunk in horror, her heartbeat already quickening and her breathing getting shallow. She refused to look at him. She would not let him see her panic at the mere thought of being locked in the trunk. Peter produced a roll of duct tape and wrapped it around her wrists, behind her back, before he shoved her in. Tessa did her best to keep from hitting her stomach on the car as she fell. It was her head that hit instead and this time when she heard the roaring in her ears, it was almost with relief she felt herself blacking out.

* * * *

Seth drove like a maniac taking the two people riding with him back home. As soon as they were out of the car, he broke every speed limit to get back to Flamingo Road.

Tessa was working at a strip club? His hands clenched on the wheel. He'd wanted to throttle every man who had looked at her, even though she had made it crystal clear she didn't want him. He thought about the outfit she'd worn. It left little to the imagination. No, it left nothing to the imagination! He could still see her slipping that twenty between the creamy curves of her breasts. His Tessa. His sweet, innocent, stubborn Tessa! His throat tightened in pain. He couldn't believe how blind and stupid he'd been.

She hadn't gone from him to some other man; everything she had done was because she loved Zach, just as it always had been. It was what had brought her to Barrett to begin with, and what still drove her when she'd left. She would do anything to protect her little brother except compromise her professionalism. So yeah, he believed what Zach had told him about who was responsible for the travel account fiasco. Seth knew his one moment of doubt might very well have cost him any chance with Tessa. Already leery of giving her trust, she was even less likely to give it now.

He was so intent on getting back to the club, he almost missed her car headed in the opposite direction. He pulled into a parking lot of another business and whipped the Escalade around. He caught the car at the next stoplight and looked over, preparing to get her attention. The man behind the wheel looked at him and then back at the road.

Was he mistaken? The light changed and Seth was getting ready to turn back around when he noticed the small sticker for Zach's school on the back bumper. That was too much of a coincidence.

It was Tessa's car, but where was she? He dropped back far enough to keep the car in sight but not so close that it would be obvious he was tailing it. He began to worry even more when the vehicle headed for the interstate instead of the side streets that would take it back to Tessa's house. He saw nothing to indicate Tessa was in the car. But as it exited onto a state highway, Seth continued to follow, his concern growing. What the hell was going on? Tessa would never go somewhere and leave Zach any longer than she had to at this time of night.

* * * *

Tessa didn't know how long she had been out. As soon as she opened her eyes, the old panic welled, making her throat tighten so it was hard to breathe and her heart pound until it was all she could hear in her ears. She closed her eyes to shut out the confined space, but it did little good. She couldn't fool herself because she already knew where she was. Trapped, until Peter let her out. If he let her out, because he knew how frightened she was of being closed in. She'd always suspected he was behind her getting locked in different places when she was a kid.

This couldn't be happening. She moved, testing her restraints, but couldn't even straighten her legs or roll over. She had hoped she could try to kick the trunk lid. Panic threatened to overwhelm her. I'm okay. I'm okay. She had to keep calm for the baby. Panicking couldn't be good for the tiny life growing inside her.

She would think about the beach. Better, she would think about sailing with Seth. As she pulled up the mental images of their last sail, her breathing eased a little. The car slowed down some, but the road also got rougher. Her shoulder, hip, and head bounced on the hard floor of the trunk.

Where was he taking her? Would there be any chance to escape? It would be so much harder now he'd bound her hands, but she might still have an opportunity if she could keep her head. When the car stopped, she expected Peter to get out and open the trunk. When that didn't happen, she couldn't stop the low whimper that escaped her. What if he forgot her? Would her air run out?

She had to get out for the baby. Tessa struggled again to free her hands, but the duct tape was a whole lot stronger than her. Grinding her teeth in frustration, she kicked out at whatever she could reach, but the walls of the trunk didn't give.

* * * *

Seth followed Tessa's car until it turned down an old gravel farm road, a knot of tension in his stomach. All his instincts told him she was in that car somewhere. Knowing stealth was important, he stopped the Escalade, threw it into park and turned off the ignition. Pressing down the emergency brake a couple of clicks disabled the automatic headlights. After restarting the engine, Seth let the SUV creep in low gear down the narrow lane. Ahead of him, the car's brake lights glowed. Seth eased his foot off the gas, but didn't dare touch the brake for fear of tipping off whoever was up there. He shifted into neutral and gently pressed the emergency brake until the Escalade slowed to a stop right at the edge of a small copse of trees.

Tessa's car was about a hundred yards ahead, near an old farmhouse. The driver got out and slammed the door, but there was no sign of Tessa. Was he wrong? The man entered the farmhouse alone.

Seth used the opportunity to follow on foot. Keeping to the brush and trees near the edge of an old pasture fence, he eased his way forward. He was almost to the car when the driver returned. Seth dropped to his haunches as the other man reached across the driver's seat and lifted up the big leather bag Tessa always carried.

Fear shafted through Seth. Where was she? Had this man already done something to her? He might have made a colossal mistake. Visions of Tessa lying injured somewhere around Flamingo Road spun through his brain. As he forced himself to calm down, his head cleared. He heard a faint thumping. He listened first with relief then with growing horror as he realized the noise came from the trunk. Had that man locked her in there? Tessa, who was so afraid of confined spaces she could hardly get on an elevator?

The man returned to the small farmhouse, this time carrying Tessa's bag. As soon as the door closed, Seth ran forward. He crouched near the trunk and put his hand against it as if he could touch her.

"Tessa?"

The movements inside stopped, and then started again in earnest, frantic and panicked. Seth closed his eyes.

"Hush, sweetheart," he soothed. "Don't attract his attention. Let me see if I can get you out of here."

Seth eased around to the driver's side and opened the door. He located the trunk release near the door and popped it before hurrying back. He pulled up the trunk lid. The light was smashed so he couldn't see her, but he heard her frightened whimpering and her shallow, panicked breathing. He lifted her out and had just set her on the ground when the door to the house opened.

"What the hell are you doing?" her abductor yelled, racing toward him. He skidded to a halt as Seth jumped up and stood to his full six-feet-five-inches.

"Shouldn't that be my question?" Seth asked, just managing to keep his hands from throttling the guy and choking the life from him. "What I want to know is why you're driving this woman's car while she's locked in the trunk?"

Tessa's kidnapper tried to bluster his way through. "Just a lover's game. It wouldn't interest you. The bitch works as a stripper. You know the type. She's into the whole bondage scene."

"Really?" Seth took an easy, relaxed step toward this unknown man, hoping to catch him off guard by making him think he might be interested in finding out more. "You into that?"

The smaller man warmed to his tale. "Yeah, some of them like it rough, and even enjoy doing more than one guy at a time. I've done a few threesomes. You interested?"

"No," Seth growled, "and neither is the lady."

As quick as a snake striking its prey, he landed a punch square in the other man's face. The other man tried to shield himself, but Seth continued to pummel him, smiling in satisfaction when he heard the man's nose crunch before he weaved for a moment and dropped into the dirt. Seth cast one contemptuous look at him and spun on his heel.

"Tessa?"

She still lay curled on her side at the back of the car with her eyes closed. He untied the gag from her mouth and reached in his slacks pocket for the knife he always carried. In a matter of seconds, he'd cut through the duct tape on her wrists and chafed them to restore circulation. Even in the dark, he saw the bruising there.

She neither moved nor opened her eyes.

"Come on, sweetheart! Look at me. You're safe now."

Her eyes opened but she didn't seem to see him. Her hands wrapped across her stomach. She brought her legs up as if protecting her body.

"Tessa! It's me, Seth. You're okay."

Wide, bewildered eyes locked with his. "The baby…" She seemed to focus all of a sudden and closed her mouth.

Seth glanced around the side of the car to make sure her assailant was still knocked out.

"Do you know this bastard, Tessa?"

She nodded and leaned her head back against the bumper of her car. In the spill of light from the open cabin door, twin tracks of tears glistened. Shadows marred her forehead and her jaw. He wasn't sure if it was dirt or bruising.

"My cousin," she croaked.

Seth looked at her again, and then at the crumpled form by the driver's door.

"Peter?"

Tessa nodded.

"Bastard. I'll call the police."

"No."

Seth paused in the act of pulling out his cellphone, feeling chilled that she would not want this man locked up. "No? Tessa, you can't be serious. The guy abducted you. And from the looks of you, hit you as well."

"My relatives will try to drag my name through the muck to defend him, Seth, like they did twelve years ago when he tried to rape me."

"All the more reason he should go to jail." He started to touch the phone again.

Tessa sobbed now. "I'll lose Zach! If Aunt Kathleen and Uncle Edwin get wind of this…and where I'm working? Please, Seth. Don't take anything else from me."

Her words were a knife slicing straight into his heart. Seth was torn by the need to do what was right, and the plea in her voice and face. At last, he crouched next to her.

"Okay. I won't call the police. Just let me get someone on the way to take care of getting your car home. Stay here for a minute while I handle your cousin, then we'll get you back home."

Seth dragged Edwards into the small house, propped his bleeding, unconscious form in a chair, and duct-taped his hands and feet so he couldn't get out of it. He pulled his phone out again, away from Tessa's hearing and made a phone call to an old friend from his freelancing days who owed him a favor. When he disconnected several minutes later, he blasted Edwards, who had come to and fought the duct tape holding him, with an icy glare.

"Nice of you to wake up, Edwards. Your cousin and I are leaving. You'll stay. My name's Seth Barlow-Barrett. Ring a bell? A friend of mine will get Tessa's car and help you…home. Should you ever set foot near her again, rest assured next time you won't get off nearly as easy."

He grabbed Tessa's leather bag and headed outside. She was standing, but leaned against the car, her hands still clasped across her stomach. Without asking, Seth swung her up into his arms and carried her back down the farm road to the Escalade. She protested but without much strength.

"Put your arms around my neck, sweetheart. I won't drop you. You weigh next to nothing."

The fact that his feisty, stubborn Tessa did what he told her to without protest was another indication of how rattled she was. After they reached the SUV, he set her on her feet, not releasing her until he was sure she wouldn't fall.

"Hang on. I'll have you in the car in a heartbeat and we'll get the hell out of here."

He settled her in the passenger seat and found a blanket from the back to wrap her in. The dome light revealed the bruise on her forehead where she'd hit her head when Edwards shoved her in the car, along with a darkening swelling along her jaw line. Had the bastard hit her?

Seth slid behind the wheel and put the Escalade in four-wheel drive to turn around in the field before heading back into town. He glanced at Tessa. She stared out the side window. Her arms still rested across her stomach. As they took the ramp to the expressway, her head drooped, and by the time they reached her apartment, she was sound asleep.

Seth hesitated a moment before rifling through her purse for her house key. After finding it, he swung her into his arms and carried her inside. He entered the apartment on cat feet, knowing Zach must be asleep in his room. She felt even lighter than he remembered, and she was so bone-tired he carried her down the hall to lay her on the bed. A flick of the bedside lamp, and he was able to turn his attention back to Tessa.

Other than the goose egg on her forehead and the bruise to the jaw, she appeared to be uninjured. Her face was smudged with dirt except where her tears had left paths on her cheeks. Seth's lips compressed as he looked at her. Remembering how she'd covered her stomach, he ran his hands over her ribs and pressed against her abdomen. He slipped off her shoes before going into the bathroom off her bedroom to get a warm washcloth. He could at least wipe some of the dirt from her face so he could get a better look at her bruises. As he reached to turn on the hot water, his hand bumped a bottle of pills. He absently put them back and held the washcloth under the running water. As he registered what the bottle said, he continued to hold the cloth under the water until it got hot enough to make him jerk his hand from beneath it and turn it off.

Pre-natal vitamins.

He stared at the bottle, realization dawning. Pre-natal vitamins. Anna had taken those when she was pregnant. Seth returned to Tessa's side and wiped the dirt from her face. She stirred, but didn't wake up. In fact, she slept so heavily it was frightening. He wondered if she might have a concussion, but dismissed the thought. His eye caught a small pamphlet on her nightstand. Nutrition: The Key to Your Healthy Pregnancy.

Holy shit.

Seth stared at Tessa's stomach. The long sweater she wore hid her from view, but he'd seen her in that damned uniform at Flamingo Road. She didn't look pregnant, did she? Seth swallowed hard. He told himself he was trying to make her comfortable by slipping off her jeans. He raised her sweater and saw she had left the button at the waistband unbuttoned. A sudden memory flashed into his mind of Anna right before she decided she would have to wear maternity pants. She could never get the waist on her clothes fastened.

Seth's fingers trembled as he slid the zipper down and slipped Tessa's jeans off. The diamond stud at her belly button was gone. For some reason, that more than anything so far convinced him that all the signs he was seeing were the reality, not wishful thinking. He stared for an instant, then rested his hand over her stomach, not pushing, just feeling the shape beneath his hand. He remembered her so well, though it had been three months since he'd loved her in this very bed. Her stomach was not as flat as it had been. His gaze darted to the nightstand and memory struck him of how carried away they had been, so carried away neither of them remembered the condom that first time. There was Zach telling him how tired she was and how she was sick all the time.

He wanted to shake her awake and find out for sure. Instead he pulled the covers up over her and turned off the light. It could wait until morning. After all, the night was already almost gone. He was not leaving her after what she'd been though, nor was he leaving until he got some answers.

Chapter 13

Hunger woke Tessa three hours later. Her stomach was beginning to roll, and if she didn't eat something soon, she would be sick. Struggling to shake off her drowsiness, she swung her legs out of bed, realizing she still had on her sweater and her underclothes, but not her jeans. What had happened? She couldn't seem to get her mind around it.

She stripped off her bra and underwear and threw on an old sweatshirt and a pair of sweatpants. Even those felt a little snug in the waist. Tessa grimaced. She'd gone overnight from being able to wear her clothes to nothing fitting quite right, not even her bras. She stumbled across the hall into the kitchen at the back of the apartment and found the half-eaten sleeve of saltines she tried to keep handy. After pouring herself a glass of water, she grabbed the crackers, headed toward the living room and stopped dead.

Seth was stretched out on the couch, his dress shoes on the floor and his suit jacket and tie folded on a nearby chair. As Tessa stared at his soundly sleeping form, memory returned. Her hands shook as she remembered Peter and being locked in the trunk of her own car. She set the glass of water on the coffee table, afraid she might drop it, but kept the crackers clutched against her chest. What had happened? Why was Seth here?

He stirred, frowning as if he couldn't find a comfortable spot. No surprise there, when he was trying to fit a six-and-a-half-foot frame onto a six-foot couch.

She remembered him putting her in his SUV, but not much after that. Had he removed her jeans? Her free hand went to her stomach and her gaze settled back on Seth. Did he know? Stupid! How could he not know? She had pregnancy literature scattered around her room. And it was wishful thinking to believe he hadn't spotted the pre-natal vitamins in the bathroom.

She looked at him again. His eyes were open and focused on her belly.

"How far along are you?"

Well, that settled the question. There was no point in trying to deny anything.

"Three months."

Seth swung his feet to the floor and sat up. His eyes, bloodshot from lack of sleep, took in the crackers in her hand and the glass of water on the table nearby. He patted the couch next to him.

"Sit down, Tessa, and eat something. I assume that's why you've got the crackers. Are you nauseous?"

She nodded, unsure what kind of mood he might be in but feeling like she needed to be as careful as if she had an untamed lion in the room. "If I wait too long between eating something I get sick."

With more than a little self-consciousness, she nibbled on a cracker when what she really wanted to do was shove it in her mouth and eat it as fast as possible.

Seth stroked the hair out of her face so he could see the goose egg there. "Then eat," he said again. "Don't nibble on it. Anna could never seem to get enough salt while she was pregnant with Becca. I guess that explains the olives you had the last time I was here."

Tessa swallowed a sip of water and nodded. "I can't keep them in the house."

"When are you due?" His tone was impersonal, as if he either didn't care or he was keeping a very tight rein on his emotions.

"The end of May."

"We can go to the courthouse Monday and get a marriage license. I'm sure I can convince our priest to perform the ceremony." It was said with the same casual tone he might use to discuss weather with a stranger.

It had a different effect on Tessa. She almost choked on the cracker she was munching on. Marriage? To Seth? Three months ago she would have fallen into his arms, but that was before he'd allowed his father to fire her, before he'd believed she would steal from him.

"I won't marry you," Tessa said.

Seth ran a hand through his hair. "Tessa, you don't have much choice."

"I do have a choice! I will not bring this baby into a loveless marriage and that's what it would be."

* * * *

Seth cringed. It might be loveless on her side, but what about him? As much as he might have tried to deny it even as short a time ago as last night, as much as he might have tried to forget Tessa, he couldn't. She was locked in his heart. He had fallen so in love with her, there was nothing he wanted more than to marry her. He pushed his own feelings aside. Tessa was logical. Maybe he could appeal to her that way.

"Tessa, you have more here to consider than just the baby. What about Zach? You worried your aunt and uncle would find out about Edwards. Think what they might do if they discover you're pregnant and unmarried."

Tessa's hand shook as she set the glass of water down and stared at Seth.

"Think about it from a judge's point of view if they ask for another custody hearing." Seth continued pressing his point. "You're getting ready to add a baby to your household, with all the expenses that entails. How will you support all of you? You can't continue working much longer as a waitress at a strip club. What will you do then?"

Tessa's expression hardened. "Roberto is moving me into the office."

"But you won't be making tips anymore, will you?" Seth kept his tone neutral and logical when what he wanted to do was grab her and shake her. He could give her and Zach the moon and not put a dent in his pocket. Why were they even having this discussion? But he knew the answer. It was Tessa's damnable stubborn streak.

"No," she admitted. "I won't be making tips anymore, but I've saved money. I won't marry you, Seth. I appreciate your help last night more than I can say, but it changes nothing." She stood up and walked away from him to the window seat. "I want you to go," she said in a small voice.

* * * *

Tessa did want him to go. He was too big, too overpowering and she was afraid if he stayed, she would say yes. She didn't want to deal with any of this. She was confused and fuzzy-headed. Now that she'd eaten something, her only desire was go back to sleep. Seth would do his duty if she let him. That was one thing she could count on with Seth. He would always take care of them, like he took care of business at Barrett even though his heart wasn't in it. And she didn't want a life like that.

"Damn it, Tessa!" Seth ground out, his voice starting to rise. "You must listen to reason."

"I am listening to reason!" she snapped back. "I'm listening to all the reasons it would never, could never work. Get out, Seth. I don't know how much more plainly I can put it."

He wanted to hit something, he was so angry. She saw it in his face, recognized it from the day he'd gotten that package that had concerned his sister. Seth grabbed his shoes, jammed his feet in them, and snatched up his coat and tie. He paused at the door and glared at her from narrowed eyes.

"There's a point, Tessa, where your desire to be self-sufficient does nothing but hurt everyone around you. I'll leave, but you're going to have to ask yourself what you've really accomplished. Are you helping Zach? Are you helping this baby? Are you even helping yourself?"

Tessa stared at him, careful to keep her face expressionless. "Get out."

* * * *

His expression might be composed, God knew he'd had plenty of experience at that, but inside he was being eviscerated with a dull knife. He shut the door with a click of finality. Seth held his mouth in a thin line as he drove back to his brownstone, trying to keep his emotions in check. He was furious, and at the same time he couldn't deny the pain. She wanted nothing to do with him, wanted to shut him out of even the child they'd created together. How much clearer could she make it that she wanted nothing to do with him? Funny, he'd never considered himself to be a masochist, but wasn't that what he was making himself by continuing to beat his head against the immovable wall of her stubbornness?

Seth pulled up to the brownstone and sighed. Brandon's sports car was already out front. No doubt his younger brother had let himself in. Bran had a way of making himself at home. Seth walked in. His brother appeared on the stair landing, about half dressed in a formal gray morning suit.

"Jesus, Seth," Brandon drawled. "You look like shit. Did you have to go carousing the night before Stacey's wedding? I mean, honest to God. You're supposed to be the sane, sober, dutiful one in the family. Then you go all woo-woo on us and vanish. Was all that exposed female flesh at that club last night too much for your aging senses?"

Seth's anger flared. "Shut the fuck up, Brandon. You are way off base on this! Were you so busy ogling that statuesque blonde on the dance floor you missed Tessa?"

"Tessa?" Brandon looked confused as he came down the carpeted stairs. "Tessa Edwards? Your Tessa?"

Seth laughed, the sound harsh and humorless. "You can hardly describe her as my Tessa, at least not anymore. She turned down my marriage proposal."

Brandon stopped next to Seth and arched a thick blond eyebrow at him. "And you went from not seeing her for months to a marriage proposal why?"

Seth raked both hands through his disheveled hair. "She's pregnant."

"Is it yours?" Brandon asked.

Seth spun on him. Fury tightened every muscle in his body, and he started to bring his fists up. He would kill him! "Why do you always have to laugh at everything? Why is everything always such a big, fucking joke to you?" Bitterness washed through Seth. "It's that flippant attitude of yours that's kept me trapped in a position I hate for almost ten years."

"Don't raise your fists to me unless you mean business, bro," Brandon drawled, his eyes narrowed. "You've trapped yourself. When will you figure out that what you see as family duty allows everyone to walk all over you?"

Seth stalked toward his brother, almost unable to control the anger that tightened his every muscle. Brandon put his hands up and backed up a couple of steps. "I'm not fighting with you. Not now, right before Stacey's wedding. And I wasn't trying to be a smart ass. You haven't seen Tessa in several months. It's a logical question."

"It wouldn't be if you knew her better!" Seth snapped. His shoulders slumped. He turned away from his brother and rubbed his gritty eyes before he half-covered his face and swallowed around the ache in his throat. "You would never say that, never even think it, if you knew her the way I do."

"Seth?" Brandon's voice had gone quiet and serious. "Is everything okay?"

"Yeah." Seth's mouth quirked in a half smile, though that was the very last thing he felt like doing at the moment. He turned toward the steps. "Everything's great. Tessa's pregnant with my child, she turned my proposal down flat and told me to get out. Yeah, everything's great. I better get ready. We'll be late."

Seth sprinted up the stairs. In a couple minutes, the shower in the master bath blasted him with jets of hot water.

Nothing was okay, and it wasn't just with Tessa. Over the last six months, his dissatisfaction with his life had mushroomed. He was a journalist, not a corporate executive. The Midwest merger had reminded him of that.

He wasn't sure he could go back to freelancing. God knew those four years he'd rebelled against the family yoke had been some of his best. He'd covered every political hotspot from Central America to the Middle East. He'd known then they couldn't last, but right now, anything looked better than where he was.

As tired as he was of always bowing to family responsibility, Seth had a wedding to attend. He made it through the ceremony and the luncheon reception that followed, making all the right responses, but his mind was still on Tessa and the pain of her rejection.

Seth kissed Stacey and shook hands with Jason Winchester, her new husband. He found the groom's parents and spoke with them for a few minutes before going in search of his own. After kissing his mother on the cheek, he nodded to his father.

"I have an appointment this evening. Please excuse me," he told his mother.

"Can't it wait, son?" she asked. "The bride and groom haven't even left."

Seth sighed. Duty. The chain that had bound him his entire life. This time it would be different.

"No. It can't. I'll beg their forgiveness later."

Brandon caught up with him as he headed for the door. "You need a ride?"

Seth shook his head. "No. Thanks anyway. I'll catch a cab. I need to get away. There's nothing pending at work. I'm leaving for a while."

"Seth?" Brandon grasped his arm, not letting go.

"I can't stay anymore, Bran. I just can't do it any longer."

Brandon released him. "Be careful, man."

Seth nodded and was gone.

Chapter 14

"What happened to your face?" They were the first words out of Zach's mouth when he stumbled into the living room still clad in his Spiderman pajamas.

Tessa hadn't thought about needing to explain the bruises, and she hesitated for a second as her mind raced. She couldn't tell him the truth, not even close.

"I tripped on the sidewalk steps when I came home last night and hit my face," she said.

"Does it hurt?"

"Some," Tessa admitted, relieved Zach was still at the age where he seldom looked beyond what he was told. Still, when Tuesday rolled around, it took a considerable amount of make-up to hide the bruising. She dressed in a boxy suit with a long enough jacket to cover the fact she couldn't zip the skirt all the way closed.

Roberto took one look at her and said, "Who roughed you up? The big guy James mentioned to me?"

"No," Tessa said. "It wasn't Seth. It was that cousin of mine who's been in here a couple of times."

Roberto tilted his head to one side. "You want to press charges? Or shall I handle it with a few phone calls?"

Tessa shook her head. "No, I don't think either one will be necessary. I don't think he'll be back. I'm grateful you've created this position for me, Roberto."

He raised one dark brow. "Just so we understand one another, nina, I didn't create any position for you. I need help back here with the business end, and I'm dumping it right in your lap, or at least what will be left of your lap in a few months. Once you get a look at the books, you might be wishing you were still out on the floor."

Over the next month, Tessa remembered those words. Roberto wasn't kidding. His business office was a mess. She reorganized his files, straightened out his books, and cleaned up the office until he looked at her with one raised, dark brow. "Are you always like this?"

Tessa smiled at him. "Like what?"

"Hyper-organized and hyperactive?"

Tessa tilted her head. "I prefer to think of it as efficient." That's what Seth had always said.

* * * *

It was early December. The weather had turned cold and dreary. Tessa dropped Zach at school and headed to a local shopping center to run errands before going home to catch more sleep. As she pulled into a parking spot, she recalled how Zach had taken the news of her pregnancy. His calmness helped to ease her mind on at least one score. Seth was a different matter. She'd heard nothing from him since he'd walked out of her place after her refusal to marry him.

Christmas decorations were up everywhere, and it seemed each store had its own individual piped in holiday music. As she walked along, Tessa was having a tough time getting in the Christmas spirit. She had felt the baby move for the first time yesterday at work. She'd been alone in the back office and hadn't been able to share it with anyone. For an instant, she had longed to pick up the phone and call Seth, have him come over and watch his leonine features light with pleasure.

She couldn't get him from her mind this morning. She wondered how he would have reacted had this been a regular pregnancy in a regular relationship. She could almost feel his capable hand splayed across her belly and see the intent look on his lean face, the dimples that would have appeared with the grin when he felt the movement beneath his hand.

Tessa turned away from the display of Christmas decorations and hurried out of the store. Her eyes were downcast so she had no way of seeing before she ran headlong into a tall masculine form. Her heart skipped a beat. For an instant, hope flared, but when she looked up, it was into the face of Brandon Barrett. She sagged against his supporting hands in disappointment.

"Tessa?" he exclaimed, tone incredulous as his hazel gaze slid down over her swelling stomach.

"Hello, Mr. Barrett," she responded, feeling awkward beyond belief, not sure what Seth might have said to him. "I'm sorry. I wasn't watching where I was going."

"How are you?" Brandon asked, his eyes once again on her stomach.

"Fine. I…we're fine."

Brandon's eyes met hers. "He left, you know. Seth."

Tessa's eyes flicked up to Brandon's and skittered away.

"He quit," Brandon continued. "A few days after he last saw you." As Tessa started to pull away, Brandon held her with just enough firmness to let her know she would stay and listen to him. "They fought, he and my father, like I've never heard before. Then he left. He's in Afghanistan, as far as I know. Not that he communicates often. He calls Anna or me every once in a while."

Tessa stared at him, trying to keep her feelings from showing. "Why are you telling me this?"

Brandon let his hands drop. "I thought it might matter to you since he says he's the father of the child you're carrying." He looked her up and down again, this time with contempt. "Maybe you did him a favor. Seth needs a woman who can love him and let him know it, not some ice-queen who's too self-absorbed to even consider what's best for the brother she's caring for or the baby she's carrying."

He stalked off, leaving Tessa staring at the Christmas tree twinkling a few feet from where she stood. Afghanistan? Seth had left Barrett and gone to Afghanistan?

Later, she couldn't remember driving home, but she did remember what followed. A sheriff's car was parked in front of her house.

Tessa climbed from the vehicle and locked it behind her, dread churning inside her.

"Miss Tessa Edwards?" an older deputy asked.

"Yes."

He handed her a thick envelope. "This is for you. Have a good day, Miss."

She stared down at the manila envelope. She didn't need to open it to know what it was. Uncle Edwin and Aunt Kathleen. Like an automaton, she climbed the steps and opened the door to the apartment. She let her purse fall near the door and collapsed on the couch. Her fingers trembled as she tore open the envelope.

They were suing for custody, this time citing her place of employment and the hours she worked as contributing to an unsavory and inappropriate environment. Tessa's shoulders sagged in defeat. There would be no Seth to step in to help this time. And this time, she feared Uncle Edwin and Aunt Kathleen would win. The ultimate irony was she would turn twenty-five in one more month.

* * * *

Seth logged off and closed the lid on his laptop. He sat on a too-small chair in a cheap hotel room on the edge of Kabul. He'd found a steady market for articles that focused on the everyday lives of the people here. It was enough to pay the bills, keep working, and keep him far, far away from his old life. Most of the time he was too busy, either getting a story or watching his back, to give much thought to that other life. Tonight was different. He checked his personal email for the first time in a long while.

There were several long missives from Anna, telling him about Becca and giving him the news they were expecting another child. Seth's hands trembled as he saw that, and he clamped a firm lock on his memories. He wrapped up more tightly in the blanket he used to ward off the chill in the room, and finished Anna's email.

The next mail was from Brandon. It had come through a couple days earlier. Most of it was pretty routine, updating him on what was happening at Barrett and at home, until he reached the bottom. "I ran into Tessa Edwards outside a store in Alexandria. She's pretty obviously pregnant. I know you cared about her, bro, but I have to tell you I think you're well rid of her."

Seth sat in the dark, staring at the wall. Tessa. He'd tried to banish her from his thoughts, and he was successful most of the time. When just staying alive was a never-ending worry, it put a lot of other things in perspective. But now in the quiet darkness of the small room, he let the memories back in. Unflappable Tessa, or so he had thought until he'd pulled her from that elevator in Chicago. Then he had discovered the passion. What they'd shared had to mean something to her. It still did to him, God knew. More and more the feeling assailed him that he had given up too soon. He had walked away when what he should have done was stay to fight, to make her see they could be good together.

He started packing. It would take a while to get back, but he'd thought about returning home for Christmas anyway. As much as he loved reporting and writing, he wanted a settled life, not the constant living out of a backpack and wondering if he would be the next journalist nabbed by extremists. And whether Tessa wanted to admit it or not, she carried his child. There was more at stake now than just him. More at stake than what either of them might want.

He'd cut his blond hair short and often wore a headcloth to cover his western roots, but he knew if he stayed it was just a matter of time before someone made the connection and grabbed him. The time for freelancing all over the world was gone. Maybe he'd gotten soft, maybe he'd grown up, but he found he wanted his things, his family. He wanted Tessa, and the family they could become. He wanted his child.

* * * *

The court hearing was the following day, so Tessa visited her attorney, worried about what might occur.

"I'm sorry, Miss Edwards," he told her, "but this is not going to be like it was last time around. I'm afraid your pregnancy, on top of everything else, could be the straw that breaks the camel's back. There are too many variables that put you in a bad light."

Tessa looked out the window in his office. She prided herself on being in control, of being able to handle anything thrown at her, but she had to admit, even if it was just to herself, she was wearing down.

"I understand, but I can't change the circumstances. I provide Zach with a stable home life, and I earn an excellent wage to support us. I won't apologize for where I work, nor will I apologize for the child I carry."

The attorney looked at her solemnly. "Then you should prepare yourself, and I would suggest you prepare Zach that the possibility exists his aunt and uncle will win custody."

"Thank you."

Tessa worked that night. As a receptionist, she had to be there while the club was open, to answer the phone and process new memberships. Although the temptation to call in sick was almost overwhelming, she couldn't afford to. When she got home in the early hours of the morning, she was too wound up to sleep. As a result, Tessa had circles under her bloodshot eyes that even make-up couldn't hide when she and Zach arrived at the courthouse in Alexandria. Zach, too, looked pale and tense. She had done her best to prepare him without trying to alarm him too much. Mr. Stanley waited outside the courtroom door for them.

"Ready?" he asked, his expression somber.

Tessa nodded, holding Zach's hand in her own. He squeezed her fingers as they sat down at the table with their attorney. It was the same judge presiding over this hearing as the last one. This time his face was much sterner as he reviewed the files in front of him.

He glanced up at her. "It says here, Miss Edwards, you were fired from Barrett. For what reason?"

Tessa swallowed. "There was some question about my handling of accounts. I did nothing wrong, your honor."

He looked at her over his reading glasses. "I also see you now work for a gentlemen's club, Flamingo Road?"

"That's correct. I'm the office manager and receptionist. I answer phones and oversee the business operations."

"And what are your work hours?"

Tessa swallowed. "I work from six in the evening to three in the morning, Tuesday through Saturday."

This time the judge frowned at her. "Who cares for Zach while you are at work?"

"My neighbor, Mrs. Flores, keeps an eye on him." She answered the judge in a monotone as he continued to ask questions, but inside she was sick. She didn't need to be a mind reader, she could feel how this was going.

"How do you plan to care for both your brother and the child you now carry?" The judge glanced down at the file. "It doesn't appear from your check stubs that your income will allow you to adequately care for two children."

"I'll manage," Tessa said.

The judge stared hard at her. "What role will the father of your child play in helping you?"

Tessa's chin jutted. "None. We don't communicate."

The judge looked down at the file again and back up at Zach and her. Tessa knew what was coming and her whole world started to unravel.

"I'm afraid, Miss Edwards," the judge began, "that in looking at the changed circumstances now presented to me, I must re-evaluate your custody. It's not a matter of where you work." His hard glance rested on her aunt and uncle. "Nor is it even a matter of your status as an unwed, expectant mother. The bottom line for me, Miss Edwards, is that out of a twenty-four hour day, you are a presence in Zachary's life for roughly three to four hours. Other than that, he's in the care of either the school or your neighbor. I believe at this point in time, Kathleen and Edwin Price can provide a more stable and secure home. I therefore award custody to the Prices along with control of the trust fund left for Zachary Mallory until such time as the court deems otherwise."

"Tessa?" Zach pleaded, trying to understand. "What does he mean?"

She squeezed his hand and hugged him close. "It means you will go with Uncle Edwin and Aunt Kathleen for right now." Tessa lowered her voice to a whisper. "But I promise you, Zach. I'll get you back. I'll find a way."

"No!" Zach pushed to his feet and made a run for the door, but the bailiff caught him. Tessa started after her brother, but her attorney held her back. She watched in horror as Uncle Edwin and Aunt Kathleen brushed past her and approached Zach. Edwin Price bent down and said something to her brother. He slumped in defeat, then left the courtroom with them.

Tessa sat at the table, staring down at her clenched hands. She'd lost Zach.

"Miss Edwards?" her attorney prompted. "It's time to go. Can I get you anything?"

Tessa shook her head. "No."

She called in sick. Aunt Kathleen phoned the following morning to arrange to pick up Zach's belongings. Tessa packed them mechanically, shutting off the emotions threatening to drown her. She'd let him down. She had promised her mother she would care for him, and she had let them both down.

Tessa avoided conversing with her aunt and uncle as they loaded everything in their car. As her aunt started to get back into the passenger seat, Tessa blurted, "Please take care of him, Aunt Kathleen. Please…" Her voice trailed away and she swallowed. "Tell him I love him."

"No need to worry," her uncle said in a bracing tone. "He'll be fine with us. We registered him at the local public school this morning, and he'll do fine there."

Tessa stared after their departing car for a long time. She shivered in the cold of the December day.

Chapter 15

There were a few tense moments going through customs in Kabul before Seth boarded the plane back home. He spent the night in Beirut in a luxury hotel that he billed to Barrett following a call to Brandon to clear it. His brother was overjoyed to hear he was coming back.

"I've appreciated the use of the brownstone, but I found a place to rent and I'm ready to move first of the year."

"That's great, Bran," Seth said. "You haven't heard anything more about Tessa, have you?" There was enough of a hesitation on the other end that he prompted, "Brandon?"

"It was a small blurb under legal notices."

"What?"

"A custody hearing earlier this week. Her aunt and uncle were given custody of Zach."

Cold filled Seth. He remembered Edwin and Kathleen Price from the hearing he'd attended with Tessa. They were not interested in Zach's welfare, just their own. He knew how much the boy meant to her. She must be out of her mind with worry. After hanging up with Brandon, he tried Tessa's home phone, but it rang and rang, not even picked up by an answering machine.

It was two more days before the taxi pulled up in front of his brownstone. Seth paid the driver before slinging his backpack onto his shoulder and climbing the steps to the front door. Seth saw the twinkling lights of the Christmas tree in the living room and it dawned on him the holiday was a week away.

He'd decided on the way home he would continue with plans for a different future…one away from the overbearing presence of his parents.

He'd put a bid in on a community newspaper on the market near his beach house. The paper had never been a real moneymaker, and the family who owned it was tired of being tied to it. Seth was waiting to hear back from them, but felt like he stood a good chance of getting it. That left Tessa. What would he do about her?

She didn't want him. She had made that more than obvious, but try as he might, he couldn't get her out of his head or his heart. He would take her on any terms he could get. And right now, with Zach in the hands of their aunt and uncle, she was vulnerable. If that was blackmail, then so be it.

It was late Sunday afternoon before the effects of the jetlag faded. Seth was sitting in his study when he heard the distant sound of the doorknocker. His housekeeper had the day off. Seth knew it wasn't Brandon because his brother had a key. Half-tempted to ignore the knock, he finally padded for the door in his bare feet. A light rain fell, and he knew the weather forecasts called for the possibility of a switch to freezing rain. Not bothering to tuck his chamois shirt back into the waistband of the well-worn jeans he wore, Seth made his way down the hall. The small figure outside the door had just turned away when he opened it.

"Tessa?"

She looked over her shoulder, raising a pale, shadowed face to him. Her hair was wet and she shivered.

"Is Zach here?" she asked, a note of desperation in her voice.

"Zach?" he asked in some consternation. It was the last question he expected her to ask. "No."

If possible, her porcelain skin lost even more color. She started to sway. Seth pulled her inside and shut the door. She had a rain slicker on, but the hood had fallen back. In the light of the hallway, she looked no better than she had on his front steps.

"Let me have your coat, Tessa. You're soaking wet."

As she let it slip from her shoulders, he saw the swell of her belly beneath her thick sweater.

"He's run away, Seth. I thought maybe..." Her voice trailed off, and her chin trembled.

Seth turned her into his arms and held her shivering frame against him, trying to share some of his warmth with her. She felt cold, and her paleness worried him.

"You thought he might come here?" he finished for her.

She nodded against his chest. "He's been missing since yesterday. I'm so afraid. The police came to my house last night and then to where I work. I think they thought he might have come to me, but he didn't. I don't know why."

When her voice broke on a hoarse sob, Seth swung her into his arms and, in spite of her protests, carried her into the den, where he laid her down on the long, plush couch facing the fireplace. Picking up a poker, he stirred the fire and added another log to it.

"Stay there, Tessa. I'm going to get you some hot chocolate to help take the chill off you, and then we'll talk. Okay?"

* * * *

She nodded and watched him go. He'd changed in the past few months. He was thinner and his hair was so close-cropped it looked more like a military cut, but she noticed his eyes the most. They were shadowed and shuttered, as if he'd become a master at keeping his emotions buried so no one could see them. Not even outbursts of his infamous temper broke through his remoteness. Had she done that to him? Was he another person she had let down?

She stared into the fire, trying to feel its warmth, but not even a spark sank into the coldness at her very core. She shivered again and looked around her as she brushed a limp strand of hair behind her ear. In the far corner of the room was an elaborate model of an older sailing vessel, every detail lovingly portrayed.

"I built that with my grandfather's help," Seth said as he handed her a steaming mug of hot chocolate, "when I was not much older than Zach is now." He watched Tessa as she took a cautious sip from the mug she held cradled in her hands. Other than the swell of her stomach, she knew she looked thinner.

"Do your aunt and uncle still have custody of Zach?"

"You know?"

Seth nodded. "Brandon told me over the phone when I called from Beirut."

Tessa looked away from him. "The judge said my job took me away from him too many hours of the day. He said he didn't think I could care for Zach and the baby, but I can, Seth."

Seth's mouth thinned. "Drink the chocolate, Tessa, and warm up. Then let's focus on Zach. He's bound to be someplace he feels comfortable."

* * * *

He watched her like a hawk as she drank from the mug. In a few minutes, a small bit of color returned to her face, but she still looked exhausted. Hot chocolate and a fire wouldn't change that.

His gaze drifted down once again to her belly. She caressed the swell of her baby bump, and to his amazement, he saw her hand move as if it had been shoved by an unseen force. He was overcome by an incredible urge to kneel down in front of her so he could share the experience of the baby's movement, but now wasn't the time.

His child. The thought struck him with more force. The child growing in her belly was his child. No matter what she might want to deny, there would always be that link between them. If she was still determined to keep him shut out of the baby's life, then she'd find she had another fight on her hands. But now wasn't the time to go into that. Now they needed to find Zach.

* * * *

Tessa set the mug down. She hadn't wanted it, and had swallowed it to make Seth happy. Her mind kept coming back to Zach. She had felt so sure that if he hadn't come to her, he would try to find Seth.

"He knows how to get to the Barrett building, Seth. Do you think he might go there?"

Seth shook his head. "Security would have called someone by now if that were the case, but we can drive by if you like."

She lifted wide blue eyes up to him. "You would do that?"

"I don't know what you think I am, Tessa," Seth snapped. "I care about your brother. I'll help look for him any way I can. Now come upstairs and let me see if I can find you a sweater to wear. The one you have is soaked."

She followed him into a master bedroom almost as large as her whole apartment. It was furnished in earth tones with a plush beige carpet so thick, her feet sank into it with every step. She hesitated in the middle of the room while Seth riffled through the closet. At last he came up with a thick fisherman's sweater.

"Believe it or not, this belonged to Anna. She left it here, and I almost forgot I still had it. Try it. I think you'll find it will fit."

When she stripped off her own damp sweater, it revealed her loose pink turtleneck. She watched as Seth's eyes dropped once again to her stomach. Without the camouflage of her sweater, her swelling belly was more defined. He swallowed, but instead of saying anything, he turned away. Fatigue washed over her as she stared at the broad barrier of his muscled back.

"It fits," she said, seeing no relaxation in his tense shoulders.

"I'll get you a jacket." He found a waterproof parka almost big enough for her to use as a sleeping bag. "This will have to do. It will at least keep you dry, which is more than can be said for what you arrived in."

Tessa nodded, sensing not one bit of softening from him.

He put her in the Escalade and started the engine. "We'll try Barrett first."

"Thanks, Seth. Thanks for helping."

He grunted in reply and put the car into gear without looking at her.

* * * *

Seth's eyes narrowed as he noticed the way the rain was hardening on the windshield. The weather had deteriorated even more by the time they arrived at Barrett. Seth parked out front on the deserted street and used his key to get in. A security guard met them at the door.

"Mr. Barrett!" the guard said in surprise. "Welcome back! It's been a while."

"Thanks, Charlie. We're looking for a little boy, eleven years old with red hair and freckles. Have you seen him anywhere?"

The guard shook his head. "No, sir. And that'd be one boy it would be hard to forget. The police were already here earlier today, and I told them the same thing."

Seth put an arm around Tessa's shoulders and pulled her into his side. "Thanks, anyway, Charlie."

"No problem, sir. I'll let you know if I see anything."

"Seth?" She was crying. He heard it in her voice as she got into the SUV. He started the engine once again. The drizzle had turned into freezing rain. Seth stared out at the weather.

"Any other ideas? What does he like to do?"

"Besides video games, the only thing he's ever shown an interest in was sailing…"

They stared at one another.

"Do you think?" Seth ventured.

Tessa shook her head. "I don't see how. That's all the way over at the bay."

Seth stared at her tear-streaked face. He had a gut feeling, but he knew she was reluctant to go that far.

"I have to check, Tessa. You know that. Do you want me to take you home?"

She huddled in the overlarge parka and shook her head. "No. If he were going to come to my apartment, he would be there already." Hurt pushed through her words. Was it the pain of knowing that Zach had apparently run from her as well?

Seth drummed his fingers on the steering wheel as he looked out at the weather. The wind was beginning to come up now, almost as if what they were getting were developing into a Nor'easter. "Let me call the marina and have them check the Wistful."

Tessa nodded. "I'm petrified, Seth. Where is he? He called me from his new school to tell me how unhappy he was, but all I did was urge him to hang in there. I didn't take to heart how desperate he was to get away from Aunt Kathleen and Uncle Edwin. This is all my fault."

"Don't start trying to assign blame..." Seth broke off as his phone was answered. He explained what was going on, then waited impatiently while they checked Wistful's berth. "What do you mean the Wistful's not in her moorings?" Seth's gut clenched and he ordered, "Alert the Coast Guard. I have reason to believe she's been taken out by an eleven-year-old boy. I'm on my way, and I want someone ready with a boat to take me out."

He shoved his phone back in his pocket and looked at Tessa's eyes, wide pools of ice blue in a face so pale it looked like milk glass in the gray, wintry light.

"Seth?" she questioned. He heard the fear in her voice. It was a living thing about to consume her. He reached for her and cradled her face, his thumbs brushing at the tears that welled and ran down her cheeks.

"I will find him, Tessa. Do you hear me? I will find him and bring him back to you."

They headed for the marina, but the going was slow as the temperature continued to fall and the wind continued to rise. As the wiper blades swished back and forth, Seth watched the moisture sliding like syrup in front of them. At the edges of the window, it bunched up into a row of half-melted slush even the defroster couldn't quite destroy. Zach was out in this somewhere. Trying to sail. God, let him have enough sense to seek shelter.

Chapter 16

Zach dropped anchor in the cove they'd fished over the summer. It had been easy enough to get Wistful and head out into the bay. Everyone thought he was an idiot. It was happening all over again at this school Aunt Kathleen and Uncle Edwin made him go to, but he wasn't an idiot. Even Tessa didn't know how well he'd learned to sail at camp, but he would show all of them they needed to quit treating him like some dumb little kid. Maybe he'd sail around the world so he never had to go back to that stupid school. At least, it had seemed like a good idea when he started.

Now, he wasn't so sure. When he had gotten up this morning, the wind had begun to pick up and a light drizzle was falling. Zack found Seth's weather radio in the cockpit and fiddled with the dial until he found the marine forecast. When he heard the warnings, he swallowed. He'd never sailed in bad weather. He'd never even been on a boat in bad weather.

He ate one of the cans of Beanee Weenees he'd brought along and drank some instant coffee he'd heated up in the small microwave. Maybe if he left now he could get Seth's boat back before he got in even bigger trouble…maybe before anyone figured out he'd taken it.

Zach pulled anchor and set sail, but the wind direction had changed. He swallowed as he realized he would have to sail against it most of the way back. He chewed on his lower lip while he tried to remember what he'd learned in camp. It was slow going, tacking back and forth and always adjusting sails to keep the boat from heeling too much.

He had to stop several times to warm up. Zach had never been so wet and cold. He tried putting on the rain suit he found below, but it was Seth-sized, hanging miles past his hands, and way too big to do anything with even when he tried rolling up the sleeves.

The rain turned to ice, and Zach nearly skidded off the side of the boat when he tried to close the door to the cabin so it wouldn't get wet inside.

He grabbed the railing while he sat on his butt on deck, his stomach doing so many somersaults he thought he might barf.

What did he know about sailing in this kind of weather? And all those gadgets Seth had to make sailing Wistful a snap in good weather weren't helping him now. In the dim afternoon light, he saw a small cove. Maybe the boat would be okay there. At least it would be out of some of the wind. As the light faded, he pulled in the sails and dropped anchor. The wind-whipped water rocked the boat from side to side, but Zach didn't think it was hard enough to make it capsize. If he could wait out the storm...

He swallowed as he sat below deck listening to the tick-tick of sleet against the cabin roof. Tessa would be so worried. He hadn't thought of that to begin with because he'd been so mad, but he did now. Maybe they were right. Maybe he was just a dumb kid. Somebody smart would have realized that worrying about him was the last thing she needed. If he got home okay, he would tell her how sorry he was. If he got home.

* * * *

When they pulled into the marina, Seth left the car running and looked at Tessa. "I'm going after him."

"I'm coming with you."

"No. You couldn't stand being locked up in a cabin, and it's too extreme out there for you to stay above deck. If you won't think of yourself, think of the baby you're carrying, Tessa."

"It's your child too," she whispered. "But Zach's like my son. I know you can understand that. I watched the way you were with him. Please. I can do this. I can."

He saw the determination in the set of her jaw. Seth touched her cheek. "Okay. We'll find him, Tessa. Together."

He sheltered her from the wind as they stopped at the marina office. The owner handed him the keys to a boat.

"I got nobody to go with you, but I got you a helluva boat. The Merry Ann's not much to look at, Mr. Barrett, but she's stout and dependable. I've gassed her up and she's ready to go. God speed."

Seth took the keys and turned to Tessa. "We'll retrace our route from our trip this summer. It seems like the most logical place to start." He looked at the owner. "If you hear anything from the Coast Guard, let us know. We'll have the radio on as well."

Seth half carried her aboard, putting her with him on the bridge. While she tried to adjust to the close quarters and the rhythmic clicking of the freezing rain hitting the glass, Seth dug around for foul weather gear. He smiled when he unearthed a full set of Gore Tex raingear and high rubber boots. Once he was suited up, he was a far cry from the man whose office Tessa had first walked into last summer. It was that man she had loved, but he wasn't sure how much of that office-bound Seth still existed. The last few months had changed him. Hell, it had changed them both.

"I'll be right back."

Through the windows, she watched him untie the last mooring line before he jumped back onto the boat and all but skidded across the deck. The footing was treacherous at best. God help Zach if he hadn't already found some shelter and dropped anchor. He returned to the bridge and started the old boat's engines. They rumbled to life with a reassuring growl. Seth turned to Tessa, his hood thrown back but a thick knit cap pulled over his short hair to protect him from the elements.

"Ready?"

She tried to smile, but Seth saw the faint quiver at the corners of her mouth. She lifted her chin. "Let's do this."

Good girl. She was still the tough little fighter he remembered. His Tessa.

He checked his charts as he set the boat on a south-southwesterly course. The light was fading and he didn't have much time. Darkness would make a search next to impossible in this weather. He pressed the throttle forward, relieved when the boat responded, and gripped the wheel as the craft leaped and bumped over each swell on the bay.

Tessa stared out the windows, adding her eyes to his as they searched for any sign of Wistful. Her white knuckles grasping the ledge were all that betrayed her nerves.

Seth berated himself. What the fuck had he been thinking, bringing her out in this? The way this weather was, they would be damn lucky to not end up needing rescuing themselves. By the time they reached the cove where they'd stopped to fish, he knew they would have to go back.

He turned to Tessa, hating to break it to her, knowing how he would crush her.

"We have to quit, don't we?" Her eyes were huge in her pale face.

Seth nodded. He wasn't going to try to sugarcoat it at this point. "There's no sign of her, sweetheart. We don't have the resources to search in the dark. We'll have to rely on the Coast Guard at least until morning."

Her chin quivered, but she nodded. He'd give almost anything to be able to take her in his arms and comfort her, but timing was everything and he feared their time had come and gone.

He turned the boat around and headed back north. The going was slower, even with the Merry Ann's powerful engines. Seth kept one eye on the navigational buoys as his gaze still swept the shore on his left. The freezing rain had stopped for the time being, but the wind continued to howl, whipping salt spray into the air. He slowed his pace so he could search what little he could see.

"Keep looking, Tess. We can at least do that as we go home."

A moment later, he felt her behind him. Slender arms wrapped around him, and she pressed against his back. "Thank you, Seth."

If he'd wondered whether she could care for the man minus the suit and the power, he had his answer. Seth swallowed and had to clear his throat before he could speak. "I'd do anything for you, Tessa. You and Zach."

"I think I already knew that, even if I couldn't admit it. That's why I came to your door, praying you would be there. And you were."

"And I always will be, Tessa, but we can talk about that later, after we have Zach back with us safe and sound." He pulled her close against his side and squeezed her shoulders. When she leaned her head into him, something that had hardened around his heart began to loosen once more.

* * * *

Zach huddled in the cockpit of the Wistful. He had turned on the lights, but didn't dare run the small heater for any length of time 'cause he was scared the battery that powered everything would run down. He'd a whole lot rather be cold than sit in the dark. After pulling off his wet clothes, he dug around until he found one of Seth's thick hooded sweatshirts. Like the rain jacket, it fell to below his knees. He also uncovered a pair of heavy wool socks that came up to his knees. He looked down at himself, making a face. He looked sooo stupid, but at least he was dry. After heating up another cup of instant coffee, Zach wrapped a blanket around himself and crawled with his mug up on one of the berths in the cabin.

He worried his lower lip and stared out the small window. The rain seemed to have stopped, but choppy waves still tossed the Wistful from side to side. No matter how much he wanted to go home, he was too scared to try sailing again until it was clear. Sliding up against that railing had been enough for him. He had wanted to prove to everyone how grown-up he was, but he knew now he'd made a dumb mistake. Uncle Edwin and Aunt Kathleen might be mad, but Tessa would be worried. Would she get in trouble because he ran away? He hadn't thought about that. His uncle and aunt would blame her, even if it wasn't true. They didn't care about that...or him.

He swallowed the rest of his coffee and thought about turning out the lights inside the small cabin, but he couldn't bring himself to do that. It was one thing to sit inside the tossing Wistful when he could see; it was another to roll around in the dark.

* * * *

Seth squinted at the small cove ahead on his left. A few isolated lights outlined the shore, but for the most part it was deserted. He was about to look away when he thought he spotted a light, a bobbing light. He pulled the throttle back and the Merry Ann settled on the uneven surface of the bay.

"What is it?" Tessa asked shifting from her perch back to his side.

Seth grabbed the binoculars hanging around his neck and put them up to his eyes. There it was again.

"A light, sweetheart. One that's moving. That means it's on the water. Let me bring us about. In this weather, any indication of another boat is worth checking out."

Adrenaline pumped through him, raising his flagging energy levels. He brought the Merry Ann around and headed toward the light.

"Help me keep an eye on it."

"I will."

When they drew closer, he turned on the boat's powerful floodlight mounted on top and shined it ahead of them.

"It's the Wistful." He recognized her even without seeing her name on the stern and relief poured through him.

He heard a small, hiccupping sob and wrapped an arm around her shoulders to give her a brief squeeze.

"It's going to be okay, sweetheart. Smart boy. Damn."

Seth opened the mic on the loudspeaker overhead. "Ahoy! Wistful. Ahoy!"

He repeated it a couple more times before he saw the cabin door slide back and a small head appeared on the steps.

"Oh, Seth!" Tessa laughed. "It's Zach. He's okay!"

Seth felt a surge of gladness so strong he staggered against the helm as he brought the Merry Ann alongside and cut the engines before lowering the anchor. He turned to Tessa and leaned down without thinking to press a kiss on her cold lips. "Wait here, Tess. I'll get him on board. It's too slippery for you and the baby out there."

She nodded.

As soon as he stepped outside, Zach's trembling voice greeted him. "Seth? Is that you?"

"Yeah, son," he reassured him, his voice gruff. He couldn't let either Zach or Tessa see how emotional he was. They were counting on him to be strong. "I'm going to throw you a line. I want you to tie it to the bow. I'll be over in a minute in the runabout to get her ready to tow back behind us and get you on board. Are you okay?"

"Yes, sir," Zach said in a subdued voice. "I'm sorry I took your boat."

"Don't worry about that now," Seth told him. "We can sort everything out later. Right now we need to get you home. Tessa's waiting onboard for you."

"Man, she'll skin me."

Seth laughed, feeling some of the heart-clenching fear ease. "I doubt it."

Zach caught the line on the second try and tied it to Wistful's bow. A minute later, Seth steered a small boat over the choppy water to the sailboat's stern where he tied up and came aboard. Zach slipped and slithered along the icy deck and launched himself at Seth. After catching the boy in his arms, Seth lifted Zach against him and hugged him hard.

"It's all right, little man," he soothed. "You did all right. You might have hell to pay when we get back, once Tessa gets over the relief of you being alive, but for right now, I'm telling you, man-to-man, you did some mighty fine sailing."

Seth heard one small sob before Zach sniffed and nodded his head. He gave the boy another hard squeeze and set him down. "Let's go below for a minute and I'll make a call on the radio."

"I would have called," Zach said, "but I didn't know how it worked."

Seth ruffled his hair. "Before you ever go out again, that's one thing we'll remedy."

Zach nodded.

Seth grabbed the mic and radioed the Coast Guard base. "This is Seth Barrett, owner of the Wistful. I've located Zachary Mallory and my boat approximately ten miles southeast of Mac's Marina. Over."

"Roger, Wistful. Advise you stay put."

"Negative," Seth replied. "I will be returning on board the fishing trawler Merry Ann. Was planning on towing Wistful. Something I should know?"

"Roger, Wistful. Storm is heating back up again. Advise you batten down the Wistful and let her ride out where she is while you return to the marina ASAP. Over."

"Roger that. We should be underway aboard the Merry Ann within the half hour. Out."

Seth turned off the radio and turned to Zach. "Can you maneuver in those clothes or do you need to change back into your own?"

"I should change," Zach said.

"Get to it then. I'll get the Wistful ready to ride this out right here. Then we need to get back to the Merry Ann."

* * * *

Tessa watched Seth help Zach onto the runabout. He had secured everything he could aboard the sailboat before he untied the line linking it to the fishing boat. Something must have made him decide not to attempt towing his boat. As she glanced at the heavy sky and listened to the wind, she realized the weather was going downhill once more. She sought them out again, watching their movements and reassuring herself they were okay.

Seth looked like he always did--whether he was in a custom-tailored suit or foul weather gear--strong and dependable. He was always there for her when she needed him the most. She swallowed as she realized the truth she'd denied for far too long. She loved Seth Barlow-Barrett whether he was wearing the suit or the soaking wet storm gear. More than that, in her heart, she knew she could trust him. It was why she had sought him out today.

She had some serious soul-searching to do and some even more serious fences to mend.

As the men she loved made their way back to the Merry Ann, Tessa heard the rain on the roof of the cockpit once again take on that distinct sound of frozen precipitation. The freezing rain was starting to come down in earnest once more as Seth stowed the runabout with Zach's help. Then they were there on the bridge. Tessa hugged Zach to her, mindless of his soaking wet clothes. He could soak her through to the skin a hundred times so long as she could hold his skinny frame next to her and bury her face in his flame-colored hair. God, she had missed him so much.

"Oh, honey," she whispered next to his ear. "I've been so worried. I'm so sorry I didn't listen to how unhappy you were."

Zach hugged her and stepped back. "I wanted to prove I wasn't some dumb little kid, but I guess I messed up big time."

Tessa shook her head in dismissal. "We'll deal with that later. For now, you need dry clothing."

She eyed the stairs leading to the cabin below deck. Seth looked over his shoulder at her. "No way. You are not climbing down those steps, as rough as it is. Zach can go on his own to see what he can scrounge up. If he's big enough to sail a boat in this, he's big enough to find dry clothing and change. You, Tessa, are staying right here."

When she looked at him and acquiesced with an, "Okay," she could see it surprised the hell out of him. She was turning over a new leaf, starting right now. Tessa wasn't sure how long it would last, but she was determined to show Seth she was done making snap judgments, done mistrusting people--well, mistrusting him at least.

* * * *

Seth restarted the Merry Ann's engines. He realized as soon as the boat chugged back out into the main channel just how much shelter Zach had managed to find. He marveled again at how well the boy had thought under stress where many adults wouldn't have made decisions nearly as sound. That basic level-headedness was what had kept him alive. Seth thanked God because he didn't even want to consider what would happen to Tessa if she lost her brother. Even he couldn't bear the thought, but then, he looked on the kid almost as a son. Seth squinted into the leaden darkness and sailed for home.

There were plenty of questions they would all have to ask and answer, but right now the most important mission was to get the Merry Ann and the most precious cargo she'd ever carried back to the marina all in one piece.

Chapter 17

Tessa sagged with relief as the lights of the harbor that sheltered the marina came into view. The seas had gotten progressively rougher on their return, so that even she was beginning to feel a faint queasiness that had nothing at all to do with being pregnant. In a few more minutes, the Merry Ann bumped up against the dock, and Mac himself was there to help them tie up.

Seth insisted on carrying her inside the office before he would set her down. Zach and the older man were right behind them, stomping their feet.

"Ice is starting to stick on more than cars and windows," Mac remarked. "We need to get out of here before it gets any worse. You need a place to stay?"

"No." Seth shook his head. "We'll use the family's house. It's just a few miles down the road."

His eyes met hers, and Tessa saw the promise in his golden gaze, a promise that they would talk at long last.

"I'll need to call Uncle Edwin and Aunt Kathleen," Tessa murmured.

"We have a land line at the house, and there's a good cell signal from there. Let's get you and Zach over there and all of us into dry clothing, then you can make any phone calls you need to make."

Mac was right, the freezing rain made even walking a challenge. Seth insisted once again on carrying Tessa. When they reached the Escalade, he told Zach to get in the back as he buckled her into the passenger seat. After starting the engine and setting the defroster on high, he chipped the ice off the windshield and side windows. It took a few minutes, but they were on their way.

As Seth said, the house was a few miles down the road, but it took a while to reach it because the roads were more than slick, they were downright hazardous. A large wooden-shingled older home, it sported a wide, pillared veranda. Seth pulled the Escalade under a side portico that looked as though it had been designed for carriages. Now it offered them a dry, ice-free avenue to get inside, and for that Tessa was grateful. She'd had all of this storm she wanted.

Zach held her hand as Seth turned on the lights. Like the house's exterior, the rooms were large and airy, their high ceilings adorned with ornate fans, and decorated with antiques that looked not just old but also well-used. It was a far cry from his parents' stuffed and starched estate in the Virginia countryside.

Seth must have read her expression. "My paternal grandmother's responsible for this house, a woman about as unpretentious as there ever was."

Tessa glanced around the room, a little more relaxed once she realized this wasn't the showplace his parents' home was.

"There is one drawback to staying here," Seth continued. "The furnace was set just high enough to keep pipes from freezing when the house was closed for the winter. There is a fireplace in the living room, so I'll build a fire, and we can use that to warm up. It will be easier than trying to crank the furnace up, not to mention a whole lot faster."

He glanced at Tessa. "If you're up to it, can you scrounge around in the kitchen to see what you can find to eat? I'll take Zach upstairs and hunt up dry clothes for all of us. As many Barlow-Barretts as there've been in and out of here over the years, there's bound to be something to fit everybody."

Tessa nodded. "I'd better call Aunt Kathleen and Uncle Edwin first." She glanced meaningfully at Zach. Seth nodded in understanding. No way did she want her brother around when she made the call because she had a feeling it wasn't going to be pleasant.

"Come on, buddy. With six kids in my family, I bet we can find clothes that will fit you, maybe even some of my hand-me-downs if there was anything left after Brandon and Phillip got through with them."

As they walked toward the wide doorway leading to the staircase visible in the front hallway, Tessa heard Zach ask in a disbelieving voice, "People had to wear hand-me-downs in your family? I thought you were rich."

Tessa cringed, but she heard Seth's laughter rumble back and it helped calm her. She waited until they'd gone, then dug out her cellphone and found her aunt and uncle's number in the contacts before punching Send. Aunt Kathleen picked up on the second ring.

"It's Tessa, Aunt Kathleen. I wanted to let you know we've found Zach and he's okay."

"Where is he? We'll come get him."

Tessa rubbed her hand behind her neck. "We're south of Annapolis on the Maryland shore, and in the middle of a full-fledged Nor'easter. The streets are a skating rink. That's why we're not coming back. I think it would be better if you waited until tomorrow when we can get back to Alexandria."

"You took him across the state line?" Her aunt's tone was accusatory. "That's kidnapping, Tessa. I can't believe you would be that foolish."

Tessa squeezed her eyes shut hard. Sometimes she couldn't believe this woman had been her mother's sister. Two people so different, it was difficult to imagine.

"I didn't take him anywhere, Aunt Kathleen," she responded, trying to be patient. "He managed to get here all by himself, which says something about how well you've been taking care of him that he could get this far without you realizing!"

"Watch it, Tessa!" There was such spite in her aunt's tone that Tessa knew any hope of establishing any kind of relationship with the couple was an impossibility.

It was also the final straw. She had tried to hold her tongue through the whole ordeal of fighting her aunt and uncle for custody, but she was through trying to play the politically correct game.

"No, you watch it! Zach had enough time to leave your place, get all the way down here and steal a sailboat, which he then sailed miles down the coast. It was pure gut feeling that made Seth call the marina after I showed up at his place to ask for help, or Zach would still be out in this storm." Tessa paused long enough to get a breath. "You can pick Zach up tomorrow, because the court says you have the right to, but tonight he's not leaving my sight. And if you want to call the cops, then you go right ahead. I'd welcome another day in court. This time you can be the ones to justify your actions…and your expenditures. So bring it on."

She disconnected without giving her aunt another chance to talk. When she set it down on the table next to the couch, the nerves from the day's stress hit. She started to shake. As the first sob broke, she felt Seth's arms come around her. She turned her face into his chest. He felt so solid, and she needed that so much.

"Shh. It's okay. Zach's okay, and we're all here together."

"I can't let him go back there," she whispered. "Even if they put me behind bars. I can't."

"We won't let him go." Seth shifted, lifting one of his arms away. "We'll stay together, won't we, Zach?"

Zach's arms wrapped around her too, and she realized Seth had moved to include her brother in a hug they could all share. The arms of the two men who mattered most to her in the world wrapped around Tessa. She couldn't remember any time since her mother's and stepfather's deaths that she'd felt this safe.

"I'll get hold of our attorney," Seth reassured them both. "We'll get it handled. For now, you need dry clothes too. We brought you some."

Tessa looked down at the sweatshirt and jeans. "Anna's?"

Seth grinned. "Yeah, before she lost weight, so you might even be able to button the jeans over your tummy."

Tessa smiled. "Don't count on it. Every time I breathe, I think my waistline expands."

"Let's go raid the kitchen, Zach, and see what we can find."

Her brother followed Seth like a puppy, but somehow she bet Seth was used to that with all the brothers and sisters he had.

She stripped off her damp clothes and slipped the sweatshirt over her head. It fit fine. So did the jeans, but she still had to leave the button undone. Tessa grinned.

When she joined them in the kitchen a few minutes later, they had found some canned beef stew in the pantry. There was also pasta, but nothing to mix with it.

"What do you think?" Seth asked.

"I think we're having beef stew."

Seth grinned. "Have at it. Zach and I will get the fire going and warm things up."

It was no gourmet meal, but the stew would be quick, hot, and filling. The freezer yielded some butter and coffee that had been stored there, she supposed to keep it fresh. Her real find, though, was in the back of the freezer, where she located a bag of frozen biscuits. She rummaged through the cupboards until she found a cookie sheet and put the biscuits on first before finding a pot and a can opener. Within a few minutes, the biscuits were baking, the stew was beginning to bubble, and she had a pot of coffee going in the drip coffee maker.

Seth stepped through the door, his large size making the huge kitchen seem smaller. He crossed over to her and tilted her chin up to face him.

"Are you okay? Not too tired?" His tone was concerned, his eyes warm.

She nodded, feeling like bawling again. As if he realized that, he touched her lips with a finger.

"Don't. We'll talk a little later. Just the two of us, okay?"
She swallowed and nodded.

"I'll find Zach and let him know we're ready to eat."

He left the room again, and Tessa sucked in a deep breath. She was tired, more tired than she cared to admit, and hungry. She wasn't sure when she'd last eaten a decent meal. The day before? Tessa put a hand to the small of her back and rubbed the dull ache there. She wanted nothing more than to curl up in front of the big fireplace and prop her feet up.

After turning the heat down on the stew and pulling the biscuits from the oven, Tessa went in search of Seth and Zach. She found them just returning to the living room. From upstairs, Seth had managed to find blankets and pillows for everyone.

"Seth says we're going to camp out in here, Tessa," Zach said. "Won't that be fun?"

Tessa's gaze slid to the tall man standing at her brother's side. "Camp out?" she questioned.

Seth shrugged. "It seemed like the easiest alternative. Rather than trying to get the behemoth of a furnace cranked enough to heat the whole house, I figured it would be easier, and warmer, if we all slept in here. Zach and I can camp on the floor, and you can have the couch."

What she wanted was to be able to lie next to Seth and snuggle up against his broad chest. Tessa glanced at her brother's hopeful face and smiled. Maybe some other time.

"Suits me," she said. "Right now, though, let's eat. The stew and the biscuits are on the table. Your beverage choices are limited to coffee, tea, or water. Sorry."

There was little conversation during the meal. All three of them were hungry. After polishing off two bowls of stew and three biscuits, Seth went back into the pantry to snoop around on some of the higher shelves. He returned with an unopened package of Oreo cookies.

"How's this for dessert? Brandon keeps a stash stored up high enough where only the tallest Barlow-Barretts can reach. Boy, does that make Anna mad."

Tessa raised both eyebrows, but shook her head. "Sweets give me indigestion, so I try to stay clear of most of them." Instead, she poured Zach and Seth more coffee and heated water in the microwave to make herself another mug of tea. She had already put all the cooking utensils and pans in the dishwasher, and now added the bowls and silverware before adjusting the wash setting and pressing the Start button.

"Why don't we move into the living room," she suggested, glancing at Seth. "That is, if it's okay to take our drinks and the cookies in there?" At his nod, she continued, "I would kill to put my feet up for a while, and I think, Zach." She gave her brother a look through narrowed eyes. "We need to talk."

Seth paused in the act of adding sugar to his coffee and asked, "Would you like me to stay in here while you and Zach have that conversation?"

Tessa shook her head. "No, I'd say you have a real interest in this since your sailboat is still out on the bay somewhere." She hated her brother's shamefaced look, but he had to face up to what he'd done and the potential trouble he'd created for himself, not to mention the risks Seth had taken to find him.

She was surprised, after she sat down on the couch, when Seth tucked a blanket around her. Tessa curled her feet up next to her and leaned back with a sigh. It felt so good to relax a bit. Zach had taken a seat on the floor, not far from the fire, as if he hoped its warmth would give him a little added courage.

Tessa set her mug down on the end table and looked at her brother. "I'll let you tell this, Zach. Begin wherever you want."

Firelight glinted off his dark red hair as he sat huddled in a blanket near the fireplace. "I told the judge that day in court that I didn't want to go live with them. You were the one that had taken care of me since Mom and Dad died, and we would still get along just fine."

Tessa grimaced. She had hoped he wouldn't start there, but she had left the decision up to him.

"I think he would have left us together, except for you saying you had no contact with Seth."

She could feel Seth's eyes swivel to hers, but she avoided his gaze.

"Anyway, Tessa, on the way home from the courthouse that day, Uncle Edwin started in with how everything was gonna change. He didn't see any reason for me to go to some stuck-up private school when public schools had been good enough for him and Aunt Kathleen. Then he went off on the whole PlayStation thing, like all I do is play video games."

Tessa had to smile at that one and duck her head. The truth was that would have been all he ever did had she not stepped in to make him do other things.

Zach's brows drew together. "The first day at school, the teacher made me read aloud. Everybody laughed. So there I was, everyone treating me like I was an idiot again. I hated it, Tess. For a while at Chesterfield, I'd felt like every other kid, like I could do stuff, you know? But it wasn't just school.

"Aunt Kathleen's not at all like Mom, and Uncle Edwin was already talking about improvements to the house now they had the money from the trust fund." He stopped and looked at Tessa and Seth. "I thought the money was to help me, you know, pay for education and stuff."

"It is," Seth said in a quiet, furious tone.

"So I heard them talking about taking a vacation to Florida for a month and finding a sitter for me. And I got mad, you know? I was mad at you too, Tessa, 'cause when I called you just gave me all that stuff about giving it time... Well, time wasn't gonna help. So, I decided to run away."

"Did you go right to the marina?" Seth asked.

"No. I went to your house, but the guy next door said you were out of town. That's when I decided to go to the marina."

"How did you get there?" Tessa asked.

"Well, I took the train as far as I could, and then I got rides."

"You hitchhiked?" Tessa's voice came out as a squeak of indignation.

Zach glanced from her to Seth, who shrugged. Zach looked back at Tessa. "Yeah. So anyway, I got to the marina and snuck on the Wistful. I wasn't going to take her out, but then I decided I would show everyone I knew what I was doing, that I wasn't just some dumb kid. And when I left, the weather was okay."

"Well you did the right thing in finding shelter where you did," Seth interjected, "and you showed the sense to know conditions were beyond you and your boat's capabilities. A lot of adults don't do that."

Tessa sipped her tea as she listened to Seth. He was right. For all the mistakes Zach had made, he also made some great choices as well. She smiled at her brother. "Seth's right about that, and I'm proud of you."

"Nevertheless," Seth stated, "you ran away without telling anyone where you were going, and you stole a boat. Because the police and the Coast Guard had to get involved, we won't be able to pretend it never happened."

"Will I go to jail?" Zach's voice was small.

Seth shook his head, but he wasn't going to cut her brother any slack either. "I doubt that. But you may have to go to court. A lot of people spent a lot of time and taxpayer money searching for you."

"I don't want to go back to Aunt Kathleen and Uncle Edwin." Zach's brows drew together and his chin took on a stubborn look.

Seth glanced at Tessa and then back at her brother. "I think we'll be able to fix that, but that's not something we need to worry about tonight.

We'll handle it once we get home. Now why don't you get tucked in there good on the floor? I'll add a couple more logs and you can watch the fire while you go to sleep."

Zach stood up and came over to Seth, climbed up on his lap and hugged him. "I love you, Seth."

So simple. Zach had always made it so simple to show love. Tessa watched as the two hugged each other.

Seth's eyes closed and he swallowed. "I love you too, buddy," he whispered hoarsely.

And Tessa never doubted that. This man had always made time for Zach, had always treated him with affection no one could doubt was anything other than genuine.

Zach hugged her after that. Tessa squeezed him. "No matter what you ever do, Zach, I will always love you. You know that, right?"

He nodded against her neck and sat back. "I wish..." He looked at both of them. "I wish I could live with both of you." He stood up. "I gotta go to the bathroom before bed."

"There's a small one in the front hall, under the stairs," Seth told him.

When he left the room, the silence stretched until Tessa thought she would scream. When she could stand it no longer, she blurted, "Can we talk?"

Chapter 18

They were the words he'd waited to hear. For a change, he wasn't the
one saying them. Tessa had. Seth thought it would take Zach forever to go
to sleep. After he went to the bathroom, then he needed a drink of water,
and following that, he had to go to the bathroom again. And the whole
time, Seth could hardly keep his eyes, let alone his hands, off Tessa. She
was so beautiful in the firelight with her hair falling around her shoulders
and the swell of her ripening body, like a flower blossom on the verge of
full-bloom.

He saw her put a hand to her belly and realized the baby must have
kicked. Seth longed to be able to put his hands there, feel what she felt. He
rubbed his palm over his chest, looking around the room, its furnishings
highlighted by the dancing light of the fireplace. It felt like a home and
a family. His family. Yes, he wanted to talk to Tessa, wanted to convince
her to stay with him, marry him, let him love her like he longed to do. She
had come to him for help. He had to be able to take that as a sign she felt
something for him.

She caught him staring, and his face heated as he made himself hold
her gaze. He wanted her to see what he felt. She was his. No matter how
this turned out, she would always be his in his heart.

She didn't look away. Her cheeks were flushed. He didn't know if that
was from the fire or from her feelings. He hoped it was the latter, hoped
she was as torn out of her frame at this moment as he was. If he'd been
a boat, he'd have been floundering. Hell, he felt like he was anyway,
floundering in fifty-foot waves that were about to crest over top of him.
Seth swallowed, his nerves stretching to breaking point, and glanced back
at Zach. Much as he loved the kid, if he didn't go to sleep soon, Seth
might have to knock him out.

At last, Zach settled into sleep. Seth patted the spot next to him on the
couch, holding his breath as he wondered whether Tessa would take up

his invitation. There was such uncertainty as she moved closer to him. His heart pounded and he felt his body stir with need. God, he didn't want her to think that was all he wanted. She was so much more than a lover. Seth wanted all of her, in every part of his life she was willing to share. When her arms burrowed around him and she rested her head against his chest, he leaned his against the back of the couch and released a deep, shuddering sigh. He blinked. He wouldn't cry. Would. Not. With a bit of hesitation, he brought his hand down and stroked it over the silky curtain of her hair. He wanted her here, like this, forever, but there were things they needed to take care of. Hurts that needed to be healed, and air that needed to be cleared.

"Are you ready to talk?" he asked. His voice shook. As much as he might want to sound strong, right now he was on the edge with the knowledge that the next few minutes would change their futures.

* * * *

It felt right lying in his arms with the fire crackling, the soft sound of Zach's breathing, and Seth's warm, solid body to lean on. Tessa would have liked to stay as they were right at that moment. But she needed some answers from him, and she had things to say. Things that weren't easy for her. As she tried to figure out where to start, the baby rolled in her belly. Seth must have felt it too because he shifted and looked down at her.

"Was that our baby?"

His eyes were wide, hungry, haunted, and it made her want to cry at how selfish she had been. Tessa nodded and pulled the hand he rested on the arm of the couch over to place it on her stomach. After a minute, the baby rewarded them with a hard kick.

"Jesus!" Seth's voice held awe. His hand stroked over the sweatshirt. With his other arm, he hugged her closer to him. "That's the most beautiful thing I've felt. No wonder you look tired if all that's going on inside you all the time."

Some of her tension eased. He wasn't angry with her. Tessa chuckled. "Not all the time, but he's been very active today."

"You know it's a boy?" His wide-eyed glance dropped to his hand resting on the swell of their child.

Tessa shook her head. "No. Not yet. I…I have an appointment tomorrow for an ultrasound. Would you… That is… Do you want to go with me?"

His eyes lifted from her belly, where he was obviously still watching to see if he could see the baby move, to her face. "I can't think of anything I would rather do."

Tessa nodded. Something warm blossomed inside her. She felt as if a part of her she'd locked up for a long time, maybe since that day someone had shut her in that tack trunk, turned loose. More than that, she at last accepted what she'd suspected when she'd shown up on Seth's doorstep seeking help to find Zach. He was a man she could trust. He wouldn't betray her, and he would always be there when she needed him. He would have been there even sooner, but she was the one who'd kept pushing him away until she'd pushed him right out of her life. And still he had come back.

They were silent for a while, both staring into the fire. Seth moved his hand over hers where it still rested on her stomach and cleared his throat. "My grandfather and my grandmother bought this house not long after they got married. My grandmother said she wanted a place near the water for her children to be able to grow strong playing in the sun and the salt air. She was unlike any of the rest of my family, and I mean that in a very complimentary way. In some respects, she reminded me a lot of Anna. She was a tiny lady with a heart so big. She was not afraid to go toe-to-toe with anyone, including my grandfather. She reminds me a lot of you in that way. As much as she and my grandfather disagreed, when it came right down to it, they were friends as well as lovers.

"I guess what I'm trying to say here…" He glanced over at her with a small smile. "…is I want to find that same thing with you. I already know we're good in bed, but I also want you as my friend, my very best friend. Do you think we can find that?"

Tessa stared into his clouded, golden eyes. "I think we can. I couldn't have said that even a few weeks ago, Seth. You know about Peter. You've seen Aunt Kathleen and Uncle Edwin firsthand. So I hope you can also see why I've had a hard time trusting other people. That changed when I met you, even as much as you growled and snapped at me. I felt like I was able to put my trust in you, but then you threw it back at me. Until Zach came to you, you believed I had stolen money from you. I wanted to trust you, and that was a deal breaker."

He stirred, started to say something, but Tessa put her fingers over his lips to stop him. "No. Let me finish. It's difficult for me to talk about my emotions. I've spent so much time holding back and hiding them. You've been there for both of us whenever I've asked--like tonight--and I think my subconscious already knew that. That's why I came to you."

Seth pinched the bridge of his nose and rubbed his eyes. "I've had a hard time dealing with this because I didn't want to believe the worst of you. I also didn't want to believe the worst of my father. There didn't seem to be any middle ground. I either believed you, which made my father a manipulative liar, or I believed him--and you became the guilty party."

Seth leaned forward, staring somberly into the fire. "My father called me about the missing money while I was out of town. I told him you were responsible for making and paying for travel arrangements from that account. I also told him it must be a clerical error because you would never embezzle money."

"Thanks for saying that," Tessa said.

"You can imagine my surprise," Seth continued, "when Tallmadge called back to say you'd admitted it and she had escorted you from the building."

"What!" Tessa hissed, trying to keep her voice down so she wouldn't wake Zach. "I never admitted taking the money, but I did know about it. I had discovered it in my account and called my bank several times to have them trace where it came from. I had just discovered it was from the travel account and asked for an immediate transfer back to that account when your father asked to see me."

Seth's gaze was solemn. "And you were beginning to suspect it was Zach, am I right?"

Tessa nodded. "Yes, but I wasn't sure. And I never admitted taking it."

Seth ran his fingers over his short hair. Tessa could feel the hurt pour off of him like steam rolling out of a sauna. "I thought my father had turned over a new leaf. He seemed to, where Anna was concerned, but this convinces me I was right to quit. He'll never stop trying to manipulate us. I think sometimes he looks at all of his children, including me, as pieces on a chess board to be moved and positioned at his will." Seth shook his head and leaned it against the back of the couch. "So much wasted time. And now I sit here wondering if I've lost the woman I love..."

He turned his head to look at her and touched her cheek with tenderness. "I do love you. I think I have from the moment you first walked into my office and I realized you weren't intimidated. You were willing to stand up to me and my bullying." He sighed. "God, Tessa, even if you can't love me anymore after all that's happened, please let me help you with our baby. I promise I'll keep you away from my father, hell, from my whole family if that's what you want. I've stayed away myself the last few months, just keeping in touch with Anna and Brandon. My life's headed in a different direction, one I promise would have room for you and Zach...and our baby."

Could she open her heart and finally trust him? Love him? How could she not?

"Give me a chance, Tessa." Seth's gaze revealed a hunger, a yearning that was almost painful to see. "We could live by the ocean if you'd like. I've had this dream for a long time of owning and running a small weekly newspaper somewhere. I've put a bid in on the paper where my beach house is…"

Tessa put her fingertips over his mouth. She swallowed. "We can figure that out later. There's something else we need to do right now."

Seth turned his head to stare at her. "Is that a yes? You'll marry me?"

She nodded, feeling tears well. "I love you, Seth. I think I have from the moment I saw how torn up you were about that package. If that didn't do it, then the way you included Zach…" She swallowed and cradled his beard-roughened cheeks between her palms. "I love you, and I'm so sorry I couldn't admit it earlier. I'm so sorry I pushed you away."

He pulled her into his arms and hugged her close. They sat there like that for several minutes.

"Seth?"

"Hmm?"

"How cold is it in the other rooms?"

He glanced up at the ceiling. "Well, the master bedroom's right above us. It will get some warmth from radiant heat." He smiled. "If we had several blankets, I'm sure we could snuggle together for warmth on the bed."

"And have a little privacy."

* * * *

It was cold in the big bedroom upstairs, but that didn't matter. They disrobed each other, taking their time at it, as Seth marveled at the changes in her body and honoring those changes with kisses and caresses. Did she know how beautiful she was like this? He had loved her body before, but now he worshiped it.

"I thought you were sexy when you first came to work for me, but it's nothing compared to now. Your breasts have ripened along with your belly. You are everything that's beautiful, Tessa."

She ran her hands over his chest, and he shivered with need, his cock swelling until it ached. "Right now, what I want to feel is you inside me."

He ran his hands over her stomach. "We won't hurt the baby?"

She shook her head. He dipped his head until his mouth slanted over hers. Passion roared through him and he doubted he could hold out. It had been too long and his body throbbed with the need to be next to her, skin to skin, to be able to slide inside of her and feel her surrounding him. Seth guided her to the big bed and followed her down on it. His body quivered with desire and the control he attempted to maintain. After several long, hot kisses, during which he massaged her breasts and nipples, he knelt between her spread thighs.

"I can't wait," he admitted. "We can take our time later, but for now, I need to be inside you."

She reached up to caress his chest with her hands. "Don't wait. I want to feel you there, Seth. I need it too. Need to feel you move inside me, come inside me."

He groaned as he pushed forward, his hips moving with exquisite care as he held himself up on his arms so he could stare into her eyes. Outside, the rain and sleet tapped against the windows, and inside they both moaned with passion long denied.

"Don't hold back," she whispered. "Let me feel all of you."

His whole body tightened and his breath came out on a groan. As he stared down into Tessa's soft smile and her glowing eyes, he pushed deep and let his seed fill her. They would do this again. The future no longer seemed like one monotonous, lonely road. Tessa would walk it with him. And along with her would be their family--Zach, the baby she carried, and even more children down the road.

"Be with me, sweetheart. Walk with me the rest of our lives."

"I love you, Seth," Tessa whispered in his ear, her fingers stroking over his head.

They were most beautiful words he'd ever heard.

Meet the Author

From the moment Rhett walked out on Scarlett, Laura's been hooked on romance. Deciding truth really is stranger than fiction, she chose a career path in journalism. Laura now teaches English and has returned to her first love--writing fiction.

She lives with her husband and son in central North Carolina along with a menagerie of animals that includes five rowdy terriers and a gentle white mare named Tweed. When she's not reading or writing, Laura enjoys riding, photography, and baking the best darned cakes you've ever tasted.

Laura's Website:
www.laurabrowningbooks.com
Reader eMail:
Laurabrowning613@yahoo.com

Turn the page for a special excerpt of Laura Browning's

Remember Me

The plane went down…and took their love with it.

All Brandon Barlow-Barrett wants is a week away from his family's newspaper empire, time on the slopes to relax and refocus. What he gets is Lucy Cameron, the most extraordinary woman he's ever met.

Lucy Cameron doesn't take vacations. Not until now. Her very first vacation is full of highs--falling in love with Brandon Barrett--and lows--realizing she has to tell him she earns her living as a stripper.

But there's no time to reveal her secret. On the way back from a day trip to a neighboring Colorado town, their plane's engine sputters and stops. All they have left is the dangerous peaks of the mountains, a nearby lake for a crash-landing, and Brandon's last-minute declaration of love.

On sale now!

Chapter 1

"I didn't dump the proposal on your desk and take off. Jesus, Dad," Brandon Barlow-Barrett growled into his Droid as he waited to check his luggage. His gaze wandered to the check-in line next to him while he continued to listen to his father's biting tones on the opposite end. "I'd like to remind you I've had this vacation scheduled for more than two months. On top of that, I gave you the proposal two weeks early, so you would have time *at your leisure* to go over it in its entirety."

A curtain of long, blond hair several people ahead in the row next to him caught his eye. The owner towered above the people surrounding her. His gaze traveled from the hair to the ass, outlined in a pair of snug, faded jeans, and he smiled in appreciation. Long, long legs ended in high-heeled cowboy boots that just added to the woman's already considerable height.

"I won't listen to your response right now. You've had the proposal on your desk for all of one hour, and it's three hundred pages. I don't want you to flip through it. I want you to read it. You aren't Congress, and this isn't health reform."

Brandon ground his teeth as his father continued to insist he'd already seen what he needed to.

"Dad! Times are changing. If we don't change with them, there will be no Barrett Newspapers to pass along to anyone." He reached the counter and slapped his suitcase in the space next to the ticket agent. "Look, gotta go. I'll be back in a week. We can talk about the proposal then—once you've had the chance to *read* it."

Brandon clipped the phone to his belt. He knew better than to allow Alexander Barlow-Barrett time to respond. He handed the suitcase to the airline agent, got his baggage claim receipt and his boarding pass, then glanced around in a casual way to see if he could locate "Legs" anywhere, but she was already gone. Damn. Flirting with her could have made for an interesting flight. After locating his gate, he discovered the plane was on time and already boarding. Great. If there was one thing he hated, it was spending any more time than he had to aboard a commercial flight. Even in first class, he found the seats didn't have the leg room he needed. But, since stepping into his elder brother's role, he'd become a lot more conservative with the company's cash, so no taking the private jet for vacation.

A gate agent and a flight steward stood at the open door to the boarding ramp. When he approached he caught the tail-end of their conversation.

"God, what I wouldn't give for one night with a woman like her."

"You got that right, dude. Can you imagine those legs wrapped around you?"

"Shit, yeah!"

Brandon arched a brow. The two men grinned at him. After checking his boarding pass, the steward's demeanor became deferential. "Thank you for flying National, Mr. Barrett. Linda will be your flight attendant. Just let her know what you need."

Brandon nodded. Laid would be nice. Sex hadn't happened in months, but he doubted it was one of the choices on Linda's menu. It turned out she was younger than his mother by only a few years, so he settled for a shot of bourbon on the rocks.

* * * *

Lucy looked out the window, watching with interest the luggage being loaded aboard the jet. It might have been mundane to most travelers, but then she wasn't most travelers. In fact, this was the first flight she'd ever been on. Little Lucy Cameron was getting a vacation at long last. For a week, she would be able to leave behind Jasmine LeFleur, the name she used as one of the top dancers at Flamingo Road. The high-end strip club catered to well-heeled clients around the Washington, DC area. It also paid extremely well.

Reflected in the glass next to her, her smile gleamed. She'd earned enough dancing at the club to pay off her college loans—even the ones for her masters—in less than five years. So traveling to Colorado to go skiing was a treat she was giving herself. Sure, she would have to stick to the easiest slopes since she didn't have experience, but her primary purpose in flying there was to see the Rockies.

The baggage handlers had finished their task and were moving the ramp away from the body of the jet. The engines picked up RPMs, and Lucy looked around at her fellow passengers. Most of them looked bored or were already plugged into laptops, iPods or whatever was their technology drug of choice. No one seemed to share the excitement she experienced just being onboard. Okay, maybe she needed to dial down her enthusiasm a couple of notches so she wouldn't come off like an unsophisticated goofball.

Nevertheless, she paid close attention while the flight attendant went through all the pre-flight instructions about fastening seatbelts, getting emergency oxygen and using her seat cushion as a floatation device. Since they were going from DC to Denver, Lucy had serious doubts a floatation device would be necessary. At least she hoped not.

They roared down the runway, engines whining, and the pressure of take-off weighed on her. The whole time, she watched everything grow smaller and smaller on the ground below until it resembled the patchwork quilt at the foot of her bed, one of the few things she could say had belonged to her real family.

Once they landed in Denver, Lucy checked her schedule. She would be taking a commuter flight from there. The itinerary said it was a propjet, whatever that was. As she made her way to the correct gate, she began to suspect *propjet* was simply a synonym for *small*. Her musings about the plane ended when she reached the gate area and saw the other passengers, one in particular.

He stood out from the skiers and vacationers, his expensive suit making him look like he'd just stepped out of a boardroom, and had in all likelihood. Lucy glanced at him from the corner of her eye. In general, she avoided staring at men because they were usually staring at her. It made her uncomfortable—and wouldn't that make everyone laugh. Who'd ever heard of an exotic dancer who didn't want people watching her?

The man's gaze swung her way, so Lucy averted her eyes, studying the resort poster hanging on the wall to his left. Not very smooth, but the best she could come up with, short of spinning away from him. She'd gotten enough of a glimpse of his face to know he wasn't the type to have any trouble getting women to fall at his feet. Hazel eyes, more a combination of topaz and green, sun-streaked hair that glinted gold in the light, and a wide mouth with a full lower lip—yeah, he would make most girls' hearts throb.

"Flight 780 to Falcon's Head is now ready for boarding. Please use the door for gate 74A and follow the steps." The disembodied voice came through the public address system. This time there was no ramp. They exited the building straight onto the tarmac, then climbed the short flight of steps into the commuter plane. Propjet not only meant small—it didn't even mean a jet.

Lucy felt someone's gaze on her, so when she reached the top step and ducked through the door, she glanced over her shoulder. Mr. Boardroom was right behind her. He smiled. Lucy swallowed and turned away, almost bonking her head as she straightened. Wow! His smile was devastating. Forget other women falling at his feet, she was about to join them.

* * * *

Brandon kept his expression neutral when Legs, as he'd come to think of her, sat in the window seat next to him. The flight from Denver to Falcon's Head wasn't long, but he began to wish it was a little longer. He had every intention of leaving with Legs's name, phone and where she was staying, especially since her finger was bare of rings.

After securing his briefcase beneath his seat, he took off his suitcoat.

"Would you like me to hang your coat?" the young flight attendant asked.

"Thanks." Brandon settled his big frame into the cramped seat. There was no first class here. His long legs almost bumped the wall in front of him.

"You can angle your legs this way, if you'd like."

Brandon shifted at his seatmate's invitation, stretched and then allowed himself to meet Legs's gaze. *Beautiful* was all he could think, looking into a face with the most arresting dark gray eyes dominating it. Gazing into their depths was like staring into the ocean on a storm-tossed day.

"Thanks."

One corner of her mouth curved upward and a dimple appeared. "That seems to be a favorite word of yours."

Brandon blinked. Was she cracking on him? He held out his hand and grinned. "I have others. I'm Brandon Barrett."

When she slipped her hand in his, he sensed several things at once. First and foremost, he felt like he'd just received an electric shock. From the slight widening of her eyes, he guessed the feeling was mutual. The second thing that struck him was the strength of her grip. So many women shook hands like they were holding out a limp rag, but this woman's hands held power.

She smiled. Her hands weren't the only power she possessed. Her smile must have belonged to a model, but damned if he could place her anywhere—and he knew plenty of models, some in the biblical sense.

"I'm Lucy Cameron."

"Well, Lucy. Are you here to work or play?"

She chuckled. It was a rich, seductive sound that sent a shiver of pleasure along his spine. "I'm going to play." She eyed his attire. "Business?"

Now he grinned. "No. Vacation too. But I had a breakfast meeting and then had to race to make the flight out of Dulles." He wanted to keep her talking. "I noticed you in line there. Are you from DC?"

"I work there."

"Modeling?"

She shook her head with a smile, but didn't enlighten him. There were definite keep-out vibes coming off her now, increasing his curiosity, but he held it in and changed the subject.

"Have you been to Falcon's Head before?"

"No. In fact, this is the first time I've been to Colorado."

"Are you here for the skiing, or just sightseeing?"

"I'm going to ski, which is another thing I've never done. What about you?"

"Major vice, I'm afraid. Most of the time I ski back East because it's easier to get away for a weekend." No need to tell her he'd once been shortlisted for the Olympics, but maybe this could work to his advantage. "Have you set up lessons?"

She shook her head. "I figured I would handle instruction when I did the whole ski rental."

"I can walk you through it all. Even get you started, if you'd like."

She tucked a strand of her shiny golden hair behind her ear. It was straight, but not thin and wispy like so many blondes. "I don't know. I don't want to impose…"

Hell, maybe she was here with someone, or meeting someone. "No problem. No doubt you and your friends already have plans, and here I am trying to barge in on them."

"Oh, I'm not…" She faltered to a stop, before appearing to come to a decision. "I'm on my own."

"Then let me show you around, get you skiing."

Her smile showed gratitude, but still a little caution. "I can't imagine it would be much fun for you. You must be pretty good."

Yeah. He was, but if he could arrange to spend a day with her, he'd ski backward down the bunny slopes the entire time and grin like a kid in a candy store while he did it. However, looking at her, he didn't think it would take all day. She looked like an athlete.

"I am, but I'm also here on my own to relax. Look, I taught two of my younger siblings to ski. Up to you."

She smiled, glancing at him from the corner of those long-lashed gray peepers of hers. "I'd like that."

"Great." The tenor of the engines shifted. "We must be getting ready to descend." Brandon pulled out his phone. "What's your cell number?"

She blushed. It was just a faint rose tint to her golden skin. "I don't have a cell."

He couldn't keep the surprise from his face. Even if they didn't use it, he wasn't sure he knew anyone anymore who didn't at least carry a prepaid phone for emergencies. "No big deal. Sometimes I'd like to be a little less plugged in. Where are you staying?"

"At the lodge at Falcon Summit Resort."

He grinned. "Me too." He leaned across her a bit to peer out the window. "If you look, you'll be able to see some of the slopes from here."

He was rewarded when she laughed in that husky voice of hers. "Oh look, Brandon! It's like looking at a line of ants."

His laughter joined hers. "It is. Never thought of it that way. Tomorrow and Sunday will be even busier, but if we get out there early, we can get ahead of the crowds. Can you stand getting up at dawn on your vacation?" And, boy, wouldn't he love to see what she looked like when she woke up in the mornings.

"Sure. I'm an early riser most of the time."

Their conversation was interrupted by the captain coming over the speaker with details of their arrival and the weather forecast. Though it was late in the season, it sounded like conditions for the upcoming week would be ideal. Brandon glanced at Lucy's profile. Since she'd returned to looking out the window, her face was averted a bit. Damn, but it was almost like she'd never seen the world from this view. On first acquaintance, she appeared to be an odd mixture of sophistication and naivete. Whichever was real, it was damned intriguing.

* * * *

Lucy accepted the ride Brandon offered in his rental car. It would save her from squeezing into the resort's hospitality car—at least she kept telling herself that was the reason she'd accepted his offer. The truth was, she wasn't sure she'd ever met a man as handsome as him. If he was hitting on her, it was with a whole lot more class than the usual crowd of men who patronized Flamingo Road. And for the last couple years, those were the only men she had encountered.

When they reached the lodge, he turned to her before they got out. "Would you like to have dinner with me tonight?"

Lucy's natural caution reared up. Maybe the invitation was him looking for company, but she wanted to keep things casual as a precaution because of the way her body responded to him. She shook her head. "No. I don't think I'd be very good company tonight. Can we meet in the morning?"

He nodded. "Six thirty in the front lobby."

"I thought they didn't open 'til nine?"

"They don't, but I figured we could get some breakfast first, and I have an in with the owner." His grin was so disarming, all Lucy could do was nod.

"Let's get our bags in, and you can take it easy." When he cupped her elbow with his palm, Lucy discovered she liked the casual touch. It was a courtesy he didn't have to think about, he simply did it.

While she checked in, another clerk was helping him a few feet away. Lucy handled the registration and credit card information, overhearing the way the clerk said *Mr. Barrett*, as if he were a valued guest. He probably was. From years of counting on tips to help her make her living, Lucy had come to recognize the difference between off-the-rack clothing and clothing that was hand-tailored. There was nothing even resembling department store about anything touching Brandon's skin.

"Are you set?" He waited for her to get her bag on her shoulder. When she nodded, he took her free hand and held it for a moment. Once again, a shock of heat and awareness zinged through her at the touch of his hand. "Have a good evening, Lucy. I'll see you here. Six thirty. Be ready to ski, okay?"

"I will." He started to turn away, and she added, "Thanks for the invitation, Brandon."

His grin was lopsided. "We'll see if you still feel the same way tomorrow afternoon."

* * * *

At loose ends, Brandon called Matt Petersohn, Falcon Summit's owner, right after he'd settled in his suite.

"Hey, Matt."

"Bran!" His friend's voice was warm over the phone line. "They told me you'd checked in. Everything good, dude?"

"Perfect, as always. You free for dinner?"

"Yeah. Why don't I have it delivered to your suite around seven? We can chow down then sit and scratch while we talk about why you don't come out here to ski much."

Brandon laughed, agreed and hung up. At last, some of the tension from his work at Barrett Newspapers drained out of him. God only knew, he'd wanted to take over Seth's position, had been overjoyed when his elder brother had put his foot down and walked out the door. But in the last few months, he'd also come to realize how much of a buffer Seth had been between Alexander Barlow-Barrett and the rest of them.

Now Brandon was the one juggling his father's rigid personality against what he knew was the best interest of the company. The industry was changing at a pace far beyond what anyone could have predicted when Brandon had graduated from business school ten years ago. Seth had been quiet and dogged, but he'd been making changes during that whole time.

The problem was everything had to be ramped up big time if they were going to keep their flagship national daily a household fixture. And, damn it, he needed his father to realize the only way it would happen was without the smell of ink or the feel of newsprint. Those days were gone, but they could still compete. There was another market out there between fancy phones and e-readers, but they needed to tap into it now. The whole world was plugged in. It was time Barrett Newspapers lived the same way.

By the time Matt showed up at his door with a couple waiters pushing carts with covered trays trailing him, Brandon had showered and exchanged the suit for a pair of well-worn jeans and a thick Nationals sweatshirt. His feet were bare and he had a bourbon in his hand. He set the glass aside so he and Matt could do the back-slapping guy hug thing.

"Damn, Matt," Brandon said, eyeing his friend's thick black braid and close-cropped beard, "you're taking this mountain man thing to heart."

Matt flicked a finger at Brandon's conservative haircut. "You're the one to talk, Mr. Powerbroker. How's it feel to be heir to the throne?"

Brandon shook his head. "Some days, not a whole lot different than stepping into a pile of horse shit."

"Papa Barrett snarling again?"

"It's not the snarling. It's the rigid immobility." Brandon stared around him. "You've made changes here."

Matt laughed. "Had to. Too much competition from other places. We've added some glitz and enough luxury to make *Grossvater* Petersohn flip over in his grave, but the bookings are up—and not just during ski season. We've added guided hiking and fishing trips during the summer." Matt uncovered a couple plates and Brandon smelled the rich aromas of wine sauce and butter.

"Damn. Let's eat. I am freaking starved."

They were almost finished when Matt looked across the table with a grin. "So my concierge tells me you came in with a drop-dead-gorgeous blonde. Keeping her all to yourself?"

Brandon stiffened for a moment, then laughed. "Not sure yet. I met her on the plane. She's here on vacation. Turned me down flat for dinner tonight, but I'm hooked up with her to teach her how to ski."

"Good work."

"Can you get one of your guys to outfit us around seven thirty? I'll pay them extra."

"No problem. Scott's been looking for some OT. You sure you want to teach her yourself? I could have him give her an hour private lesson, then you could hold her hand down a couple of beginner slopes before you hit the expert runs."

Brandon leaned back in his chair, feeling full and mellow after the meal. "You know, in most circumstances I would take you up on your offer, but I have the feeling teaching Lucy Cameron to ski might be fun. She's built like an athlete."

"You going to teach her anything else?"

Brandon sipped his brandy and stared into the fire. "We're not at that point yet, but I will tell you, my cylinders start firing whenever I see her."

Matt laughed. "Well, she's safe from me, buddy. You know I have a hands-off policy on guests to begin with, but it's definitely hands off of any territory you're marking. We've been tight for too long to compete over a woman."

Brandon smiled. "'Preciate that, Matt."

"I'll say no sweat for now, but I reserve the right to change my response to an *aw shit* if she turns out to be worth the glazed look in the eyes of the front desk clerks."

www.ingramcontent.com/pod-product-compliance
Lightning Source LLC
Chambersburg PA
CBHW022151260626
47155CB00017B/1725